ENVY

THE DAMNING BOOK 2

KATIE MAY

EXPRESSO PUBLISHING, LLC

To Grandma and Grandpa. Thank you for letting me stay at your house and write without distractions

CONTENTS

I skirted the old well Z and I used to play at, now boarded up, before dashing into the forest.

The forest once brought me comfort. The trees, tall enough to brush the skyline, and the animals scurrying through the brush. Like all vampires, I was drawn to the living. Some might argue that it was merely a pull towards a food source, but I begged to differ.

Vampires loved the living because we were death incarnate.

Stumbling over the trim of my gown, I found myself in front of an unfamiliar cabin. The windows were unwashed, cracked in some places, and the wood was beginning to deteriorate with age. Still, the formidable building resembled a mansion to me and my tired body.

With considerable effort, I dragged myself up the stone staircase and onto the wraparound porch. I waited, using my vampiric hearing, but detected no heartbeats inside.

Breaths sawing in and out from the marathon I'd just run, I stepped through the door.

The inside was just as dilapidated as the outside. Worn rugs, tearing on the edges, adorned the mahogany floorboards. A single hearth was lit in the entrance, the flames flickering and casting strange shadows on the walls.

Alone at last, I settled on the ground and pulled out the arrow that had lodged itself into my leg. I'd heard rumors of the before time—before nightmares existed—and that the humans had used guns and bullets. I couldn't imagine such a weapon when something as simple as a bow and arrow was able to incapacitate a newly-fed vampire. The council was full of assholes, but they'd done one thing right when they had banned weapons worse than a knife.

Cursing, I removed the wooden arrow and tossed it into the fire. The flames hissed but eagerly ate at its treat.

I allowed my mind to wander.

How did my life get so fucked up? I'd thought I had everything—a best friend, two mates, a job. But it had all shattered around me with the finesse of a bull trampling through a china shop.

A sob lodged in my throat when I thought about Diego. His body lying limp on the ground, drenched in his own blood. The gurgling noises escaping from his lips. The tears in his eyes.

I closed my own eyes, as if that could somehow rid me of the horrendous images.

And then Z's face, the accusation in her gaze. The hatred. She could've killed me. I wanted her to.

Because of me, Diego was dead. Because of me, my *mate* was dead. Zack. The person who was designed to be the other half of my soul.

Or, at least, a third of it.

My mind flittered to Atta and the last time I'd seen her. Her red hair framing her face as she leaned down to kiss my neck. Her small hand kneading my breasts, tweaking my nipples. I hadn't been with a woman before, but she'd made it as easy as breathing. As my tongue eagerly lapped at her slit and her head rolled backwards, I'd known I was in love. That love was only reconfirmed when she'd returned the favor, our breasts bouncing against one another as our bodies moved.

I'd thought that if I were to be with any girl, it would've been Z. I would've been the first to admit that I was in love with my best friend, despite my previous conquests only being men. I would imagine her always. Under me. On top of me. Her heavy breasts bouncing in my face.

I'd been jealous when she'd started seeing the princes, irrationally so. Maybe things would've been different if I could've just supported my best friend. I'd been so bitter, so angry, that I hadn't once told her about Zack and me. When he'd been with me, he hadn't been a monster. There had been so much gentle anxiety on his face, so much reverence, as he kissed down my body.

Who would've known that a monster lurked underneath?

When Z cast me out, she'd thought she was saving me from death.

But she was wrong.

Where could a vampire that had been forsaken by her own kind go? I'd worked with the human assassins, but they no longer wanted me. My family didn't want me.

No one fucking wanted me.

A rogue nightmare was easy prey. Already, I'd had over a dozen hunters come after me—the reason for the arrow burning away in the fire.

Sobbing, I placed my head in my hands and thought of death. It was so incredibly tempting, that seductive dark embrace constantly nagging at me, and I wanted nothing more than to give in. But I knew I could never.

Atta.

Z.

My love and my best friend. Somehow, someway, I would earn their forgiveness and love. In my mind, I had a goal—to win Atta and Z back before Z's wedding to the seven princes. I chuckled yet again, slightly hysterically, as I thought of my badass, nightmare hating best friend as the lover of the seven nightmare princes. It was some cosmic joke. Fate was no doubt laughing at her.

Suddenly, the fire was blown out, and a cool wind blew through my hiding spot. I froze, knowing that I was too weak to defend myself from the hunters. As a vampire, I healed faster than a mere mortal, but the wound in my leg had been deep, cutting through bone and tendons.

"Get up, you pathetic simpleton," a strident feminine voice demanded. It was unfamiliar but still caused pinpricks of terror to race down my spine. It was the voice you would hear on a stage, innately demanding your respect.

I remained shivering on the floorboards, eyes squeezed shut.

The smell of death permeated the air. There was no doubt in my mind that it was emanating directly from this woman.

Footsteps echoed around me, surrounding me. I counted at least fifteen heartbeats.

Somebody grabbed my hair, and I screamed at the initial stab of pain. My eyes, unbidden, flickered to the woman who held me.

She was beautiful, that much was obvious. Her fiery red hair cascaded around her shoulders in soft waves. Her eyes were a beautiful shade of blue, that exact color of the sky when the sun began to peek through the boughs of trees early in the morning.

Her hand curved around my face, and a delicate smile touched her red painted lips. She looked as delicate as a snake, however. No amount of smiling could pacify the rage in her eyes. The darkness.

"My poor dear," she cooed. "Cast out. Abandoned. Alone." She shook her head in mock apology, and my temper flared. That condescending little bitch!

"Who are you?"

"I think the better question would be, what do I want?" She laughed, and the sound made goosebumps erupt on my skin. Fear penetrated my defenses, and it took considerable effort not to curl into a fetal position and cry. "Your name is Mali."

"No shit," I sniped back, resisting the urge to spit on her smug face. Her smile never wavered at my small act of disobedience.

"My name is Aaliyah," she said calmly. "And you're going to help me."

ONE

Z

The throne room was...underwhelming.

That was not a term I would've thought to associate with such a room. The connotations of the word 'throne room' would suggest intricately carved chairs raised on a dais and three-tiered chandeliers. What I found, however, was something else entirely.

It had once been beautiful, the opulence even now undeniable, but time had tarnished its beauty. The chandeliers were covered in dust and spiderwebs. The thrones themselves were cracked in more places than one.

I tried to mask my expression of shock, but a tiny gasp slipped out unintentionally. I shouldn't have been surprised.

This room was just one of many throne rooms for the seven kings. They barely ever traveled to the capital unless there was an important event transpiring, like the Damning—a fight to the death between one hundred of the worst criminals and assassins. At the end of the day, there was only one winner. One person to claim the title of the kings' private assassin.

A title that currently belonged to me.

I could feel the phantom remnants of blood slithering over my skin like a snake, and the screams of the men I'd killed contaminated the air until I was practically choking on them.

Nobody expected a person like me to win. A girl, for one, and a human—an insignificant bug in this fucked-up world of predators. I was expected to be squashed by more than one foot, not emerge victorious. I blamed it on dumb luck.

The seven nightmare species were descended from the Seven Deadly Sins. It hadn't always been that way. Hundreds of years ago, humans had ruled the world. There had been skyscrapers and presidents and jobs that didn't involve groveling. When the sins descended like damn vultures, they gifted certain families with ethereal powers. Powers that defied the natural order.

Humans had feared these creatures, coined as nightmares, but they were a dying breed. It became apparent that no amount of fighting could quell the growing plague of supernatural monsters. They were stronger, better, smarter—or so they claimed—and we were helpless to escape their keen claws burrowing into our sides.

For the first time in forever, the humans found themselves near the bottom of the food chain.

Lifting my head up imperiously, I took the final steps into the desolate room. It was still beautiful, there was no denying that, but it was apparent that it had been forgotten. The room was actually a fitting representation of myself in that respect.

My eyes latched onto the shifter king first. He sat in the center of the room, penetrating eyes aimed directly at me. At his gaze, I straightened imperceptibly. I wouldn't allow him to intimidate me.

Shifters were descended from Wrath. They were volatile by nature, jumping to violence as a form of resolution. They tended to see the worst in people and were quick to anger and slow to forgive. The current king was also a major asshole, no surprise, and was the most avid proponent of human work camps.

Behind him, standing abnormally still with his muscular arms folded in front of his chest, was the king's son, Lupe.

My heart hammered when I met his blue eyes. His hair was disheveled, as if he'd run his hand through it one too many times, but his eyes were kind. Sympathetic. Compassionate.

My lips pursed.

I didn't deserve his pity, nor did I want it. He may have been my mate, the other half—or at least a seventh—of my soul, but he didn't understand me. He couldn't possibly understand how it felt to lose your two best friends in a matter of days.

My stomach was a clamorous mixture of dread and an almost incandescent fury. I kept envisioning Diego's face...

His eyes had been wide, staring blankly at a spot on the ceiling. I'd heard that you were supposed to close the eyes of the dead, but I couldn't bring myself to do it. After all, they weren't Diego's eyes. Not anymore. His eyes had always been alight with laughter and mirth. His lips had always been curved into a perpetual smirk. There hadn't been blood on the Diego I remembered. No, the man lying on the ground, dead, was a shell of the man I'd known and loved.

The solution to everything was simple—I would never love again.

Everybody I'd ever loved was brutally taken from me. Death had claimed them all, and I was helpless to stop it.

My parents, murdered in front of my eyes.

S, the man I'd loved, killed by rogue shifters.

Diego, stabbed trying to protect me.

Mali, my best friend, who'd betrayed me by quite literally falling into bed with the enemy—Zack. The last man I killed with a single, unceremonious stab to the heart.

Even Devlin, despite him sleeping soundly in my room, had left me. He was the first man I'd ever loved, the man I'd thought I would make a life with, and he'd left me under this delusional belief that he needed to protect me. It was only a few days ago that I discovered our entire relationship was built on a lie. He'd been Devlin, the Crowned Prince of Genies, not Lin, the man I loved.

And I was Z, the human assassin who killed his kind for a living, not the timid, innocent girl he'd believed himself to love.

There was nothing beautiful about our relationship. It was a ferocious snowstorm with no hope of relief. It was tumbling in a riptide, desperate for fresh air before you were pulled back under. It was death in the truest form.

I ripped my eyes reluctantly off of Lupe's, surveying the rest of the men in the room. Of course there were only men. Of freaking course.

The mermaid king caught my eye. He was sitting directly beside the shifter king, lips curved up into a malicious smile. His glacial eyes grazed the other kings before landing and staying on me. His smile grew significantly. He might've been handsome, with his golden hair and lightly tanned skin, but there was something cold in his eyes. Something that made the hair on the back of my neck stand on end. I had the sudden urge to escape, to run, to leave this hellish room with the many eyes that seemed to see too much. I felt vulnerable standing there. Not at all like the fierce warrior I was expected to be. In that moment, I wasn't Z the assassin, but Zara the fragile human girl.

There were three men surrounding the mermaid king. They all had the same golden-spun hair and ocean blue eyes. There was no doubting the similarities between them and the king. Them and Dair.

My heart kick-started at the thought of my sweet, gentle mate. He wasn't present in the room, but I could sense him nearby, perhaps a few rooms over. I didn't know how I knew it, only that I did. That damn mate bond between us. The bond that I somewhat refused to acknowledge.

This bond didn't guarantee love, but it was almost always present. And love, I'd come to find out, was immensely dangerous. It strangled you, choked you.

Falling in love with one person made me off-kilter, but falling in love with more than one was damn near suicidal.

Briefly, my eyes flitted around the remaining kings. Besides Lupe, none of my princes were present.

Not my *princes*, I scolded myself.

The shadow king was clothed in darkness, hidden in the corner of the room. I wanted to chuckle at the similarities between Ryland and his father. As descendants of Pride, they refused to show their faces to people they didn't deem as worthy—a word I hated intensely. That definition was skewed by bias and prejudice.

A female and a human? Most definitely *not* worthy in their eyes.

The incubus king, descended from Lust, sat directly beside him. On his other side was the King of Vampires, whose line originated from Gluttony.

With a confidence I didn't feel, I turned my attention towards the King of Genies. As a descendant of Greed, he fed off the selfishness of others. My heart hammered at the similarities between him and his son, Devlin. The same olive-toned skin and violet eyes, shining as if there was a candle lit beneath the surface. The same curly brown hair. The same broad shoulders leading down to tapered waists. The king, however, had streaks of gray in his shoulder-length hair.

And his eyes...

They were what I imagined standing in freezing water would feel like. Numbness would begin in your toes, slowing snaking upwards until it clamped around your heart. Your breathing would turn shallow, just as unconsciousness claimed you.

While the mermaid king's eyes were malicious, the King of the Genies' were empty. Cold. Frigid. The eyes of a man who'd had his innocence chipped away by time and environment.

Would that happen to Devlin?

The mere thought filled me with unease.

I tried to picture Devlin as cold, untouchable, evil... but the thought eluded me. It just didn't fit with the man I knew and once loved. *Still* loved. Maybe.

"So this is the winner," the mermaid king said, diverting my attention. He was watching me with narrowed, piercing eyes. I was fully dressed, but it felt as if I was naked. With one glance, I could tell he wanted to tear me apart, rip me to shreds. Piece by piece.

I resisted the urge to bow sardonically. The last thing I wanted to do was show any type of reverence to these monsters.

Planting my hands on my hips, I waited, a quirk to my brow.

It was the vampire king that moved first, gliding across the distressed wood until he was nose to nose with me. Out of my peripheral, I noted Lupe stiffening imperceptibly. His nostrils flared at the other man's proximity to me. It wasn't jealousy. No, it was *fear*. Fear for me. There was no mistaking the predatory intent in the king's beady black eyes, such a contrast to Jax's own striking shade of green. It was rumored that the more someone fed, the darker their eyes became.

He resembled the demons I had read about as a child.

He leaned forward until his face was in the crook of my neck and inhaled deeply. My jaw clenched.

"She doesn't smell like much." His voice lilted with an unfamiliar accent. It wasn't one I had heard before. Native to the Vampire Kingdom?

"She doesn't have to smell like much to still be our assassin," the incubus king drawled lazily.

"I still don't understand how that can be!" This outburst was, of course, from the mermaid king. Envious bastards. I knew they would be upset that a mermaid hadn't won the competition. Though, if I wasn't mistaken, a mermaid hadn't even made it to the top ten.

"What's your name?" This next voice was not belligerent but not necessarily kind. I swiveled my head towards the shadows, somewhat surprised that the shadow king was speaking to me directly.

From the gaping mouths of the other men present, they felt the same.

I quickly caught my bearings, standing straighter.

"Z," I answered firmly.

"Z..." He said my name as if he was testing it, tasting it on his tongue.

"Not Zara?" The genie king's voice was tinged with amusement.

Zara was the name of the woman I was impersonating—a blonde bimbo that served as the assistant and lover of Z. Basically, I was the perceived lover of myself.

Diego had had a field day with that knowledge.

At the thought of my best friend, my mood instantly turned somber.

"My name is Z," I said sharply. I thought I'd overstepped when the genie king's eyes flared brightly, but the shadow king merely threw back his head in laughter. It wasn't entirely unpleasant. It sounded almost...normal. As if he was familiar with laughing.

"I like her. She has fire."

"She's a female." I didn't even have to look to know that it would be the shifter king who'd spoken. "And she's a human."

"But she won the Damning," the shadow king pointed out. Was I mistaken or did he sound...smug?

"That she did."

Silence, sudden and pronounced, seemed to suffocate me as if I were buried below twenty feet of black, sticky tar. I resisted the urge to fidget.

I was in a room full of my enemies, the monsters I had been tasked to kill, and there was nothing I could do about it. The knife in my sleeve suddenly felt ten times heavier.

How easy it would be to slice through flesh and tendon and bone...

There was a certain way you had to hold a knife for maximum impact. Lightly gripped between your fingers, the copper handle resting on your palm, an extension of your hand. A fluid flick of your wrist...

"The situation is different," the incubus king agreed with a nod. My eyes, unbidden, flickered towards him, and I sucked in a breath. He was gorgeous. I hadn't expected anything else from a descendant of lust, but it wasn't even his unnaturally good looks that caused my heart to hammer. It was the power he exuded in waves. Even from where I stood, liquid heat settled in my core. I had the need to rub my thighs together to alleviate the ache.

I noticed Lupe sniff, eyes heating with lust. No doubt, he could smell my arousal. If he could smell it...

The Vampire King laughed giddily, slapping his thigh for emphasis.

"Better tone it down a bit," he said, turning to smile at the incubus. "We don't want her to jump you."

The incubus king's grin was satisfactory, eyes brewing with wanton desire. His hair was a shade of garnet, darker than his son's, and his chiseled cheekbones made his face even more striking. What I wouldn't give to lick...

I shook my head, clearing my lust muddled haze. Anger replaced it, and I glared at the king.

How dare he use his powers on me?

The man who had hurt my mate! I recalled Killian's story, how this despicable man had tried to force him to have sex with a woman he considered a mother. When Killian refused, he'd raped her in front of him. And then killed her.

Anger burned me from the inside out, like molten lava brewing just below the surface. I had the sudden urge to leap the few feet separating us and jab my knife into his head. No, that would be too quick of a death. He deserved to suffer. Bleed.

Lupe's expression was positively murderous, and his hands clenched and unclenched at his sides.

"She has to prove herself," the mermaid king interjected. It was apparent he was jealous that the attention was no longer on him. Resisting the urge to roll my eyes, I reluctantly turned in his direction.

My brow furrowed when I caught his son's eye over his shoulder. Dair's brother. The man was handsome, with lightly tanned skin and golden blond hair, but he didn't hold a candle to my mate. My mate...

I still hated those damn words.

The man—Tavvy, if I remembered my facts correctly—was watching me with rapt attention. His head tilted to the side as if he were contemplating a difficult math equation. I pulled my eyes from his, focusing on his father, the mermaid king.

"A task. One chosen by each king." There were a few mutters of approval before they were silenced by a wave of his hand. The shifter king growled harshly at what he perceived as a slight from the mermaid. I had a feeling he would've attacked the envious ruler if not for Lupe's hand on his shoulder, restraining him. My mouth flattened at their touch, hating to see Lupe with such a monster.

"A task?" the shadow king parroted, amusement evident in his voice. The mermaid's smile was positively gleeful.

I couldn't help but compare it to the smile of a sociopath seconds after a kill. It was a smile not intended for comfort.

"A task. To prove your worth and loyalty to the seven ruling families." He nodded towards the mage king, descended from Sloth, who lazily lifted his head. Had the asshole been asleep?

When he turned half-lidded eyes towards me, smiling indolently, I realized that yes, yes, he had.

Procuring a small flask from his pocket, he tossed it to me. I scrambled to catch the bottle, eyes scanning the inscription on the label with unease. The last thing I wanted to do was put an unknown substance into my body, as the kings seemed to be implying, especially something gifted from the King of Mages himself.

"Drink it, whore," the shifter king demanded. I glared at the crude acknowledgement, and I could've sworn I heard Lupe growl from behind his father. If the king heard it, he didn't acknowledge it.

"What will it do?" I asked. I tried not to let them see how frightened I actually was. Surely they weren't going to kill me with poison. Right?

Right?

I would be ashamed and embarrassed for them if they lacked the creativity to kill me with some pizzazz.

It was Lupe that caught my attention. Fur had grown on his face and forearms, teeth elongated.

The last thing I wanted to do was out Lupe's and my relationship to the kings...or lack thereof. I didn't know how the kings would feel if they discovered we were soulmates.

Actually, I imagined they would be pretty pissed off. The type of pissed off that usually ended with dead bodies and heads on spikes.

Deciding quickly, I chugged the contents of the drink before Lupe could shift fully.

And then the pain began.

TWO

Z

The pain lasted for only a second. Enough time for me to scream in agony as my bones ripped apart and then fused themselves back together again. Enough time for Lupe to partially transform into his bear, body turning larger, hair growing once more on his forearms, lips curling backwards into a snarl.

In all honesty, the kings should've been grateful that I was able to snap out of it. I wasn't sure if even they were immune to a grizzly attack.

Gasping, I glanced through my fringe of lashes. Somehow, I found myself on the floor, keeled over as vomit churned in the back of my throat. My stomach threatened to expel the contents of my dinner, but I held it in. The last thing I wanted to do was give the assholes the satisfaction of watching me squirm.

Granted, I was on the floor, a shivering, sobbing mess, but throwing up was the final straw.

"Impressive," the shadow king said brightly. "The last one passed out for hours."

"The last one was a wimp who didn't last five minutes," drawled the incubus king.

"Semantics."

"What...what was that?" I asked, struggling to take in that precious air. I clutched my chest, afraid my heart would be ripped from it. Unbidden, my eyes flickered to Lupe's. Claw marks marred the pillar he was leaning against, and sweat beaded on his forehead. I gave him a subtle nod to let him know I was okay, that I was alive, that I was still breathing and ready to kick ass. He looked as if he was seconds away from lunging towards me and carrying me out of the room, caveman style, but he managed to nod.

Trusting my judgement.

The shifter king laughed, the unpleasant sound grating on my nerves. I wondered if he saw the exchange between his son and me. If he did, he didn't comment. I worried, briefly, that he would take out his anger on Lupe later before quickly dismissing that thought in a tidal wave of anger. From what intel I'd gathered, the shifter king had never laid a hand on his son, which was surprising, given his wrathful nature and bigoted ideologies. He just took his frustration out on everyone else instead.

"That, my dear child, was a binding spell." This came from the mage king.

Had he...?

Had he brought a pillow?

One glance confirmed that, yup, he was lying sideways in his throne, a pillow under his head. His half-lidded eyes met mine.

He wasn't as handsome as his son, Bash, but I could

definitely see the similarities. The same pale skin and ash blond hair. The same dimples that appeared when they smiled.

Not that Bash smiled much, mind you. The asshole was more stubborn than I was.

He hated the mate bond with a passion. In his mind, the mate bond equaled a loss of free will, a loss of freedom. I didn't entirely blame him. To know that there were seven people made perfectly for me, made to soothe the jagged edges of my soul, made me uneasy. I wasn't good at relationships or love or any of that shit. I was more of a *stab first, ask questions later* kind of girl.

I knew I didn't love them. Not even Devlin, the man I'd once loved with my entire heart.

At least, I wasn't certain if I loved him.

They were strangers to me, and I still struggled to differentiate them from my enemies. I had been programmed my entire life to be wary of the nightmare princes. The prophecy itself had stated that these princes, these seven men who'd slammed into my life like a wrecking ball, were designed specifically to either end the world or save it.

No pressure.

Realizing my thoughts had drifted from the matter at hand, I lifted my chin imperceptibly and met the mage king's light, playful eyes. It was just another distinction from the brooding, serious Sebastian.

"The binding spell assures your loyalty to the seven crowns," the mermaid king said. A cruel, taunting smirk pulled up his thin lips.

"With it, no harm may befall us either by your hand

or your mind," added the incubus king. He pointed to his head for emphasis, as if I really needed him to spell out where the mind was.

Well...shit. That put a damper on the whole "kill them all" plan.

"What would happen if I break it?" I asked. If it were possible, and I didn't think it was, the kings appeared even more amused. The shadow king went as far as to throw back his head in laughter.

"My dear child..." Gliding towards me, the shifter king rested a heavy hand on my shoulder. His nails broke through clothes and into skin. I knew it was going to leave a nasty bruise. "If you break the oath, the spell, then you die. Simple. You are dismissed until we call upon you for your first task."

His words echoed in my ears. Reverberated through my body.

Simple.

Then why did it feel as if I were walking to my execution?

DEVLIN WAS STILL ASLEEP when I snuck back into the room. I hadn't made him aware of my meeting with the kings, knowing for certain that he would demand to go with me. Whatever secrecy our relationship had would no doubt shatter the second he entered that throne room.

He looked peaceful as he slept. Serene. His abnormally long lashes fluttered against his olive-toned skin, and his disheveled curls fanned out on the pillow. Tiptoeing so I wouldn't disturb him, I perched on the edge of the bed.

How did I feel about Devlin Genie?

There was no easy way for me to answer that question.

One part of me remembered our time together, the love we'd shared, the way he'd held me with reverence and tenderness as if I were the only girl in the world. The other half of me balked at the idea of reentering a relationship with the man who'd broken my heart. Trust had to be earned, and once you broke it, it was impossible to fix completely, like trying to capture raindrops in the palm of your hand.

Add on the fact that he was my fated mate, one of the seven men designed specifically for me, only made me more cautious. We'd spent years together, and he never bothered to tell me.

I'd even fallen in *love* with another man, and he'd still remained silent.

At the same time, I'd lied to him too. My name, when we first met, had been Susan, and I'd posed as a helpless damsel in distress. I had never nor would ever be that woman. Time may have cracked away at my innocence, but I'd always been hard. Glacial. Not even cannons could tear down the walls I'd impeccably crafted, brick by brick.

He stirred, muttering something beneath his breath. Glutton for punishment, I leaned closer, pressing my ear against his parted lips.

"Z..." he whispered sleepily. Dreamily.

My heart thudded in my chest before dropping through the floorboards. A fire built in my stomach, setting me ablaze.

Why did the thought of him dreaming of me fill me with both dread and excitement?

Unable to answer that, I settled on stroking his hair.

Being with Devlin...it had once felt like coming home after trekking through an atrocious snowstorm. The wind howling, the snow assaulting my face, the water seeping through the legs of my pants. Once I entered the house, warmth emanated from the lit fire and the smell of baked cookies wafted from the oven, the smell pervasive. It was the feeling of wrapping your favorite blanket around your shoulders to curb the frigid air. Home. He'd felt like home.

Now? That home had cracks that brought in the snow, and the fire had long since turned to embers.

"Z?" a tired voice whispered

It took me a moment to realize that Devlin wasn't just sleepily mumbling my name. He opened one eye lazily, a content smile fluttering on his face. Before I could say something, perhaps explain why I was sitting there staring at him like a stalker, he reached a hand out and pulled me towards him. My body bounced against his hard, muscular one, and I tensed instinctively.

I didn't...cuddle.

But I also couldn't deny that being in his arms felt right.

"When did you get up?" he whispered, nuzzling my hair with his nose. I heard him inhale deeply, breathing in my scent. I prayed that I didn't stink of...well, blood. Or whatever else assassins would stink of.

"Um...just a little bit ago?"

Was this the new pillow talk?

"Liar," Devlin said suddenly, catching me off guard. When I merely tilted my head up to stare at him, blinking rapidly, he grinned down at me. "You have a tell, my love. You stiffen."

"I stiffen?" I asked in disbelief. I catalogued my body, somewhat pissed when I noticed that my limbs *were* abnormally tight. "That's probably because you pulled me on top of you," I deflected.

He snorted, hand coming down to brush at my thighs. Now, my body stiffened for an entirely different reason. Damn feminine hormones. And damn him for having a magic hand. I'd lived on only *my* hand for a year, thank you very much, and the last thing I needed—

I gasped as his fingers fluttered against the seams of my pants, directly over my core.

"Where were you?" he repeated. "Were you with one of the others?"

He didn't sound jealous talking about my six other mates, his brothers in every way but blood, though I imagined it couldn't have been easy for him. He'd had me all to himself once upon a time, and now...

I knew I would go quite stabby if he had six other lovers.

Nope. Not going there.

Bitches would be stabbed.

Painfully.

In the boob.

"What are you thinking about now?" he asked. He pressed his lips to the crown of my head before moving lower, across my cheekbone, and finally resting on my jaw. His scruff tickled my sensitive skin.

"Boobs," I answered honestly. At least that was one thing I *could* answer. He chuckled, the sound making my body tingle. Unlike his father's, it was a genuine, amused laugh.

"Should I be jealous?" he asked teasingly. Those damn lips of his rested on my earlobe, nibbling softly. The barest graze of teeth.

"As long as you don't think about boobs, we shouldn't have a problem," I said breathlessly. I blamed it on the jog I hadn't taken. Yup. That five-mile nonexistent run through the woods.

"Is that so?"

Devlin's hand snaked upwards before resting on my heavy breast. Squeezing softly, he began to knead the mound, fingers tweaking my nipple through my thin shirt.

"Yup."

Make that a ten-mile jog.

"Now are you going to tell me where you were...or who you were with?"

His hand left my breast, and I practically cried out at the loss of contact. That cry turned into a gasp of pleasure when it crept under my shirt, beneath my bra, and touched my bare skin. His thumb rubbed back and forth over my aching, beaded nipple.

As always with Devlin, I felt too much, too soon, too

deeply. He made me feel as if I wasn't broken but instead a work in progress.

And I hated it.

I hated the vulnerability he evoked from me. The love I inherently felt when I looked into his violet eyes. The way my defenses crumbled around me, piece by small piece, but still enough for him to slip through.

"I met with your dad," I blurted, and his hand froze on my breast.

Yup. That did it.

Ways to kill a mood—talk about asshole fathers.

With great reluctance, his hand left me, and he flopped onto his back. I didn't even have to see his face to know that he was wearing his customary scowl heavy with disapproval.

"Why didn't you wake me?"

"Because it wasn't your business," I retorted automatically, sitting up.

"Wasn't my...motherfucking... You *are* my business!" He propped himself onto his elbow to stare at me. *Glare* at me would be a better description.

"I'm nobody's business but my own," I countered, sitting up on the bed. "I've been taking care of myself just fine for the last few years."

His eyes hardened, hand reaching out to twine his fingers through my own. I let him, knowing that he needed the contact.

"You don't have to face this alone anymore, my love. That's what you have me for, and as much as I hate to admit it, that's what you have the others for. We're your mates. We're designed—"

"Blah. Blah. Blah," I said, cutting him off, and untangled my hand from his, placing my fingers into my ears. Childish? Yes. Effective? Also, yes. When I was sure he'd stopped spouting off nonsense, I removed my fingers and placed my hands on my hips. "The last thing I want is seven men who feel obligated to be with me. To take fucking care of me when I am more than capable of taking care of myself."

He opened his mouth to no doubt protest, but I cut him off with a wave of my hand.

"Look at Bash, Lin! He can barely look at me, and he's my mate! Look at Jax... He's engaged to be fucking married!" Shaking my head, I stood from the bed and took a step backwards. And then another one. And another one. My back rested against the door, and I leaned heavily against it. I wanted nothing more than to escape. To leave and never look back.

But I couldn't.

Because despite everything I claimed, the damn assholes each held a tiny sliver of my heart. I didn't have a lot to offer, but what I did, they took. Greedily, if you asked me. Lapping it up like famished vampires finding the holy grail of blood.

It scared me.

Absolutely terrified me. I'd faced countless monsters, countless nightmares, and never once had I felt this unhinged.

When Devlin continued to stare at me, violet eyes warm with understanding, I just about exploded. I had the distinct feeling he could see me clearer than I could see myself.

How much of that was real, and how much of that was the mate bond?

I didn't dare look too closely at that. I knew I wouldn't like the answer, no matter the verdict.

"I need to go...stab things."

"Z..." He trailed off helplessly, forking a hand through his brown curls.

Before he could say something else, before he could completely unravel me, I hurried out the door. I had no destination in mind, only away. Away from him. Away from my feelings.

Away.

THREE

KILLIAN

I'd never masturbated before. Honestly, there hadn't been a need. As an incubus who relied on pleasure but had never been sexually attracted to a male or female, I was content with just sitting outside doors, listening to their sated moans, and pretending that I wasn't a screw-up of a nightmare.

I wrapped my hands around my rock-hard cock, perching myself on the foot of the bed. I wasn't even sure if it would work, if it would relieve the tension that was skating that precarious line between pleasure and pain.

Once you found your mate, the incubus was only ever able to receive pleasure from said mate. Which made what my father did to my nanny years ago even more fucked up—he'd known that sleeping with her wouldn't get him off, yet he'd done it anyway because he was a sadistic asshole who lived to torture people.

I closed my eyes, envisioning Z's dewy, heart-shaped face. Those glorious golden tresses, untamed and wild. Just like her.

Her eyes...

It wasn't even the color, but more so the expressions in them. She may have believed she'd hidden herself away, but I could see her. I always saw her.

And damn if she wasn't beautiful.

I didn't think it was possible to have your breath taken away. I'd read about it in books but laughed at how absurd that was.

Yet when she looked at me, I crumbled. With only a look, she had me on my knees.

I palmed my balls before starting at the tip of my cock, using my pre-cum as lubrication. Steadily, I began to jack myself off. Sweat beaded on my forehead, and my breathing was uneven.

Her breasts, bouncing with each breath she took. Those rose-colored nipples just begging to be sucked. That pussy...

Her taste...

I worked myself into a frenzy, cussing up a storm as I reached that pinnacle. That peak. That clifftop, before I flew over—

"WHAT THE FUCK ARE YOU DOING?" a voice yelled in horror. I jumped, removing my hand from my cock and turning to face the intruder.

Bash stood in the doorway, a stunned and slightly disgusted expression on his face, before giving me his back.

"For fuck's sake, man!" he snapped.

Cheeks flaming, I struggled to find something to clean myself up with. Seeing nothing and not wanting to stand with my dick out a moment longer, I wiped it on the edge of my blanket before shoving it back into my pants.

Still painfully hard.

"...have to fucking bleach my eyes out," he was muttering when I finished.

Heat blossomed in my cheeks, embarrassment causing my stutter to come out in all its stutter glory. "W-What-t-t d-do you-u w-wan-nt-t?"

"You dressed, asshole?" he asked, still refusing to look in my direction.

I nodded before remembering he couldn't see me. "Yeah."

He spun on his heel, jabbing a finger into the air as he spoke. "Rule number one for masturbation—you fucking close and lock the door. This wouldn't have happened if you'd done the damn sock rule."

"Sock rule?" I lifted a brow. Was I supposed to masturbate wearing socks? I couldn't see how that would add to the experience, but I was a novice. There was still a lot I had to learn.

"For the love of..." Bash gripped his hair, pulling at the strands. "Just don't fucking masturbate with the door open, man, and don't fucking scream her name!"

Ah. That was the root of the issue.

Bash was jealous.

I tried to hide my smirk as his chest heaved and color rose to his cheeks. It wasn't anger, not entirely, but an envy that ran soul deep.

After all, I hadn't been the one to reject our mate. I hadn't run her away.

I *had* been the one to taste her sweet nectar, feel her heavy mound in my hand, listen to her soft cries...

"Fucking dammit!" Bash kicked at the door frame. "You're thinking about it again! Fucking asshole. Dick. Vagina." What his curses lacked in creativity, they made up for in gusto. "I can't get her fucking body out of my mind! The way she looked when you went down on her. The fucking noises—"

He cut off suddenly, as if aware of what he'd unintentionally admitted to.

I was a sexual creature by nature, and even I was shocked. Motherfucking Bash had *watched*. Bash. Of all people. The same man who spent most of his days having orgies because he hated sitting on the sidelines. He'd watched, and if the heat in his eyes and the tent in his pants was any indication, he'd gotten off on it.

I didn't know whether I wanted to blush or ask him if I'd done a good job. That would probably be weird. Right?

Men did not ask other men if he did a good job sucking on the clit of the girl they had both mated with.

"We're not talking about that," Bash said, for once not sounding smug and confident. I wasn't used to Bash being anything other than a drunk asshole.

Blinking at him, I agreed, "Okay. Sure. Z's orgasm is off the table for discussion. Got it. Not one word on her delicious taste. Or the feel of her nipple."

His eyes narrowed, and I blanched. What the hell had I said now?

Smoothing his features, Bash entered my room fully and went to sit on the bed, grimaced, and then sat in the plush armchair. He kicked his feet up and rested his arms behind his head.

"I talked to my father today, and he gave me some interesting information about our little assassin."

I squinted, wondering if I'd heard him right.

Bash *hated* his father. The only time he would ever willingly talk to him was if he was desperate. After what he'd done...

Anger burned briefly in my stomach before I smothered the flames.

The kings were assholes. It wasn't just known but expected.

If they didn't do one asshole thing a moon cycle, I would question their sanity. And if it wasn't practically psycho, I would assume they were having a good month.

"What did he say?" I stuttered out, mentally cursing my disability.

I hated my stutter, hated how less of a man it made me feel.

Z noticed it, but she never made feel less for it. She reminded me repeatedly that my stutter was a part of me, a part she cared for, and shouldn't be reprimanded.

"Stop with the fucking dreamy smile and listen!" Bash snapped his fingers in front of my face. The asshole was especially moody today.

Probably because he couldn't get hard if his life depended on it.

I smirked, glancing down at my own erect cock. Yup. Still got it.

"For the love of..." Bash jumped from the chair and

hit me on the back of the head. "Stop thinking about your damn dick."

Wincing, I lifted my gaze to him once more.

"Sorry."

"Brothers..." a lilting, musical voice said from the doorway. Cloaked entirely in shadows, features inscrutable, Ryland glided through the door, taking residence in his usual corner of the room. "Did you hear the news?"

"About Z?" Bash asked, quirking a brow. "I was just telling Killian."

I tapped my fingers against my thigh. I couldn't deny that I was worried. Now that she was the official assassin of the kingdom, her life had only gotten worse. She would be forced to fight repeatedly and not just for her life, but for the lives of all the people she hated. The spell Bash's dad placed on her assured that she would not only be loyal, but be compelled to do their bidding.

"What's going on?" I stuttered. My nerves always made my stutter more pronounced. And what was more nerve-racking than hearing dire news about your mate?

Ryland made a noise, as if he was about to speak, but was cut off by Bash's grunt of impatience.

"For fuck's sake! Stop trying to steal my spotlight and let me talk, dammit!"

Even when we were kids, Bash was a drama queen. Nothing changed with age, it seemed.

Ryland chuckled softly from his usual stalker corner.

"A test," Bash blurted, as if afraid Ryland was going to try once more to take over this conversation.

"A test?" I echoed.

He nodded curtly. "One from each of the kings, designed to prove her competence and loyalty to the kingdoms." This was all said with a sardonic twist to his lips. He knew as well as I did that Z held no loyalty to those sick, sadistic bastards. Only the spell would stop her from killing every last one of them.

My hands clenched into fists, knuckles whitening and veins protruding. What type of test would they put into place?

This wasn't a test to prove herself, not really. It was a test designed for her to fail.

"She's heading to the Mermaid Kingdom first," Bash said with a pointed look.

Cold sweat broke out on my skin.

I'd never been to the Mermaid Kingdom before, but I'd heard rumors. They were wolves in sheep's clothing, monsters disguised as humans. They used their siren songs and ethereal good looks to lure you in...before they killed you. The mermaids were cut-throat, each trying to get the upper hand on everyone else. Envy was funny in that respect.

You couldn't just be good. You had to be great.

If you were perfect? They ate you alive.

And if you weren't? You ate yourself alive.

"Do you know what the task is?" I asked Bash urgently. There were thousands of things the mermaid king could ask her to do, each one worse than the last. A pounding headache reverberated behind my eyes, and I brought my hand to my forehead.

Why couldn't fate have given me an easy mate?

As quickly as I thought that, I dismissed it. I didn't

want easy, not anymore. Not after I'd met and held Z. I was even willing to share her, just on the off chance she'd grant me a small piece of her heart. I knew she was capable of it, despite her beliefs. She may not have loved often, but when she did love, she gave everything she had. Being loved by her was worth more than a thousand females, a thousand easy mates.

"No idea," Bash answered. "Ryland?"

"He's planning on announcing it tonight," the shadow answered demurely. No doubt, he was thinking about the same thing I was—the fragility of our human mate.

"We're going with her," I said. It wasn't a question, despite my need for confirmation from the other two. If they weren't joining her, then I would go by myself. Either way, she was not leaving my sight again.

Before they could respond, the door was pushed open and Devlin entered, breathing heavily. My stomach tightened when I caught the heady remains of his lust and desire wafting off of him. Jealousy briefly speared my chest before I pushed it down. I had no right to be jealous of these men, my brothers. Z was their mate just as much as she was mine.

"What's going on?" Bash asked lazily, flicking his eyes towards the genie. There was no missing Devlin's unkempt, disheveled appearance, but if Bash knew the cause of it, he didn't comment. That was a first.

Progress.

"It's Z," Devlin said breathlessly, and my breath left me. Icy dread slithered down my spine.

Danger. Danger. Danger.

That single, repetitive thought hummed through my mind.

"Is she okay?" I asked anxiously. Bash tried to look nonplussed, impassive, but I could see the tightening of his eyes and the stiffening of his shoulders. He had a lot to do to win over our little mate, but I knew he would try.

He just had to get his head out of his ass first.

"I think so..." Devlin trailed off, running his fingers through his curls, a gesture he always did when he was anxious.

"You think so?" Ryland asked darkly, and Devlin jumped. It was surprising he hadn't noticed the shadow when he initially entered the room. He must've been really distracted. Or nervous.

My heart, which had already been beating erratically, now picked up speed.

"She's gone."

Devlin's words doused me in cold water.

"What?" Bash asked, raising a blond brow.

"She's gone," Devlin repeated. His nails dug into the palm of his hand, a coping mechanism he'd done since we were children. "She left."

Z

The air was crisp, unnaturally chilly, as I walked down the dirt streets of my hometown. The skeletal branches of trees clawed at the sky, and wispy clouds did little to block out the sun.

It was a beautiful day, despite the chill, and I couldn't help but smile. Contentment coursed through me in waves.

The last time I'd been back here...

It was when I'd first heard about the Damning. I'd been instructed by B, the leader of the Alphabet Resistance, to kill a mage who'd murdered young children. The mage had been initially selected for the Damning, but when I killed him, the magic had transferred itself to me.

My life had changed dramatically since then. No longer was I merely Z, the poor assassin girl. I was Zara and Susan as well. The competition had brought me to my mates, seven men who I still didn't fully understand, but it had also inevitably led to the death of my best friend and the banishment of the other.

Children giggled, racing past me, and an older woman asked me to sample her freshly baked bread.

Everything was familiar. Simple. Exactly as I remembered it.

But also painfully different.

The girl I'd once been, the girl who'd wandered these streets, was dead. In her place was someone designed to be a killing tool for the monsters I'd once hunted. What would B say if he saw me now? What would S think?

My heart hurt thinking of my dead lover. The pain was softer than it once was, a mere wrenching. It no longer overwhelmed me as it used to. I supposed the saying was true—time healed broken hearts and all that shit.

A smile, unbidden, broke free when I caught sight of a small bakery. It was in there, surrounded by the pervasive scent of stale bread and cheeses, that I'd met Devlin. I remembered his violet eyes glimmering with barely suppressed amusement. The curve of his lips. Those soft curls I desperately wanted to run my fingers through.

The smile left my face when I stopped in front of a dilapidated house, ivy and vines clawing upwards. The windows had been broken, and graffiti covered every spare inch of cream-colored walling.

It was in this house that I'd first confessed my love to S.

It was in this house that I'd watched him die.

Trembling, I burrowed my face further into my coat, inhaling the unique, pine scent I'd come to associate with

Lupe. I hadn't even realized I'd stolen his coat until I was already in town. Not that he would mind.

"What are you looking at?" a voice whispered in my ear, and I screamed, spinning with my hands raised.

A vampire stood inches from me, hot breath fanning my face. He had short brown hair and a handsome, chiseled face.

I recognized him. The vampire who I'd dreamt about. The vampire who'd crawled into my bed with me.

The vampire I'd allowed to crawl into my bed with me.

From what little I'd gathered from the other princes, this was my mate. Jax.

But of course, we'd never been properly introduced.

He stared at me as intensely as I stared at him.

"It tingles," he whispered hoarsely, scratching at his arm.

I raised my brow before understanding dawned. According to lore, when a vampire met his mate, his skin began to itch. It was what had happened to Mali when she first came into contact with Atta...and Zack.

"It tingles. My blood tingles like fairies spelled me. Why won't it stop?" Almost absently, his nails dug into his skin, hard enough to draw blood. It was only then that I noticed the numerous scars adorning his pale arm.

Did he do that to himself?

Horror filled me, immediately dissipating any ill feelings or fears I felt towards the vampire. I grabbed at his hand, the one scratching his skin, and held it between both of mine.

"Stop that!" I demanded.

He froze, muscles contracting, before his eyes met mine. They were alight with wonder and awe. Reverence. All of which I didn't deserve.

"Z?" he croaked out. As if he couldn't help himself, he reached with his free hand and brushed at my mane of curls. It took him a few tries, since his hand kept shaking, but finally, he was able to push a lock of my golden tresses behind my ear.

"Jax?" I said his name hesitantly. For the first time, there was coherence in his eyes. It was as if the pieces to the puzzle clicked. He stared at me as if I held all the answers to his questions, as if I were shrouded in a golden light.

Instantly, self-consciousness filled me, and I stepped away.

The coherence disappeared from his eyes immediately, and he, too, stepped back.

"I have five fingers on one hand. Four on the other. Five plus four equals nine. And nine is the number. I heard the devils talking. Five plus four equals nine. Nine fingers. We need nine fingers," he rambled, pulling at his hair. His eyes flitted from my face, to my shoes, to the building behind me, before resting once more on me. This time, he didn't meet my eyes. He seemed to be looking anywhere but.

When his eyes lowered to my cleavage, I knew he didn't mean it as sexual. He was just desperate for something, anything, to stare at.

What the hell had happened to him?

"The voices keep talking. And talking. And talking." In a blur of movements, he whacked his closed fist against his head. "Stupid. They call me stupid. But I need them to stop."

Tears welled in his eyes, and he finally met my gaze pleadingly. "Please make it stop."

We were garnering attention from the humans and the few Nightmares scattered about. Frowning, I gripped Jax's hand and pulled him into the house. As I stepped over the threshold, taking in the empty room and peeling wallpaper, the memories didn't bombard me as they once would've. They would no doubt come in time, but right now, I needed to focus on Jax.

He'd stopped babbling and now followed me wordlessly into a room that once served as a living room. There was only one window, facing the alleyway, so I didn't have to be afraid we would be looked in on. Surprisingly, the ugly floral couch S had bought still sat in the center of the room, collecting dust on the silver tarp. I'd thought for sure it would've been stolen or destroyed.

Releasing Jax's hand, I removed the tarp, coughing at the onslaught of dust particles hanging stagnant in the air.

"Sit," I instructed Jax. He muttered something under his breath, something about toenails, before tentatively perching himself on the edge of the couch. He held himself rigid, back straight, as if he feared what his proximity would do to me. I appreciated his consideration.

There was no denying I was still wary around nightmares.

"Um..." What did one say to an obviously crazed

vampire? I couldn't just damn well ask if he wanted a refreshment.

The thought made me snort out a laugh. I pictured myself bleeding over a coffee cup, a serene smile on my face as I discussed mundane things like the weather with the Crowned Prince of the Vampires.

"The voices whisper," Jax said urgently. He shifted closer, his knee a hair's breadth away.

"The voices?" I asked slowly.

One thing was becoming abundantly clear—Jax needed help. More help than someone like me, a mere human with no substantial knowledge of the nightmare world, could give him.

"Nine fingers. Five fingers plus four fingers equals nine fingers."

"Jax," I said soothingly. I was momentarily startled by my own voice. When had I ever sounded that... loving? "I don't understand what you're saying. You have ten fingers. See?" I took his hand, absently stroking each finger. Once I reached the tenth, I dropped his hand.

He let out a grunt of impatience.

Speaking slowly, deliberately, as if talking to a child, he repeated, "Five plus four equals nine."

He reached for my hand once more, and I let him, mentally reveling in how small he made me feel. How delicate. His calloused hand engulfed my little one. That wasn't to say I didn't have calluses and scars of my own, because I did, but he made me feel...vulnerable. Innocent.

His breath left him, and his ramblings ceased. He

stared down at our clasped hands, several emotions flashing across his face—shock, astonishment, excitement.

Clarity.

"Did I ever tell you that I hate being what I am? Who I am? Or is it whom?" I rambled. Putting a finger to my chin, I waited a beat before continuing. Outside, the rasping wind toyed with the shutters, opening and closing them at intermittent intervals. "Did you notice how many people were outside? How many doors? How many windows? How many vehicles?"

His nose crinkled adorably. That was not a word I would normally associate with any male, least of all a nightmare, but it fit him.

"Who would notice that?" he asked somewhat dazedly.

"Twenty-four people. Seven doors. Eighteen windows. Two vehicles," I said, ticking them off on my fingers. "It's my job to see everything. To know every-thing. To hear everything. And..." I shrugged helplessly. "It's daunting."

"Daunting?" he parroted. Once more, that delicate brown eyebrow arched.

"Daunting," I said with a firm nod. "I feel like I have the weight of the world on my shoulders, now more so than ever." Throwing my head back, I released a humor-less laugh. Jax continued to watch me, eyes narrowed, but didn't interrupt. "I hated you guys for as long as I could remember. The seven princes. Now look at me. You guys are my mates."

The world really did have a sick sense of humor.

His thumb swiped against my knuckles, the barest of

grazes, as he stared upwards. His expression was almost contemplative, as if he were attempting to solve a difficult chemistry formula. After a moment, he lowered his head and met my eyes. I couldn't quite read the expression on his face.

"I understand what you're saying," he said after a long moment of silence. It wasn't uncomfortable by any means. Just long.

"Huh?" I asked.

A brilliant grin took over his face. "I understand what you mean," he repeated. And then he laughed, a jovial sound that went straight to my core. "Tell me more!"

The poor vamp really had lost his mind.

At a loss for words, I gestured around me with my free hand.

"I used to live in this house," I admitted.

"Did you, my love?" he asked, that smile still firmly in place.

What was even happening?

It felt...natural speaking with Jax. As if we were long-time friends instead of virtual strangers. I knew it was the mate bond causing that inherent reaction, but it still unnerved me. It wasn't normal to feel this comfortable with a vampire.

Then again, nothing about my life had ever been normal.

"With S," I said with a nod. It no longer hurt to say his name.

I envisioned his face then, eyes crinkling with his smile and his shock of brown hair.

"S..." Jax said the name, face twisting oddly. It wasn't

jealousy necessarily, I wasn't sure if he was even capable of feeling such a normal emotion, but something that made me almost suspicious. "Was that your human lover?"

"I don't want to talk about him," I said stiffly. Maybe I should. Maybe I should air my dirty laundry for the entire world to see. Maybe I should tell him I killed the last man I loved and to stay clear of me.

I should...but I was selfish.

From outside, muted voices reached me. Their words were mostly inarticulate, but I managed to gather a few important words and phrases.

Z. Prince Jax. Aaliyah.

Releasing Jax's hand, I jumped like my body was on fire. Before he could protest, I grabbed the blade out of my shirt sleeve and held it up, aiming it towards the door.

"Monsters are coming," Jax whispered softly. He began to mutter under his breath, but I no longer heard him. Instead, I focused on the door. Waiting.

Ready.

It blew off its hinges, shattering against the back wall.

A young man entered, eyes livid and a cruel grin on his face. Immediately, I catalogued him as a mage.

He lifted his hand, and I was thrown across the room, back ricocheting off the wood. Pain erupted in my spine, but I shakily got back to my feet.

There were a few rules when fighting a mage, but I only ever focused on one.

Take him out as soon as possible.

The longer you remained fighting, the more power he was able to collect and use. Mages, unless they were using potions and talismans, relied heavily on internal magic. They could gather this magic from anything— nature, sex, blood. It all depended on the type of magic they wielded. It was for this reason, I suspected, that a mage couldn't get erect after he'd come into contact with his mate. The powers that be didn't want them replenishing their magic with anyone other than their fated mate.

Before the asshole could draw more power into him, I charged forward, knife raised. Quickly, I slammed the blade into his shoulder. I'd meant to hit his heart, but he'd moved at the last second.

Grunting, he pulled the dagger out of his skin, blood dripping down the blade. I kneed him in the stomach, simultaneously reaching for my second dagger in my other sleeve.

Dimly, I was aware of Jax fighting against two vampires behind me. With vampires the rules were different—don't get too close, especially if you were human. One blow to the head with a vampire's strength had the capacity to decapitate you.

"What does Aaliyah want with me?" I asked, blocking each blow. I had no doubt the she-bitch had sent them like she'd sent Zack. He swiped a knife at me, the knife I'd used on him, and I deftly backed out of its offending arc.

Balancing the copper handle of my second knife in my palm, holding it the way one would hold a violin bow, I jabbed it into his stomach when I saw an opening. He grunted, doubling over.

"Why are you fighting?" he hissed, slamming an

elbow into my side. I made an *oomf* sound, pain coursing through me in tangible waves.

And the asshole wondered why I was fighting?

We parried, each consecutive hit causing my strength to wane. There was always one immense problem when fighting nightmares—they were supernatural beings, descended from the Devil himself, and I was only human.

A particularly hard hit sent me staggering backwards, landing on a pile of cut glass.

His hair was blowing rapidly in a breeze I couldn't feel, his power manifesting itself physically. I knew I was seconds away from dying...or whatever else was going to happen to me. This Aaliyah chick was persistent, I'd give her that.

I snapped my eyes shut, awaiting the inevitable pain, before I heard a cuss and a gurgle. Unbidden, one eye opened as I took in the room. Almost immediately, I saw Jax, panting heavily. Two vampires lay dead at his feet. He looked unscathed, thankfully, but slightly tired.

But it wasn't him who'd saved me.

My eyes flickered past the mage, now spitting out blood as his hands desperately grabbed at his throat. He fell to his knees, eyes blank, before falling over.

Dead.

T smiled at me, spinning a long katana sword.

"Well, well, well. What do we have here, little sister?"

FIVE

Z

T smiled at me, showcasing row after row of perfectly white teeth.

He was handsome, with auburn hair and two dimples that appeared when he smiled. It also didn't hurt that he looked similar to his brother, S.

Despite the similarities, T and I had never had a romantic relationship. Maybe, at one point, we each had feelings for the other, but they never happened at the same time. He quickly became a close friend of mine, if not a brother figure to me.

Seeing him standing there, a singularly beautiful smile lighting up his face and blood dripping down the sword he held, caused my own grin to widen.

"T," I whispered, pulling myself off the ground and wrapping my arms around him. He staggered under my weight before returning my hug enthusiastically. His arms comforted me, warmth emanating in palpable waves through his black shirt and skintight jeans. Just as quickly as he grabbed me, he released me, shoving me behind him. He raised his katana and brandished it threateningly.

At Jax.

My vampire mate's head was tilted curiously to the side. His wild eyes flickered from my face to T's and then to the body on the ground, never staying on one area longer than a second. His perfect, cherry red lips tilted up.

"I see there is a dead body," he mused, carefully stepping over said dead body. Before I could scream—whether it would've been directed at Jax to stop moving or T not to hurt him, I didn't know—T exploded. My fingers feebly grasped at air as he charged at Jax, knocking him to the ground.

"STOP!" I screamed, running forward and grabbing T's shoulder. The sword paused mere centimeters from Jax's neck.

T threw me a bewildered look over his shoulder.

"Don't hurt him," I said, kneeling down. My hand, with a life of its own, stroked Jax's hair. My eyes catalogued each and every injury on his body, mentally planning how I would make the already dead vampires pay. There were two bruises on both of his arms and a nasty cut beneath his eye. His leg oozed blood, but I was unable to see the extent of that injury. Other than that, he appeared fine, if not slightly confused with the sword dangerously close to his artery.

There were only a few ways you could kill a vampire, but a beheading was one of them. Most nightmares were able to heal themselves, particularly shifters and vampires, who had a higher resilience against certain weapons. But a head shot? Even a heart shot?

Fatal.

I didn't want to think of that word. And I didn't want to think of *why* I didn't want to think of that word.

"Who the hell is he?" T asked, but he finally relented and removed his katana, placing it in the sheath behind his back once more. Jax's breaths sawed in and out, and he scrambled backwards, away from the offending object. He began to mutter under his breath, words inarticulate. I could've sworn I heard him whisper a name, a female's name, and jealousy roared inside of me. I quickly smothered that emotion down, focusing instead on T.

"His name is Jax," I said breezily, willing him to drop the topic. Unfortunately, I'd never been that lucky. T's eyes widened imperceptibly, face tightening. It didn't take long for understanding to dawn, and his expression turned from contemplative to murderous. I was unfamiliar with seeing such an emotion on his face...directed at me.

"Jax," he repeated snidely. "As in, the Prince of Vampires?" Without waiting for me to respond, he advanced on me. "The one you were supposed to fucking kill?"

Well, when he put it like that...

"It's complicated," I said, hating how much of an excuse those words seemed to be. But what else could I say? It *was* complicated. This mission went from being black and white to many shades of grey. No, not grey. The world had suddenly turned colorful, like a brilliant rainbow obscuring my vision. I hadn't realized how long

I'd been living in the darkness, seeing things through tunnel vision. S's death had killed me, but slowly, these men—my mates—were piecing me back together.

And I fucking hated it.

"It's complicated," T mocked. He ran a trembling hand through his hair. With a shuddering breath, he focused back on me. "Where's Diego? And where's Mali?"

His words were the wakeup call I needed. Immediately, my muscles tensed and my hands clenched into fists. Try as I might, all I repeatedly saw was the blade meant for me running through Diego's chest. The tears in Mali's eyes as she realized her mate had killed one of her best friends. The fear contaminating the air.

"Fuck," T whispered, reading my expression without me having to say a word. "I'm so sorry, Z."

Instinctively, he reached for me.

And instinctively, Jax pounced.

The vampire stood between me and T, eyes blazing. T staggered back a step, and his hand gripped the hilt of his sword.

"Don't touch her," Jax hissed. I couldn't see his face, but he held his body rigidly. The muscles in his back jumped as I placed my hand placatingly on his shoulder.

"Jax, it's okay," I whispered soothingly, aware that T was watching our exchange with narrowed eyes. "He's not going to hurt me."

Jax's breathing was heavy, erratic, and he still did not relax. It was moments like that when I remembered Jax wasn't just my mate, but a predator. A nightmare. A vampire. His entire species was designed to hunt and kill prey. He was the monster that would hide in the shadows, lurk beneath beds, sink its fangs into unsuspecting humans.

It was times like that when I remembered he wasn't human.

Stories had one fact wrong.

Vampires *were* able to stand in sunlight, despite contrary belief. They just preferred the darkness. No one knew for certain, but it was rumored that their powers became stronger at night, under the watchful eye of the moon. Not even Mali could confirm or deny this. The rumor solely focused on the royal family. For normal vampires, night or day didn't make a difference.

As the sunlight streamed through the window, highlighting the golden streaks in Jax's hair and the muscles accentuated beneath his thin shirt, I wondered if those rumors were true. In the day, Jax was powerful, a beast of a man just waiting to run rampant on the unsuspecting population. I couldn't even imagine him with more power.

A hiss escaped him, even as his body leaned further against mine, seeking my comfort. T's eyes fixed on that diminutive movement, and his brows drew together.

T wasn't stupid. He could read between the lines easily enough. He might not have known the extent of my relationship with Jax or any of the princes, but he could see that something was up.

Without a word, he dropped his katana to the ground, followed by the daggers he always kept in his sheaths. Weaponless, he held his hands up like a prisoner approaching an officer.

"I'm not going to hurt her," T said soothingly. Despite speaking to Jax, his eyes remained fixed on me. "I care about her."

Jax growled low in his throat, and I curled my body against his, pressing my cheek to his back.

I didn't know why I did that. I wasn't the *cuddling* type, but something about Jax called to me. It could've been how broken he was, or it could've been the damn mate bond. Either way, I hated seeing him distressed.

"Not like that," T said, reading something in Jax's expression I couldn't see. "Like a sister. I care about her like a sister."

"Jax," I whispered into his ear. At my voice, his body wilted against mine like a neglected flower. I wrapped my arms around him, holding him to me from behind. "Calm your ass down."

Not the most romantic statement, but it seemed to work. Jax turned in my arms, blinking down at me rapidly. I hesitantly reached to grab his wrist, my fingers brushing bare skin. The fog receded from his eyes, and a tentative smile touched his lips.

"Are you okay?" he asked.

I reached up to trace the cut beneath his eye, ignoring T's snort of disgust.

"I'm fine. What about you?"

Before Jax could respond, the window shattered, glass piercing the opposite wall. I jumped, even as both Jax and T moved to stand in front of me.

I grabbed a dagger off the dead mage's person, facing the now opened window. I didn't know what I expected to see, but it wasn't a creature with dark green skin, leaves for hair, and a circular mouth showcasing large, sharp teeth.

"What the hell is that?" T whispered, echoing my own thought. The figure didn't walk into the room. No, it *crawled,* abnormally long arms and legs supporting a small body.

The creature was unlike anything I'd ever seen before. It wasn't a mage or a shifter. It wasn't a vampire, an incubus, or a shadow. It wasn't a genie or a mermaid.

It was something else, something other, something that instilled fear deep in my heart.

The creature lunged at us, mouth opened, and I stealthily sidestepped out of its path. Jax was not as lucky, falling to the ground as the creature pounced on him. T raised his sword, slamming it into the monster's side. For most creatures, it would've been a killing blow.

However, it merely raised its head, eyes glinting like rubies in the dim lighting, before pulling the blade from its skin. Black blood gushed out of the hole.

"That wasn't supposed to happen," T mumbled, already reaching for his dagger on the ground.

Jax bucked beneath the creature's weight, propelling it off and against the wall using his vampiric strength. The entire house shook as it slid down the wall, blinking its red eyes wildly.

"They come from the trees," Jax whispered. His shirt was in tatters, hideous gashes from the creature's claws taking up the majority of his chest. I gasped at the sight, my protective instincts rearing.

Without thinking twice, I charged at the creature. It roared, those keen teeth inches from my face. I avoided its clawed hand, rolling out of the way. Just as it came after me a second time, I lifted my dagger and jammed it through where I assumed its heart was.

It released a roar but didn't let up its assault. Blow after blow was delivered to me, but I parried each one. It pounced on me, snapping its jaw inches from my neck. I let out a cry as its rancid breath polluted the air around me. My nose began to bleed, but I couldn't lift a hand to scrub it away.

The creature froze suddenly, teeth inches from my bare skin, before its head was ripped from its body. Black blood coated my skin, my clothes, my hair, and I blinked rapidly.

What the hell just happened?

Lupe stood above me, eyes feral as he held the creature's head in his clawed hands. His face was contorted, fur growing on his forehead and cheeks.

"What the hell is that thing?" Devlin. I would recognize his voice anywhere.

My genie mate was kneeling beside Jax, checking him over for injuries. Killian and Bash stood in the doorway, eyes wide and wary, while Dair had rolled his wheelchair to T. I didn't spot Ryland, but I knew he would be in one of the corners, a constant shadow.

"It shouldn't be possible," Jax was mumbling, sitting up.

"What shouldn't be possible?" Bash asked, voice tight with irritation. And disgust.

Pretty boy probably didn't want to get blood on his new shoes.

"He's right." Lupe's voice was a growl, his bear still

fighting for control. He took a calming breath, reeling himself back in, and I watched in rapt fascination as his face changed once more. Gone was the beast, and in its place was a handsome prince.

I felt something touch my forehead, checking me for injuries, and I smiled reassuringly at Killian, wiping the blood from my nose on my sleeve. Bash still stood in the doorway, arms crossed over his chest.

"Will you stop speaking in riddles and tell us what the hell happened?" he barked, and I resisted the urge to roll my eyes.

I'd been the one mere inches from death, and Bash was the one demanding answers.

"This right here is a fae," Lupe answered dizzily. Face twisting with disgust, he dropped the head onto the ground. It rolled, landing an inch away from T.

"Fae?" I parroted. I'd heard the word before, had read about them in history books. Lupe must've been mistaken. "The fae have been extinct for hundreds of years."

"They're coming back," Jax muttered beneath his breath. "They're all coming back."

Ignoring him, Lupe focused on me. The hardness in his features softened when he took stock of me. I could see instant relief when he spotted no new injuries.

"What are you saying?" Killian asked, wrapping an arm around my shoulder. I shoved him away, ignoring the flash of hurt in his eyes, before scrambling to my feet. I didn't want to look weak with the seven princes surrounding me, regardless of them being my mates.

"What he's saying is impossible," Bash snapped like

the asshole he was. From my history lessons, I knew that there were once hundreds of other supernatural creatures, each descended from lesser known demons. When the Seven Deadly Sins came to the world, they eliminated all of them, determined to be the most powerful creatures on the planet. Besides the humans, of course.

They needed someone to be their slaves.

"Are you saying that I was just attacked by an extinct supernatural creature?" I asked in disbelief. I couldn't even begin to wrap my head around it. My eyes fixed once more on the dead fae, if it even was that. For all I knew, it could've been a shifter or something in disguise. Anything seemed like a more rational explanation.

Lupe's jaw clenched. "I don't know."

T's voice had us all turning towards him. I could see my mates stiffening, muscles flexing dangerously as they surveyed the human. T, for his part, looked more annoyed than scared, though there was still a healthy dose of fear in his eyes. He lifted his hand as if he were in a classroom.

"Please, for the love of all things holy, tell me what is going on?" Turning towards me, he quirked an eyebrow. "Z, my dear sister, you have a lot of explaining to do."

Z

By the time we made it to the small, bungalow style house T had been staying at, the sun had fallen, disappearing behind boughs of trees.

My mates were uncharacteristically quiet, sullen almost, as we skirted past the remnants of an old school. Vines and ivy crawled up the brick sides, and the windows had long since been shattered. I spotted a tree growing from one of the windows, its branches wrapping around the huge white pillars adorning either side of the entryway.

As T scurried ahead, barely sparing us a glance, I turned towards Dair, who was wheeling himself beside me. His forearms strained as we climbed the steep hill, blond hair glinting in the waning sunlight. He was so handsome, so perfect, that my breath caught.

"Don't pity me," he murmured softly. We'd somehow found ourselves in the middle of the group. Bash and Jax walked in front of us, eyes warily fixed on T as if he were a monster they needed to smite. Devlin, Killian, and

Lupe held up the rear. And Ryland? Who the hell knew where he went. Probably lurking on a tree branch or something.

"Pity?" I echoed, raising a brow.

Dair's handsome face pinched slightly—a furrow of his brow, a crease between his eyes, the scrunch of his nose. It was an expression I was beginning to read easily on my mermaid prince, one that hinted at the unease he wished to remain hidden. But he couldn't hide things from me, whether or not he liked it. I was his mate, dammit, the other half of his soul.

Releasing a breath, Dair continued to roll himself up the incline, his powerful muscles bulging with each movement.

"I'm not stupid," he said quietly, succinctly. "Everybody looks at me like that."

"Like what?"

Like they want to jump his fine ass? Because if that was the case, I might get a little stabby.

"Like they feel bad for me." His voice was resigned, holding no anger or resentment. It was as if he were reciting a fact, like the color of the sky. My heart clenched. "And it's funny. I never considered myself lesser because of my disability. I never considered myself as anything other than a person." His tongue snuck out to wet his lips, and my eyes fixated on that seemingly innocent movement. "I'm used to it, you know. The pitying stares. The whispers. The disgust. It's rare to see a nightmare with a disability, let alone a prince. I never asked to be confined to this damn chair."

As if the universe had a twisted sense of humor, even

more so than I originally thought. his wheel got caught on a particularly sharp rock. He murmured something unintelligible beneath his breath, desperately attempting to maneuver his chair over this obstacle.

"Let me—" I took an automatic step forward, arms extended to push him farther, but he leveled me with a glare. It hardened his features. Instead of the angelic prince I once thought him to be, he looked dangerous, every inch the nightmare prince I'd originally imagined.

"I've got it!" he snapped. Though his tone wasn't belligerent, it wasn't kind. In those three words, I could hear years of pent-up anger and aggression. Not directed at me, I knew innately that he would never harm me, but at the world. At the injustice. At the unfairness of being stuck in a chair while the rest of us were able to run and walk and dance. I could see it all clearly.

Devlin stepped up behind me and placed a hand on my shoulder. He quirked a brow, glancing from me to Dair. At his unasked question, I nodded for him to go on ahead. He hesitated only a moment before kissing my cheek and following Killian and Lupe farther up the path.

The overprotective fools leaned against a tree, far enough away where they weren't in hearing distance but close enough to jump to my rescue if the need arose.

As if I would need them to rescue me. They were sorely mistaken if they thought I was the damsel in this story. Hell, in Killian's case, I'd saved him more often than not.

Shaking my head, I focused back on Dair, who was still struggling to move his chair. It might've been the mate bond speaking, but I knew he needed me. To talk to him. To comfort him. To do whatever the hell it was mates did.

"I don't think you're lesser, Dair," I said hesitantly. My fingers thrummed against each other, desperate for something to do. I never knew I would be the type to twiddle my thumbs, but there I was, twiddling my damn thumbs.

Feeling ridiculous, I grabbed my dagger out of my waistband and spun it between my fingers.

Much better.

"What can I do?" Dair murmured bitterly, self-loathing evident in his voice. "I can't protect you like the others. I'm not as smart as Lupe. I don't have history with you like Devlin. I'm not awkwardly adorable like Killian."

I snorted, endeared at hearing Dair call my incubus prince awkwardly adorable.

He smiled softly at me before his smile faded. "I just..." With a growl, he shoved at the wheels once more.

"Dair..." Tentatively, I crouched down beside him. I didn't know quite what to say or how to comfort him. In my past relationships, I'd never focused on feelings. That wasn't to say that I didn't have that, because I did, but I never needed to talk about my emotions.

But Dair wasn't Devlin or S, and I cared about him just as much. Different types of relationships required different efforts.

"Look..."

"Z!" T poked his head out of the doorway, ignoring the growl from Lupe. And myself, if I was being honest. There I was, trying to be all serious and romantic and shit, and my ex's brother had to go and ruin it.

Snapping my teeth at him, I shouted, "What?"

"You have a visitor!"

I frowned, sifting through the people I knew in my life who could possibly be visiting me in the middle of fucking nowhere. Frankly, I wasn't the most friendly person. The list was small.

"I don't have any friends!" I retorted. Bash, leaning against the fence of the old school, snorted out a laugh, and I gave him my finger.

"Go ahead," Dair said tiredly to me, nodding towards the house wearily. Still, he flashed me a smile, though it didn't reach his eyes.

"Dair..." I murmured, hating his attitude. There was probably some profound saying that could be used to help him, something about changing his outlook on life, but I couldn't articulate it without sounding like an imbecile. Instead, I settled for awkwardly patting him on the shoulder.

He blanched, and I internally groaned.

Fucking shit. I sucked at this whole mate thing.

My thought process was interrupted by a willowy man appearing in the doorway. Lupe snarled, claws extending, and Devlin's eyes burned a brilliant violet. Even Bash raised his hands, an incantation on his lips.

The man was short, smaller than even me, with a shock of dark hair and tanned skin. He wore wire-framed glasses that slid down his nose and skintight jeans.

His eyes slid over the men without sticking before focusing on me. He nodded his head once in what I supposed was a nod of solidarity. Even so, my throat clogged tight with emotion.

"Come," he said briskly. "I made tea."

When no one seemed inclined to move, he grabbed a dagger out of his waistband and tossed it in the air. It flew, hitting a tree trunk inches from Killian's head. The incubus stared wide-eyed at the protruding dagger before whipping his head to face the tiny little man and then focusing back on the dagger once more. He turned his helpless eyes onto me.

I shrugged.

"The man said he made tea."

Ignoring Dair's protest that he didn't need my help, I lifted the chair over the rock and wheeled him the short distance to the tiny house.

"HH," I murmured, instantly wrapping my arms around the smaller man. He stiffened imperceptibly, and I immediately pulled back. "Sorry."

"HH?" Killian asked, a red eyebrow raising. "Diego's...?"

He didn't need to finish his sentence.

Diego's mate.

Who no doubt felt the exact moment Diego died. Had felt the life bleed from his one true love.

Heart tightening and stomach plummeting, I walked inside the sparsely furnished room. Aside from a sleeping bag in the corner and a pile of canned fruit, the main room was empty. T was currently sitting on the sleeping bag, sorting through the collection of food.

"Is this where you're staying?" I asked in disbelief. T barely looked up.

"Yup."

"Why?" Why not at the headquarters? I wanted to ask but remained tight-lipped. I trusted my mates to an extent, but they were loyal to the kings first and foremost. I didn't know if that loyalty would exceed their loyalty to me.

T met my eyes with understanding.

"Mali visited our house," he murmured. And by house, he meant the compound that housed the resistance. It couldn't be called a building, since it was located deep beneath the ground in a series of tunnels. A part of me missed the dripping gray walls and sparse lighting the farther you ventured through the labyrinth.

"Mali?" I whispered hoarsely. I didn't know why saying her name hurt as badly as it did. But damn, that stung like a bitch. I rubbed at my heart as if that could somehow soothe the ache her absence caused me. "What happened?"

"What do you think?" T continued his perusal of the food, voice dry. "B kicked her out. I didn't know why at the time. I kind of assumed she'd wanted to stay with you and B hadn't allowed her to, so they argued and B booted her."

I wasn't surprised, not entirely, but it still hurt to hear. Where would she go? She was considered a traitor to her own kind.

The vampires would never accept her back, and the humans would love nothing more than to hunt her.

"And then what happened?" I asked.

He sighed heavily, but was saved from explaining by HH returning. He carried a tray with ten teacups and a kettle. Without a word, he placed the tray on the table and began pouring tea into the cute, ceramic cups.

Bash held it up distastefully, lips curling.

"It's not poisoned, is it?" he asked. HH leveled him with a long, impossible to read look. Almost absently, his hand rested on his dagger's hilt.

The meaning was clear—drink the fucking tea.

"Is the big, bad mage afraid of a little tea?" I sang mockingly. Bash tossed me an acrimonious glare before downing the drink in one go. HH watched him impassively.

"The poison should take effect in five minutes," he deadpanned, handing the next drink on the tray to Lupe.

The expression on Bash's face as he sputtered, brown tea dripping down his chin? Priceless.

T chortled, and I threw back my own head in laughter. The rest of my mates were glancing at me as if I had lost my mind.

"He's fucking with you," I assured Bash, though a part of me really wanted to see what he would do.

Bash wiped his mouth with the back of his hand. "That's not very nice," he muttered, and his petulant attitude only made me laugh harder. He flicked a fireball at me, and I let out a screech as it heated my ass.

HH handed me my own cup before sitting down beside T on the small bedroll.

"Anyway," T murmured, getting back on track. I remained standing, my mates surrounding me. If HH was shocked to see the seven princes with me, he didn't show it. I wouldn't have been surprised, however, if Diego had found a way to communicate with him ahead of time about my predicament. "We were attacked. About a week ago."

"Attacked?" I asked, gasping. "What happened?"

"Nightmares. Dozens of them." T's eyes flickered warily to the men behind me, but he continued talking doggedly. "Slaughtered everyone. Women. Children."

I could see the anguish in his eyes, the agony, and I knew my own eyes were a mirror image. I could also see the guilt brewing just below the surface. His next words confirmed as much.

"I was on a mission when I got the message," he said softly. His eyes latched onto something over my shoulder. I could tell he didn't want to meet my eyes, didn't want to see the pity in my gaze. The anger. The pain. "By the time I arrived..."

HH nodded stoutly. He didn't have to say anything for me to know his story would be somewhat similar. In all actuality, he was probably on his way to the capital to find Diego. Or at the very least, his body.

"The survivors got separated," T said. "With the numerous safe houses throughout the area, I was lucky I was able to come into contact with HH. We've been visiting each house in the hopes of finding more survivors. He hadn't told me about Mali and..."

And Diego.

He gave me a knowing stare, and I nodded. That was how he'd found me. The house S and I had lived at, the house we'd made our own, was now a safe house for the resistance. An unused one, by the look of it.

"Are we going to talk about what happened back there?" Devlin cut in crisply. Even after the fight, he was as impeccably dressed as always in an ironed black suit and white collared shirt. His dark curls were brushed away from his face.

"About this supposed fae attacking us?" T murmured bitterly.

"Not attacking us," Dair countered. "Attacking Z."

At this turn of conversation, HH dropped his teacup, eyes sparking with interest. It was the first genuine emotion I'd seen on his face since I arrived.

"Are you sure that was a fae?" Bash drawled, and Lupe nodded.

"I would have to do more research, but yes, I'm sure. Nearly positive."

I wasn't surprised. Despite looking like a lumbering giant, Lupe was nothing more than a giant teddy bear. Literally. As in, he was a big ass bear when he shifted.

He also preferred hiding away in his library instead of facing the world head-on. It was a shock to see him kill that creature in the first place, to put it mildly. Lupe was a lover, not a fighter.

I knew that a shifter's protective instincts went into overdrive when their mate was involved, but to see it in person was overwhelming. I hoped he would grow out of it and fast. I didn't need some man to protect me, someone I barely knew but who thought they knew what was right for me. I still hadn't decided what I was going to do about these mating bonds, but you could bet your ass I wouldn't put up with being kept locked away like some dainty princess.

If he wanted a princess, he could have one. That would never be me.

Realizing my thoughts had drifted from the conversation, I focused on the matter at hand.

Lupe was arguing with Bash over the logistics of an extinct supernatural creature coming back from the dead. I heard words like "colonies" and "possibilities" as well as curse words from Bash ranging from "anal plug" to "ass wiping vagina."

And then I heard a soft murmuring, directly behind me.

"They live in trees. They live in trees. They live in trees."

"Jax?" I whispered, taking a step closer to the vampire. His wild eyes rapidly moved around the room in a calculating manner, and he continued to mutter nonsense beneath his breath.

"Not nonsense," Ryland whispered in my ear, and I shivered. The shadow moved with grace until he was directly beside me, his fingers interlocked with my own. Until that moment, I hadn't even realized I was thinking out loud.

"Then what the hell is he saying?" I asked him, eyes locked on Jax. He began to pace, running a hand through his short brown hair in agitation. With each word, his voice grew louder and louder until he was almost screaming, garnering the attention of the rest of the men in the room. "Jax," I whispered, taking a step closer. Ryland moved with me until we were face-to-face with the erratic vampire. His wide eyes pleaded with me, but for what, I couldn't discern.

"They live in trees," he said earnestly.

"The fae?"

"That's true," Lupe murmured from behind me. "I remember reading about that in one of my books. I'd have to look at it in more detail..." He trailed off, mind already wandering to what new discovery he could make.

"Not nonsense," Ryland repeated. He gave my fingers a quick squeeze. "Jaxie here knows more than he lets on. We just need to figure out a way to get the information out of him."

SEVEN

LUPE

The library was my favorite room in the entire capital.

It was a good combination of old and modern, elegant and simple. Three-tiered chandeliers shone down on the mahogany shelves. Row after row of dusty, centuries-old books sat on the distressed wood, their spines creased and faded with age. It carried the pervasive scent of old books—a heady mixture of dust and mold.

Still, the library was my sanctuary, my escape. In the shelves, with sunlight streaming through the floor to ceiling windows, I felt like I was home.

I perched myself on the wooden bench of one of the tables, a stack of books piled high. The librarian had been quite helpful when I had inquired about ancient texts and mythological studies. After a moment of careful perusal, she handed me a stack the size of my arm. Throughout the day, she'd repeatedly added to the pile.

My eyelids drooped heavily, fatigue and hunger

dominating me. Still, I charged on, my eyes rapidly moving over the faded text.

"You need a break," a soft, familiar voice said from behind me. Electricity coursed through my veins at her presence. Her distinct scent of roses and pomegranates wafted to my nose, and I inhaled deeply. I would never admit to anyone my obsession with her smell, least of all to her. She would think I was weird, or at the very least, weirder than she already perceived me as. Still, I couldn't help but inhale deeply as she ventured forward.

"No break," I muttered gruffly, focusing back on my latest text. It was an old mythological book, written before the Seven Deadly Sins appeared on Earth, that detailed the supposed supernatural creatures on the Earth. Of course, everything was merely a theory. Humans hadn't known about the supernatural world at the time this was written.

Z was silent, and I was afraid she'd left.

A moment later, a small hand rested on my shoulder, followed by a steaming bowl of soup. I glanced at her in surprise...and more than a little bit of disbelief. I couldn't remember the last time someone had taken care of me. My mother had died when I was a child, and my father hadn't been the nurturing type of parent.

"Eat," she said stiffly, crossing her arms over her chest. I noticed that she was no longer wearing those frilly, silk dresses she'd been forced into when posing as Zara. Instead, she wore black pants and a tight, black shirt. Her blonde curls were pulled back into a high ponytail.

Though I loved how she looked in dresses, I preferred

her in pants. It was obviously what she was most comfortable wearing, and the pants accentuated the muscles in her legs. Those damn perfect legs...

With a murmured thanks, I blew on the soup before swallowing a bite. It was delicious, the creamy broth heightening the flavor of the chicken and vegetables. Who knew Z could cook?

She must've read something on my face, as she laughed. It wasn't a giggle—I wasn't sure if Z knew how to do something as dainty as that—but a full-on belly laugh. Tears welled in her eyes, but she brushed them away.

"God, no. I didn't make that. Devlin did. I don't fucking cook."

Smirking, I took another sip of soup. Now that I was looking for it, I could clearly tell this was a masterpiece created by my genie brother. He had a certain fascination with cooking. As he said, it was a way to create, not destroy. He also preferred spices over bland favors.

Z sat beside me, eyes carefully roaming over the various books.

"What have you found?" she asked, grabbing one. She held the book with reverence, fingers flipping through the pages with a touch as light as a moth's wing. It was a book about underwater creatures. Sirens, water fairies, and the most dangerous, krakens.

I watched her work, mesmerized, before I cleared my throat.

"The fae creatures were descended from one of the lesser known demons. They had an affinity for nature and tended to live in forests and fields." My finger moved over the words I'd already memorized. "Jax was right—they *do* live in trees. Or flowers. Or grass."

"And they're extinct, correct?" Z asked, head bent over her own book. A strand of blonde hair escaped its ponytail, and I had the irresistible urge to brush it behind her ear. I had to physically clench my hand into a fist to keep from touching her.

"Yes," I agreed. "All of my research is consistent with that fact. They became extinct hundreds of years ago when my ancestors first arrived."

Z nodded, brow creased. She appeared to be deep in thought.

Sitting in the library, that adorable crinkle between her brows and a book in her hands, I'd never seen anyone more sexy before.

"So how is it possible?" she blurted out at last. Finally, she turned to face me, and I was momentarily lost in her eyes. I wanted to reach out and touch her, trace those high cheekbones and those abnormally long lashes. Curve my hand around her neck and pull her towards me.

"How is what possible?" I asked stupidly. She smirked, no doubt knowing the direction of my thoughts.

"How can an extinct supernatural creature come back from the dead?" she asked, spelling it out to me. "Unless..." Her finger tapped the bottom of her chin. "Unless they were never truly extinct. Maybe they somehow survived, living in hiding."

Even before she'd finished speaking, I was already shaking my head.

"That's impossible, my love." The endearment

slipped out before I could reel it in, and I watched as she grimaced. I tried to ignore the brief stab of pain spearing my chest at that, but it felt like someone had rammed a burning iron rod straight through my heart. Clearing my throat, I continued before she could notice. "The Seven Sins made sure of it."

I pointed towards another book, this one detailing the plague.

The plague had killed all the other creatures, all the other demons. A plague that was created by the one of the Four Horsemen himself.

Her lips pursed as she read the words I knew by heart. When the plague struck, it killed millions instantly. There was no warning. One second, they were alive, and the next, they were dead. Humans, at the time, blamed it on a medical ailment brought about by mosquitos. It would take only a few years until they learned the truth.

"So this fae shouldn't have been alive," she deduced, and I nodded in confirmation.

"It's quite literally impossible," I answered.

For a moment, we were both silent, the only sound the occasional crinkle of paper or heavy volume landing on the desk. Z worked diligently beside me, scanning the words and making notes on a sheet of paper

I, too, attempted to work, but I couldn't help but focus on her. In my element, she was glorious.

"What?" she asked sharply, glancing up. My face burned when I realized I'd been staring at her. "Why do you keep looking at me?"

"Because you're beautiful," I answered immediately.

Unashamedly. When I was old enough to understand what mates meant, I made a vow to myself that I would constantly shower my own with love and affection. I'd seen what happened when there was no love between mates. And, on the opposite spectrum, I'd seen what happened when there was too much. My father was a prime example of the latter.

All I'd ever wanted was to meet my mate, to fall in love and have her love me back unconditionally. I wanted to treat her like a queen, *my* queen.

At my confession, her own head ducked down sheepishly, the tips of her ears burning. She mumbled something unintelligible beneath her breath.

"You don't like compliments," I noted, somewhat amusedly. At that, her head snapped up and she glared.

"I don't mind them," she stressed. "I just... They make me feel uncomfortable."

"Didn't Devlin or S compliment you when you guys were together?" I asked, quirking a brow. The flush burning her cheeks was answer enough. "They didn't, did they? I'm going to have to talk to Devlin about the proper ways to woo a lady."

At that, a smile cracked through her icy exterior. It was there and gone, the briefest flash of white teeth, before I could comment on it.

"As you've probably already noticed, Lupe, I'm anything *but* a lady."

I waved a hand dismissively. "So you like to stab people and kill things. Why does that make you less than a proper lady? You deserve to be lavished with attention and gifts and crowns."

"Crowns?" One side of her lip curved upwards in a crooked smile. I wanted to see her smile more often. Every day, if I had my choice. She was stunning normally, but when she smiled, she was positively ethereal.

I'd once tried to draw her, but even my artist's hand failed to recreate everything that was Z.

"Crowns," I said with a decisive head bob. "Because you're a queen."

A laugh, unbidden, escaped her, and she brought a hand to her mouth to muffle the sound.

Well, that wouldn't do...

Taking her small, dainty hand in my own, I marveled at how little she was compared to me. Her pale hand was entirely engulfed by my own darker one. I wondered how she would feel lying in bed, her body against my own and her head in the crook of my neck.

"You need to do that more often," I murmured, tracing patterns on her palm. She shivered delicately, and I resisted the urge to grin like a fool at the effect I had on her.

"Do what?" she asked.

"Laugh."

I was afraid she'd run away, that I'd pushed her too hard, but instead, she tilted her head to the side curiously. I could feel her eyes grazing my face, but I focused instead on the veins running through her wrist.

"And you need to get out of this library more often," she reasoned. I shrugged a broad shoulder. In a flash, she'd jumped to her feet, hand still woven with mine. I glanced at her curiously but allowed her to pull me up.

"Where are we going?" I asked, my feet moving of their own accord. But damn if I wouldn't follow her anywhere and everywhere, even off a bridge.

"You need a break," she insisted. We reached the large double doors of the library, and she shoved them open without preamble. "And I, apparently, need to smile and laugh more. Did I get that right?"

She didn't sound mad at my assessment of her. Still, my cheeks burned, and I muttered something beneath my breath.

"HH and T are searching the various safe houses for survivors," she said, still pulling me along. "They should get back to me in about a day. If I'm even still here." Her lip curled. "Heaven only knows when Asshole Extraordinaire—aka the mermaid king—will call me for the next fucking game."

"I like that nickname," I mused. "It's fitting."

Again, she gifted me with that laugh-snort mixture I found so attractive.

"In the meantime..." She trailed off, stopping in front of her desired location. Releasing my hand, she pushed the door open, and I followed after her, gaping at my surroundings. "We're going to have some fun."

EIGHT

Z

Lupe eyed me as if I were a poisonous scorpion preparing to strike. I wanted to laugh at the disbelief in his expression, but I managed to hold it in.

"This is your idea of fun?" he asked in disdain.

I'd found this gem when I was exploring the capital after the Damning had ended and I couldn't stand to be in the same room with any of my mates. According to one of the servants roaming these halls, the room had once served as a training facility for cadets and other governmental agents. When the training center got relocated, nobody bothered to clean up the room.

A large, wooden obstacle course sat in the very center over a collection of blue mats. Chipped white paint added color to the dreary structure and battered wood. To start the course, there was a gray rock climbing wall stopping seven feet above the ground. That led to monkey bars and a simple wooden block the participants had to climb or jump over. From there, you had to army crawl beneath barbed wire to a rope swing. The rope swing led to tires you had to crawl through, until finally, you reached the finish line.

Lupe's wide eyes surveyed the room.

"Super fun," I quipped, walking to the beginning of the course. Lupe, with great reluctance, followed me.

He mimicked my stretching, large muscles bulging beneath his shirt. He wasn't dressed for this type of excursion, wearing a long-sleeved thermal sweater and jeans, but he didn't complain.

I grabbed my elbow over my head and nearly laughed when he did as well.

"Stop it," he said, eyes glinting with amusement.

"Stop what?" I asked innocently.

"I know you want to laugh." He poked a finger into my side, and I swatted his big hand away.

"Do not," I protested half-heartedly. "That would be horrible. I'd never laugh at you."

When he merely raised a brow, eyes narrowing, I couldn't keep my laughter in check. Clutching my stomach, I keeled over.

"Okay, okay, but you have to admit that it's funny," I said with a snort, wiping a stray tear away. "You're like this big ass man with more muscles in your pinkie finger than I have in my body, and you hate exercising. It's funny."

His lip quirked upwards.

"I love that sound," he said seriously, and my laughter dissipated.

"What? Me teasing you?" I asked, though I already knew his answer.

Why did it feel so weird to laugh with him? To smile? Why did it feel like I was disrespecting Diego's memory? I knew it was irrational, but the thought remained, hounding me like a barrage of assaults against my mind and heart.

It felt wrong to be happy when he was dead. When my parents were dead. When S, my second love, was dead.

And I hated it.

I didn't know if I hated my self-loathing, my inability to hold onto happiness, or the fact that I was happy in the first place. My stomach was a tumultuous mixture of grief and confusion. I knew that it would be nearly impossible to get my emotions pacified.

"I get it," Lupe said suddenly. His face brightened like a lightbulb glowing beneath the surface. I resisted the urge to squirm uncomfortably at his knowing, all seeing stare. "You don't think you deserve to be happy."

"I don't know what you're talking about," I snarked, feeling abnormally vulnerable. In a matter of seconds, Lupe had stripped me bare, revealing all the broken and twisted parts of me to his inquisitive eyes. Was this what having mates meant? Would I always feel like that?

I didn't know if I loved it or hated it.

Loved him or hated him.

"I think you do." One of his big hands captured mine. "You're still grieving Diego and even Mali. You miss S and your parents. Hell, you even miss the simplicity of your relationship with Devlin. I get it. I do. This all happened so suddenly, and you don't know up from down. Z, I *see* you. I understand."

I wrenched my hands free from his, trembling. "I don't want you to fucking see me. I don't want anyone to see me. Don't you get that? Don't you understand? I never asked to be your mate, and I already suck at it."

"Z..." he whispered helplessly. I knew he was going to try to reassure me, tell me that I was a perfect mate, that I was deserving of his love, even though it would be falling on willfully deaf ears. "You're right."

"I'm right?" I asked, raising a brow.

Well...that wasn't what I'd expected.

"You don't know how to be in a relationship, and you sure as hell don't know how to love someone."

His words stung, slamming into me with the force of a mage's spell. I physically staggered back a step.

"Gee, thanks," I said dryly, turning away. I refused to let him see that his words had hurt me.

"Z, just listen for a damn minute!" he snapped, and I paused, my back to him. I could hear his heavy breathing accompanied by loud footsteps. In a matter of seconds, he was directly behind me, the heat from his body warming my own. "You talk too much."

"Some people say it's part of my charm," I deadpanned.

Ignoring me, he placed a large, callused hand on my waist. I'd always wondered what he did to cause such calluses and peeled blisters. From what I'd gathered and knew of him, he spent very little time outside of the library.

"None of us know what it's like to have a mate. To be

in a relationship. Do you think I know? Do you think any of us know? Devlin fucked it up the first time. Before you, Killian hadn't been able to last more than five minutes alone in a room with a girl without blurting out anatomy parts. Bash has had more lovers than I could ever count." I stiffened at the last statement, the ugly green monster coming out to play with a vengeance. The last thing I wanted to think about was my mate with another female.

Especially Bash, which surprised me.

I hated him, but at the same time, I sort of liked him. Maybe. Just a smidge.

"What I'm saying is, we can work on this together. This relationship thing. Z, you deserve to be loved."

"Wow," a sly voice said from the corner of the room. I jumped, recognizing the lilt and husky tone immediately. "That was deep. You changed my entire outlook on life and love."

"Ryland," I said, peering into the darkness. His shadowy form moved until it was hovering at the very top of the wooden wall, dark legs dangling. The shadows clung to him, black tendrils that obscured his features from view.

Except for the one time I saw his face...

"Princess," Ryland replied immediately. He moved once more, jumping from the wall and swinging on the rope swing. The shadows moved with him, curling upwards, until he was directly in front of me. The wispy shadows danced in the skylight roof.

"Were you spying on us?" I asked, cocking my hip to the side. I shouldn't have been surprised. Ryland had a strange fascination—read as fetish—with watching people. Lurking in the corners of rooms, the rest of the world oblivious. Listening but never speaking.

Shadows were descended from Pride, and it was rumored that they hid their faces because the rest of the world wasn't allowed to look upon them. With Ryland, I believed he hid his face for an entirely different reason.

A reason I was determined to get to the bottom of, even if it killed me.

"I like spying on you," he said easily.

"Creep." I smiled to soften the word.

"Only for you."

"If you're done now..." Lupe's voice was tight with irritation. "We were talking."

"Excuse me for interrupting your moment. What was next? Romantic stories? A love poem? Ohhh! Maybe you planned to show her that portrait you made of her when she was sleeping."

Lupe's face turned red at Ryland's words, and I turned to face the shifter with a hand on my hip.

"Really? When I was sleeping?"

"So when *he* stalks you, it's romantic, but when I do it, it's creepy." He threw his hands up into the air. "I can never please you, woman."

Rolling my eyes at his antics, I slapped him on the chest.

"So are we doing this?" I asked, nodding towards the obstacle course.

Lupe grimaced, but I imagined Ryland would be smiling brightly.

"A woman after my own heart," he cooed dramatically.

Without another word, I threw myself at the course.

HOURS LATER, I found myself dripping sweat. It clung to my skin like a glossy sheen. My body felt unnaturally heavy, weighted. Halfway through the obstacle course, my nose began to bleed, but a quick trip to the bathroom had stopped the heavy flow. Sweat and copper from my nosebleed permeated the air. Poor Lupe and his keen shifter senses. I probably smelled something awful at the moment unless he switched it off.

Fortunately, he wasn't faring much better. His dark hair was plastered to his forehead, and his breathing was ragged.

"Never again," he huffed, flopping onto his back and extending his arms. I moved to sit down beside him, wrapping my arm around my knees.

"Baby," I said with a smirk.

"Trust me." He tilted his head up to meet my eyes, smile devious. Devilish. "I am nothing but man."

Heat pooled in both my cheeks and core.

"And I'm disgusted," Ryland quipped from where he was sitting opposite us. The shadows were still pulled tightly around his person, but I could see a flash of icy blue eyes peering through the tar-like blackness. "That was an awful pickup line."

"Pickup line?" Lupe retorted, still grinning at me. I liked seeing him smile. He always looked so serious, as if he were weighed down by the entire world. I wasn't sure if he would ever be carefree, but I enjoyed seeing this side of him. "I was only speaking the truth."

My dumbass mouth blurted out the first thing I could think of. "Prove it."

Totally didn't consider the implications of such a statement.

Lupe's eyebrows touched his hairline, even as his smile broadened.

Ryland chuckled.

"I think she wants us to whip out our dicks," he said to Lupe.

"What is it with females and their fascination with male dicks?" the burly shifter mused. I had no doubt that it would be just as big as the rest of him.

"Females?" I asked teasingly. "As in, more than one?"

Okay, half teasingly. I would probably maim any female who dared get too close to my males, let alone see their dicks.

A large hand cupped my breast from behind, and I hissed slightly in pleasure. This touch was followed by the lightest brush of lips against my neck. Eagerly, I tilted my head to grant him better access.

"Only one for me," Lupe murmured. His tongue snuck out to lick my skin, a growl rumbling in his chest. "And you, Ryland?"

The shadow materialized inches from my face. Those blue eyes stood out like a white dot on a black sheet of paper. They were so blue, like waves cresting against the shoreline, and I knew I could get lost in them. I could tumble head over heel in a riptide, drowning. It would be the sweetest death imaginable.

"One for me as well, brother."

Lupe's fingers pinched my nipple through my thin, black shirt and bra, and I practically purred.

"I don't think there has ever been a girl as beautiful as you," Lupe murmured into my neck. His hot breath fanned out against my skin.

"You're so full of shit," I murmured.

"Nope." Ryland popped his p. "But we are biased."

"Rightfully so," Lupe added. His lips moved to my earlobe, tugging it between his teeth. I groaned low in my throat.

The feel of his hard, muscled body behind mine...

Desperately, I grabbed his neck and brought his lips to my own. He conceded without a fight, opening his mouth to devour me completely. His tongue tangled with mine, and I felt his hand push up my shirt and bra, revealing my breasts.

The cold air had already made my nipples hard, but his touch brought the sensation to almost decadent levels.

His fingers pinched and tugged, his thumb circling my peak. His free hand crept lower, towards the waistband of my pants, before thrusting inside. I gasped as his finger entered my already wet slit.

"You're so wet for me, baby girl," he whispered, pulling his lips from mine. "So fucking ready."

His lips trailed down my neck, across my shirt that was pushed up to my neck, and then landed on my breasts. His tongue snaked out and swirled over my nipple before pulling it completely into his mouth. I gasped, arching my back at the sensation.

Down below, his finger began its relentless pursuit, bringing me to that edge of oblivion. A second finger joined the first, and I thought I would orgasm then and there. The feel of him inside of me, even if it was just a couple fingers, was very near overwhelming. I felt so safe in his strong arms. So loved. Electricity shot through my nerves, lighting me up.

Movement captured my attention.

The shadows around Ryland had receded slightly, revealing a dark hand around a straining cock. I wondered if he even realized he was doing it as he stroked himself in tandem to Lupe's fingers fucking me.

My lips parted, and a breathy exhale left me.

As Lupe continued to lift me higher and higher, I kept my focus on Ryland.

His large, dark hand moved erratically over his length. Another hand cupped his balls, fondling them.

He made a noise, a combination between a groan and a howl, before he came, spilling his seed across the mat.

That was my undoing. I stumbled face first over that cliff I'd found myself on, a scream lodged in my throat. I came around Lupe's expert fingers, tears in my eyes and inarticulate praises escaping me.

Ryland pulled the shadows around him once more, hiding his cock from my eager eyes, and I wanted to pout in disappointment.

Lupe continued to finger fuck me through my orgasm, finally pulling out when I was well sated and spent. Almost absently, he placed his fingers into his mouth and began to lick them clean. I watched it all with hooded, lust filled eyes.

These men were going to fucking destroy me.

"Well..." Ryland chuckled breathily. "That was fun."

I collapsed against Lupe's chest, my breathing heavy and my mind spinning.

Yup. Destroy.

NINE

Z

Devlin was once again on my ass.

And not in the good way.

The second I walked into my room, the post orgasmic bliss washing over me, he pounced. His immaculately pressed suit was unbuttoned, showcasing a healthy layer of chest hair. Dark bruises rimmed his violet eyes, and his pouty lips were pursed.

"Where were you?" he asked instantly. It looked as if he'd worn a hole in the rug from his repeated pacing.

"Why?" I asked, full of snark. "Are you my keeper now?"

His lips tightened into a thin line.

"You disappeared. Again. Without even a fucking note."

"So you *are* my keeper," I mused. I stepped around him, towards the immense shower in the bathroom. It was able to fit approximately three people and had jet streams that could massage your ass. Diego had loved this damn shower, probably more than he loved me.

Ignoring the probing gaze I could feel on my back, I slipped out of my sweat soaked shirt and pants. Dressed in only my panties and bra, I turned to look at him, placing my hands on my hips. The anger in his eyes diminished instantly to be replaced by a carnal hunger. Heat radiated from his eyes, warming my skin and seeping through to my very bones.

"I was worried," he said cautiously. His eyes continued to mentally, relentlessly, undress me. Normally, I would've ripped him a new one, but I was still riding the wave of my last orgasm. If Devlin—handsome, perfect Devlin—wanted to give me another? Who was I to complain?

"I'm not stupid," Devlin continued as I turned on the water. I tentatively placed a hand beneath the spray, gauging the temperature, before deciding that it needed to be warmer. "I know about your past."

"My past," I said succinctly. "What do you think you know?"

"That you worked for the Alphabet Resistance." He took a step closer. The heat in his eyes belied the coldness of his words. My body tensed, electricity shooting through my nerves, and not in a good way. Instead of answering, I shoved my hand back into the water. Perfect temperature.

"I killed people, you know," I whispered, reaching behind me to absently unhook my bra. I heard his sharp intake of breath, but I ignored it. Ignored him. "Killed people that you might've known. Genies, for one. Other nightmares. I was supposed to kill you and your brothers, but I think you already know that."

Slipping the straps down my arms, I turned, holding the gauzy fabric to my chest in order to keep some semblance of modesty. Who was I kidding? When it came to these men, I had not one modest bone in my body. Still, it felt odd to confess this to him completely naked.

Devlin watched me for a long moment, an undefinable expression flickering across his handsome face. When the silence became unbearable, suffocating even, I turned around. My bra fell to the ground unceremoniously, and I leaned down to remove my underwear as well. Through it all, I could feel his eyes caressing my bare flesh. The wanton desire in his gaze was impossible to ignore, evident despite my confession.

Despite the fact that I'd murdered people.

"I don't care," he answered at last, voice terse.

A laugh bubbled out of me, but I tampered it down with a hand to my mouth. There was no joy, no mirth, in that sound. It was cold and heartless.

"How could you not?" I whispered, finally stepping beneath the spray. I leaned over to grab my body wash, the heady scent of pomegranates invading my senses. This particular soap always appeared in my room. I had a distinct feeling that my mates were behind it...or at the very least, one in particular. I wasn't completely oblivious to Lupe's sniffing tendencies.

"I've killed too." His voice was a whisper. He still didn't move closer, his silhouette visible through the steamed glass of the shower. "I've murdered, Z. I'm not innocent."

"I never said you were." The last word I would ever

associate with Devlin Genie was innocent. My heart rico-cheted, one beat away from completely breaking free of my ribcage.

Why was everything so difficult with him? Why was I so determined to break things off before they could even begin?

I knew the answer to those questions, though a part of me wished I didn't. It would be much easier to live in my oblivious, diminutive bubble, unaware of the rest of the world and my own damn feelings.

The truth was, Devlin had hurt me once. Hurt me beyond repair. What little pieces of my heart I'd given him, he had shattered. Did he think of me as I'd thought of him when we were apart? Did he regret breaking me, breaking my heart?

"Those men we met..." Devlin took a step closer. His black jacket fell to the floor beside my clothes. "They're assassins too, right? They're a part of the resistance." Though it started as a question, it ended as a statement of fact. There was no denying it—somehow, Devlin knew everything. No surprise. We weren't exactly subtle about it.

"Yes," I answered evenly. I rubbed the soap across my body, down my arms, and over my breasts. I paid extra attention to my nipples, pulling them between my soapy fingers.

I heard the sound of his belt coming undone.

"You scared the shit out of me when you left, you know that?" I didn't respond to him, focusing instead on my shampoo. I massaged it into my scalp, tilting my head up to catch the blistering hot water on my face. "Why would you do something so fucking stupid? Especially when you know you have a target on your back."

The shower door opened and closed, and Devlin moved to stand in the spray beside me. Rivulets of water dribbled down his naked, chiseled body, and his cock was already half erect. Without a word, he stepped closer, replacing my hands in my hair as he rubbed the shampoo into my scalp. I very nearly groaned at the sensation, at the feel of him.

"It was stupid," I admitted. "But I couldn't stay here."

"Because you run." Again, it wasn't a question.

"And you're afraid," I retorted. There was no malice in my statement, though, only understanding. For the first time, Devlin wasn't difficult to read.

"I'm fucking terrified, baby girl," he whispered. "I can't lose you again."

I spun in his arms, memorizing his features. God, he was so fucking perfect. And he was mine. All mine. My eyes traced over his olive-toned face, those high cheekbones, those penetrating violet eyes that always saw through me. My gaze drifted lower, over his chiseled abs to his straining cock and down his toned, muscular legs. Perfect didn't even begin to describe him. Even with water streaming down his face and his hair disheveled, he was as beautiful as always.

"Prove it," I whispered hotly, stepping closer. My breasts brushed his chest, and I heard him inhale sharply. "Prove how much you love me. Prove that you're mine."

His breathing was ragged, but his eyes darkened with

barely constrained lust. Reaching forward, I interlocked our hands together before moving it over my breast. Not touching, just hovering over the sensitive skin.

He waited. Always waiting.

"You can touch me," I whispered breathily. When he eagerly began to lean in, I stepped back, tsking disapprovingly. "Only here." I nodded towards where his hands hovered about my breasts.

With renewed vigor, he palmed my heavy mounds, twisting my nipples between his fingers. I melted under the feel of his ministrations, the feel of him, the possessiveness and ownership with each flick of his wrist. He ducked his head, breath fanning over my tips, and raised one brow in question.

Giving him permission with a decisive bob of my head, he began to lick and suck on my boobs. His tongue swirled over my nipple the way he knew I liked, a growl reverberating in his chest. I panted, arching, but he didn't let up. His hands desperately gripped my hips, pulling me even closer to his rock-hard cock.

"Stop," I instructed, and with a whimper, he backed away. He stood still, watching me with heavily lidded, lustful eyes. "Don't move."

Keeping my eyes on him, I dropped to my knees. He waited patiently, but his chest had stopped moving. The poor man wasn't even breathing.

With a coy smile, I cupped one of his balls, testing the weight. A moan echoed in the small shower and through me with the strength of a drumline. Instinctively, he began to rock his hips, but I slapped one of his ass cheeks.

"No," I growled, and he stopped immediately. Taking my time—punishment was a bitch, after all—I ran a nail down his length. He was long, longer than any of the other men I'd slept with, and thick. The first time I'd taken him, I was afraid he wouldn't fit. I shouldn't have been surprised when we came together like two pieces of a puzzle. After all, the fates wouldn't have given me a mate I couldn't take.

Even if I did lose my ability to walk for a week afterwards.

When his breaths continued to deepen, erupting in quick spurts, I replaced my nail with my tongue, licking his thick underside and the throbbing vein. Adjusting my hand around the base for easier access, I wrapped my mouth around his tip, using my saliva as a lubricant.

"Fuck," he whispered harshly, hands tangling in my hair.

I immediately pulled away with a frown, once more slapping his ass.

"No touching," I hissed. When I was sure he would be compliant, I happily pulled him back into my mouth. He was long, but I knew I could take him. Once he was fully in my mouth, I began to hum. His gasp made my insides tighten deliciously, heat pooling low in my core.

With practiced efficiency, I sucked him in and out of my mouth repeatedly. Through it all, he whispered my name, told me how much he loved me, and begged me for more.

When his cock began to quiver, I pulled away, wiping my mouth with the back of my hand.

His eyes were very near pleading with me. Begging me.

Standing on my tiptoes, I brought my lips to his ear, relishing the way he shivered.

I did that. Me.

"Fuck me, Devlin. Fuck me and show me that you're mine."

Taking my words as permission, he hoisted me up, and my legs automatically wrapped around his waist. In this position, I could feel his cock directly against my aching core. In one, firm thrust, he was sheathed inside of me.

I moaned, feeling utterly full to the point of breaking.

He waited, still inside me, until I nodded.

"Move." He began to rock his hips, fucking me in earnest, and I matched his movements. Our lovemaking became erratic, in tandem to our racing hearts, but still, we didn't let up. His lips clashed with mine, tongue prodding my seams. I opened to him immediately, taking him in. Loving him.

Showing him exactly who he belonged to.

I gasped his name seconds before I reached the precipice, then I exploded, my pussy clenching around his cock. He continued thrusting in and out of me before chasing his own release, my name a prayer on his lips.

My legs quivered, and I quite literally needed him to stand up. Even when he placed me on trembling legs, I found myself leaning against him, pressing my forehead against his chest. Overcome by emotion, I pressed a soft kiss there. I felt unnaturally dizzy, a feat that had never happened after sex before. Why was the world spinning?

I blinked rapidly to clear the sluggish fatigue from my mind.

"I love you," I whispered. The words felt foreign on my lips. Unfamiliar. They weren't words I'd ever thought I would use again romantically. I'd thought that type of love had been driven out of me, cut out with a keen blade.

I couldn't deny the truth of the words, though, no matter how much I wished to deny them. They surrounded me like a warm blanket, leaving me comforted and loved. Cherished.

God, he made me feel cherished.

And a part of me hated it, hated the way he made me feel, while the other part of me clung to it desperately. Pathetically, if I was being honest with myself.

At my confession, Devlin went still. Only his heart told me he was still alive, still breathing, as it thumped beneath me.

"Say it again." His tone dropped to a hushed murmur, almost as if he were worried anything louder would break the glass globe we'd found ourselves in.

I finally lifted my head, placing my chin where my forehead had once rested. His violet eyes were staring down at me as if I'd hung the moon and stars. If I'd ever doubted his love for me, one look into his eyes contradicted that thought. There was no denying he loved me. Was it crazy, this relationship between a genie and an assassin? An assassin and seven men? Yes.

Did it feel right?

Yes.

Mustering my courage, I whispered, "I love you,

Devlin Genie. I love you so fucking much that I don't know what to do with myself at times."

The smile that erupted on his face was brilliant. It made it worth saying those dreaded words.

I could only hope I wouldn't regret them.

TEN

Z

The mermaid king could suck my nonexistent dick.

The pompous asshole remained rooted on his throne while his indolent eyes, the same shade of blue as his son's, ensnared me. No matter how hard I tried, I couldn't look away.

The other six thrones were empty, but that didn't abate how stifling the room felt under the many watchful eyes. The king's sons, Dair's brothers, stood in a semi-circle around their father, eyes intently trained on me. I could feel their caress like a branding iron, burning my skin until it touched my bone. The heat threatened to burn me from the inside out, threatened to burn me alive. It wasn't a pleasant feeling.

Behind them, Dair sat in his wheelchair. His azure eyes, the shade of water cresting the shoreline, were also trained on me. I avoided eye contact with a vigor that surprised me. Somehow, I knew that meeting his searing gaze would clue the others in on the nature of our relationship.

"Your Majesty," I said with a sardonic curtsy, breaking the silence that had stretched for five long, tedious minutes. The mermaid king's lips twitched, but he remained silent. Watching. Calculating. Those pinprick blue eyes of his seemed to stare into my very soul.

After a long moment, he nodded towards his eldest son. I couldn't recall the name—something with a T—but he had the same golden hair and sun-kissed skin as my mate. His smile was coy though as he handed me a slip of paper.

I couldn't help but note his hand brushed mine a second longer than propriety allowed.

I wrenched my hand away, and a frown carved itself into his handsome, marble features. Still, he didn't press as he strode back towards his father.

Dair was glancing between me and his brother, expression inscrutable.

Feeling as if I were being analyzed beneath a microscope, I unfolded the sheet of paper and smoothed out its creases. My brow furrowed as I read through what I'd been given.

It was a map of an unfamiliar landscape. From the large expanse of water taking up three-fourths of the map, I deduced it was a part of the Mermaid Kingdom. The back had handwritten notes about an unnamed man. A brief description, biography, and his last known location.

Reading the words once and then a second time, I

quirked a brow. I knew it might have been considered rude of me, but my emotions were already at an all-time high. Unease skittered down my spine at what was very obviously an assassination assignment.

Don't get me wrong—I wasn't opposed to killing. I couldn't have won this competition, nor have been one of the best human assassins, if I were. I was, however, against killing people I knew nothing about. Who was this male with green eyes and red hair, according to the report? What had he done?

"You want me to kill him," I said tersely. It wasn't a question.

When the king continued to smirk mockingly, the unease turned into a rock-hard ball churning in my gut. I was discomfited by the prospect of doing something to help this evil asshole.

And that was what he was—evil. There was no doubt about it in my mind. He was an evil I was chained to, unfortunately. Somehow, he'd crawled inside of me, infesting me like a damn parasite. The spell prohibited me from harming him or allowing others to harm him. I was trapped, and he was one of seven who held the chains.

Grappling with my own emotions, I nodded once. Innately, I knew it wasn't one of agreement. Did they even have nods for 'I want to kill you, but a spell prohibits me from doing just that'?

"What did this man do?" I asked the king stiffly.

Nothing. Just another curl of his lips.

"We will have a ball to celebrate your...position," he replied at last. His words took me by surprise, and I physically staggered back a step. The king's lips twitched.

"A ball?" I parroted in disbelief.

"A ball," he repeated with a decisive head bob. Behind him, Dair's lips thinned, as pleased by this development as I was.

And the smile on the mermaid's king's face?

I had the distinct feeling the ball was just one of his many tests.

THE DRESSMAKER WAS A SHREWD, tiny woman with coiffed gray hair pulled tight on her head and beady brown eyes. She moved with an otherworldly elegance that hinted she may have been a vampire or even a shifter.

A familiar head of orange-red hair appeared next, smiling brightly.

I recognized Lupe's sister immediately. Mali's mate.

And Jax's fiancée, though I didn't want to think of that. Her smile widened when she took stock of me, white teeth flashing.

"You look beautiful," she gushed, gliding into the room and perching on my couch. The dressmaker barely spared her a glance, despite Atta being a princess. Her entire focus was on me and making me as miserable as possible.

That macabre thought was only reinforced when a knife—read as a needle—was jabbed into my side, making me wince.

"This is hell," I replied, my tone snarky. I'd been poked and prodded to within an inch of my life. Each stab of the needle felt like a sword through the chest.

As soon as that petty thought came to me, I felt guilty, a depthless ocean that threatened to swallow me whole.

Atta continued on, oblivious to my inner turmoil.

"As is the price of beauty, my dear friend," she said lightly. She leaned farther back on the couch, folding her hands beneath her ample breasts. If I didn't know that she preferred females, I might've been jealous of her engagement to Jax. Even knowing what I did, my stomach clenched and tightened whenever I thought of the two of them together.

Even if it was only for show.

Her words registered a second too late.

"I'm not your friend," I sputtered out.

If I'd expected her to be upset by my words, I was poorly mistaken. She merely grinned cheekily.

"We're practically family," she cooed, tossing me a sultry wink. "Especially since..."

I helplessly glanced at the dressmaker, willing Atta with my eyes to shut the hell up.

"I was going to say because you're my family's assassin, but whatever toots your horn."

I rolled my eyes at her cattiness, just as the seamstress stabbed a particularly sharp pin into my side. I yelped, jumping, but she merely tsked her tongue in disapproval. Atta just laughed. There was obviously no help coming from her.

"I can't stay for long." Atta gracefully moved to her

feet, every inch the refined, dainty princess. "I just came to deliver a message."

"A message?" I asked, but my attention was on the wretched woman kneeling before me. I snapped my teeth at her, and she responded with purposefully shoving a damn needle into my thigh. "Motherfucker—"

"She says she's sorry." Atta's calm voice broke me off mid curse. "And that she loves you. Very much."

Her words made me freeze, my muscles locking. The seamstress's hand on my thigh prohibited me from looking directly at Atta, so I settled for moving my eyes only.

"What?"

There was only one person she could be referring to. One woman who she could be talking about.

Mali.

Her message delivered, Atta stalked out of the room, her long, peach dress trailing behind her. I was left numb and trembling, her words replaying in my head.

Sorry.

Sorry.

Sorry.

Mali, I miss you.

I forgive you.

Those thoughts diminished, buried beneath weeks of anger and pain. She could be sorry all she wanted, but there would be no forgiveness from me.

I hardened myself, emptied myself, so I would feel nothing at all.

Z

Tflashed me his signature smile, looking so much like S at that moment, it was a physical pain slashing my chest. His reddish blond hair was shorter than when I'd last seen him, only a few days ago, and his pale face betrayed his strain despite the easy smile.

"Any updates?" I asked.

We stood in a cluster of trees two towns over from the capital. In the distance, I could see the shambles of faded russet-colored roofs that made up the cozy, minuscule human town T had instructed me to go to. I'd found him initially inside a tavern, drinking happily and flirting with the pretty waitress. When he saw me, he'd jumped to his feet and guided me into the surrounding forests with a simple come-hither crook of his finger. The skeletal branches grazed my cheeks, and the bitter wind contradicted the bright sun overhead.

I pulled my jacket tighter around my shoulders.

"Nothing," T said. His nervous eyes flickered, taking

in every shadow and every hidden crevice of the dark forest. The canopy of boughs obscured the sunlight, minus a single strip that lit where we stood. "We checked every safe house in Sector One and Sector Two. They're gone, Z. All of them."

I processed his words for a moment in silence. It just didn't make any sense. How could over a hundred people magically disappear without a trace? How could over a hundred *assassins* disappear? My stomach churned, tightened, perilously close to losing the contents of my early morning breakfast.

"It just doesn't make any sense," T said, echoing my thoughts. He forked his fingers through his hair.

"Nothing about this makes any sense," I agreed. Movement in my peripheral captured and ensnared my attention. I frowned, pulling my lip between my teeth when I recognized the figure crouched behind a trunk.

"I should go," I continued, cutting off whatever T was going to say. He raised an eyebrow suspiciously but didn't comment.

"Okay?"

"Okay."

When he continued standing there, staring at me as if I'd grown wings and horns, I shoved his shoulder.

"Trust me, okay?" Canting my head to the side, I nodded at the "hidden" figure. T's eyebrows raised, confusion being replaced by amusement. He shook his head once in disbelief, muttering beneath his breath.

With a chaste kiss to my cheek, he hurried out of the forest. I could've sworn I heard his chuckle long after he disappeared through the thicket.

Alone—correction, semi alone, I placed my hand on my hip.

"You can come out now," I called, not bothering to turn towards the intruder.

I heard the shuffle of leaves, a muffled curse, and then a warm body was mere inches from my back.

"How did you know I was there?" Bash asked, and I finally looked back at him. His blond hair was wildly disheveled, with a few loose leaves stuck on his head. Dirt covered his high cheekbones and nose, and his clothes were ruffled. I'd never seen Bash so unkempt before, and I couldn't help but flush, white hot, at the onslaught of dirty thoughts assaulting me. Namely, other ways I could ruffle his clothes and mess up his normally impeccably styled hair.

There was no denying that Bash was a handsome man...and that I was attracted to him in a carnal way.

But then he had to open his damn mouth.

"Apparently, I'm your babysitter for the day," he said with a sly tilt to his lips. Those damn kissable lips with a plump, full lower one and a small upper one. I couldn't help but imagine pulling it between my teeth.

And then his words registered.

"Babysitter?" I asked in disbelief. When he continued to stare at me, I huffed, placing my hands on my hips. "I don't need a fucking babysitter."

"Try telling that to your other six mates." He leaned back against a tree trunk, arms crossed over his chest. "Personally, I think you're kickass enough to handle things yourself, but I'm outnumbered."

That was...surprisingly sweet.

"You're more man than female anyway," he continued. "I wouldn't want to be locked in a room with you for more than an hour."

Or not.

"Oh fuck off, Bash," I hissed, stomping through the forest and back towards the town. Foliage and dried leaves crackled beneath my feet with every step. I heard, rather than saw, Bash move behind me. He didn't seem inclined to stand beside me, despite his long legs easily being able to eat up the distance between us.

"Trust me. I wish I could *fuck*." I didn't even have to see him to know he was scowling. "Anyone and anything. Besides you, of course, *princess*."

I stopped mid step, glancing over my shoulder to meet his eyes.

"Is that an endearment?" I cooed mockingly. "That's so sweet. I knew you cared."

His nostrils flared.

"Why would I call you by an endearment? I don't like you." He spoke these words candidly, the sincerity in them almost impossible to deny. Almost. But I was his mate, after all, and I knew his tell.

The slightest hitch of breath was definitely one of them.

Ignoring it, I continued walking, purposely pushing branches out of my way, only to have them hit Bash square in the chest. I smiled in satisfaction when he grumbled.

"So do you have another lover we need to know about?" Bash inquired, his tone snarky. "You seemed awfully close to that human." Why couldn't he just shut the hell up for more than a moment? For fuck's sake...

"Jealous?" I quipped.

"Disgusted would be a better word. I never knew you to be a cheater on top of—" Before he could even finish his thought, I had him pinned to a tree, my arm at his throat. He blinked rapidly at me, heat rising to his cheeks.

Was he...?

There was no mistaking the heat emanating from his eyes as I held him hostage. His breaths shuddered in and out.

"Don't talk about me like that," I hissed. "I didn't want this mate bond either, asshole. But the last thing I would ever do is cheat on them...or you, for that matter. Though sometimes I want to fucking stab you."

"Oh, how you flatter me," Bash drawled dramatically.

"Go have an orgy or something and leave me alone," I snapped, my already thin patience splintering like a ball being thrown on a slate of ice. When the ice broke, I was immediately submerged in icy cold water that made goosebumps erupt on my skin. "Wait. You can't have one. Because you can't get fucking hard."

We were both breathing heavily, and I saw Bash's pupils dilate.

He leaned over me, and I knew he was going to kiss me. I couldn't decide if I wanted him to...or if I wanted to knee him in the balls. All I knew for certain was that his hot breath fanned over my face, smelling distinctly of peppermints, and I was slowly losing all mental capabilities. When he exhaled, those damn lips parted seductively. He was so handsome, and it fucking bothered me.

How could such a dick be so beautiful? How could such a dick be my mate?

"I can't fucking stand this," Bash whispered hoarsely. Huskily. "I don't want to be a puppet in fate's grand plan, you know? I don't want to be fated to love someone."

He leaned even closer, a trickle of blond hair caressing my cheek. His forehead rested against mine. If I didn't know Bash like I did, I would've almost described his eyes as tender. Reverent. Loving.

But I did.

"Z..." His eyes flickered upwards, over my shoulder, and in a span of seconds, I was falling to the ground, Bash standing protectively in front of me. Before I could even scream at him for shoving me, I took stock of who he was protecting me from.

Or *what*.

It was unlike anything I'd ever seen before, with decaying flesh and milky, sunken eyeballs. It was completely naked, revealing withered, gray skin that reminded me vaguely of a raisin. Its nose consisted of two large holes directly in the center of its face, and when it opened its mouth, head canted to the side, I saw row after row of sharp teeth. More teeth than should've been possible. I counted at least three rows, formed in a circle in its mouth

The creature's nostrils, *holes*, expanded, and it tottered forward when it caught a scent—my scent, if the direction of its eyes was any indication. It let out a guttural scream, lunging forward. It didn't walk. The combination of abnormally long legs and a small upper body made it seem as if it was flying, leaping, propelling itself off its back legs.

Bash muttered something beneath his breath, an incantation, I realized, and extended a hand. Golden sparks flickered to life, and he directed it towards the creature. His hand still raised, he pushed the sparks towards the monster.

I watched in rapt fascination as fire engulfed the creature immediately. Glorious red flames spread from its head to its small, naked torso, down to its legs, and finally rooted itself at its feet.

Scrambling to my feet, I released a knife from its customary sheath at my side. I didn't know if Bash's hand on my shoulder was meant to be restraining or comforting, but either way, I pushed it off and marched towards the withering creature.

Up close, even with the flames charring the skin, I could see how hideous it actually was. Mottled, gray skin and wispy black streaks of hair at its head. Those unseeing white eyes. The pervasive scent of urine combined with burning flesh.

Disgust churned in my lower belly, but my hand was steady as I tossed the dagger into its head.

The monster collapsed to the ground, the dagger protruding from its forehead and flames continually eating away at its sunken skin.

I exchanged a glance with Bash, both of us breathing heavy from adrenaline and, in Bash's case, overexertion. I noted sweat dripping from Bash's forehead—a byproduct of the spell he'd cast. Still, he managed to level me with a glare that made the fire burning appear cold.

"What the hell were you doing?" he snapped, stalking up to me. His hands grabbed my shoulders and gave them a shake. I eyed his hands through a slitted gaze, and he dropped them immediately.

Good choice, since he probably wanted to keep those limbs in the first place.

"I had it taken care of," he continued curtly. "You didn't have to jump in there like some motherfucking hero. You could've been hurt. The fire could've burned you!"

I rolled my eyes. At this point, I wouldn't have been surprised if they remained glued to the back of my head.

"He, the creature, was in agony, Bash. What was I supposed to do? Allow him to burn a slow and painful death while I watched? Believe it or not, I'm not a monster." My tone was more defensive than I wanted it to be, bitterness seeping through, despite my best efforts. Bash's face softened considerably, and he hesitantly placed his hands back on my shoulders. This time, I let him.

I didn't know why, only that a part of me craved the comfort he offered. I knew he wasn't the type who would hold my hand and tell me everything would be okay, so the comfort he did offer, though scarce, I lapped up greedily.

"I know that," he said softly. "And I know you could've handled it yourself. It's just...seeing him—it come at you... Fuck! I don't know."

He released me as if I'd burned him and started pacing. His eyes occasionally flashed towards the decaying corpse.

"What the hell even is that thing?" I asked, nodding towards the disgusting creature. His—I was under the impression it was a male—features were unrecognizable now, the fire completely eating away the rest of his skin to reveal the brittle bone beneath. That must've been one hell of a fire. Even where I stood, now a few feet away, I could feel the heat it emanated in blistering waves.

"I'm not certain...but..." Bash trailed off, casting a scathing glance once more at the corpse. I raised a brow at him to continue, and he sighed resignedly. "It reminds me of a story my dad used to read to me before bed. About a princess, a prince, and the monster that attacked and killed her. The prince killed himself in grief."

"That was the bedtime story your dad told you?" I gasped in disbelief, heart breaking for younger Bash. "That's fucked up."

He tossed me a glare.

"Not important. Anyway, the creature was described exactly like the thing that attacked us. Holes for a nose. Circular mouth with hundreds of little teeth. Gray skin. It scared the shit out of me when I was younger."

"What is it?" I repeated. There were minuscule pains all throughout my body, but I couldn't tell the source. The fight hadn't been too strenuous, so why did it feel like I'd run twenty miles? I absently rubbed at my nose, shocked when my hand came away stained with blood. I hid it behind my back before Bash could notice.

"A revenant." Bash's voice was quiet, but it carried easily through the suddenly stilled forest. Not even animals wanted to bear witness to what had transpired.

The tranquility was nothing more than an illusion, betraying how fucked up everything actually was.

Bash sighed once more, a hand combing through his blond hair. "They've been extinct for years now," he admitted. "That...*thing*...shouldn't exist."

TWELVE

DAIR

ather stared at me over the dinner table, fork partially lifted and a contemplative expression on his face. I squirmed, unease prickling my skin at his undivided attention. Even Tavvy noticed my father's uncharacteristic interest in me, skin wrinkling around his eyes and brows in irritation.

Poor, envious bastard. For once, he wasn't the center of attention. You couldn't begin to imagine the rage Tavvy experienced when the other kings declared him mentally unfit to be the crowned prince and next in line for the mermaid throne. My father had argued too, but it was no use fighting against the other kings. They saw Tavvy as a threat to themselves and their rule, too unpredictable and volatile, and as such, fought against giving him any crown.

Which put me in line for the throne.

What Tavvy didn't know was my willingness to sell my soul to escape my father. I didn't *want* his attention. I didn't want those crystal-clear blue eyes, the same shade as my own, to be fixed on me with an interest that made my hair stand on end. I didn't want to be on the receiving end of his punishing hand, his cruel words, his excessive games.

But freedom was a foreign concept, one grafted from this improbable ideology that we were actually made to be free. That was a lie. We were born only to serve those in power. To bow down to those higher than us, stronger than us, faster than us. It wasn't so much a hierarchy as it was a way of life.

You were either born with power, or you weren't.

But every person, my father included, had a weakness. His weakness wasn't physical, but mental. It was the same affinity that plagued the rest of my family and species—envy.

It was for that reason alone Father had numerous wives, each one a different age, a different skin color, and a different body type. His favorite wife at the moment, Marcella, sat in the seat beside him, dark skin and dark hair a contrast to my mother's own golden hair and golden skin—a trait that I had inherited.

Marcella, noticing my stare, leaned over, revealing her ample breasts and cleavage. Disgust filled me instantly, and I turned away. Tavvy had no such qualms, flashing Marcella a sultry grin and unabashedly staring at her breasts. No doubt, he would track her down and fuck her later.

As was always the case with Father's new wives.

Tavvy got jealous, fucked them, and then let Father know. More than one woman had paid the price for

Tavvy's transgressions, even if the woman hadn't been a willing participant.

More than a few of Father's wives had come onto me as well, despite my disability. I knew they only wanted me to prove a point, to mark me off their list, put a notch in their bedpost, to tell the world that they'd conquered the impossible. I hadn't ever been inclined to indulge myself in such scandalous—and frankly, disgusting—activities, but that distaste had turned into complete and utter revulsion now that I'd found my mate.

Of course, the rest of the world didn't know about that. It was a secret I would take to my grave until the time was right.

My father...

The cold-hearted bastard would steal her before I could stop him. Before any of us could stop him. We may be the princes, but we were suffocated by the rules and regulations of the courts. That wasn't to say that we wouldn't break all of them for Z, we would, but it meant having a relationship with her was slightly more difficult than one would anticipate after meeting his mate.

Not one of us was against running away with her. Leaving the capital and never returning.

But we knew Z would never stand for it. As crowned princes, we had the capability to actually make change. To fix this world that our parents had broken. Between the human work camps, the resistance groups, and Aaliyah, it wasn't practical to run from our problems. Not yet at least.

"What did you do today, son?" Father asked. It took me a moment to realize he was talking to me. It took me another moment to lift my jaw off the ground at the realization that he'd addressed me for the first time in forever.

Tavvy's jaw tightened.

"Um..."

"Hid away in the water, probably," Tavvy sneered. My other two brothers, twins, snickered, despite the fact there was nothing remotely funny about that statement.

"Are you excited for the ball?" continued Father, stabbing his fork into a fillet of fish.

"Um..."

I was at a loss for words on how to respond. I couldn't remember the last time I'd my father's attention besides when he was harming me. I wasn't dumb enough to believe he held actual interest in my welfare or feelings. If anything, this was a trap.

He was just waiting to ensnare me.

I remembered when he used to set up traps in the fields surrounding our castle. For rabbits, he'd said.

Of course, no rabbits were ever captured. Instead, my father carried in armed resistance leaders and assassins.

Fear tightened my throat muscles, clogging my airway. All I could do was stare at my father with barely concealed resentment and confusion, waiting not so patiently for the other shoe to fall.

"As this party is to celebrate Z's accomplishments, I've decided it would only be fitting for one of my sons to escort her." His lips curled, resembling a sneer more than an actual smile. "What would the kids say? A date? Yes, a date. One of my sons shall be her date to the ball."

Once again, he threw me a pointed stare.

Understanding didn't just dawn on me, but pelted

me in the face with the strength of a mountain, smothering me until I could barely breathe let alone speak. My heart clenched painfully in tandem to my fingers clenching around my fork. My knuckles were white, the veins beneath my skin visible.

Somehow, someway, my father *knew*. How he'd discovered it remained a mystery, but there was no denying the telltale glimmer in his eyes, privy to a joke the rest of the world hadn't heard.

Father pulled his focus away from mine, and it felt like I could breathe again. My breathing stuttered, nerves thrumming, I focused back on my meal. Father's next words effectively suffocated me once more.

"Tavvy, it would make me a proud father to have you escort Z to the ball."

The world spun rapidly, dizzily. The floor dropped out from underneath me, and I was spun head over heels. Pounding reverberated in my brain, and even my deep breaths did nothing to dispel the growing panic.

Dozens of emotions slammed into me, like physical blows—anger at my father, distress, jealousy so potent that it contaminated the air like an acidic fog. The earth continued to disappear from under me, a gaping chasm that consisted of nothing but emptiness and darkness. A sickly tar that clung to my skin and hair, as black as night.

Trying to stop these emotions was like trying to stop the waves from touching the shoreline with my bare hands. They overwhelmed me in their intensity, pulling me deeper and deeper into the swirling whirlpool with no hope of escape.

Tavvy sat up straighter, an imperious set to his chin

that hadn't been there previously. His smile was malicious and cruel, eyes glimmering like beaded jewels.

"I would be honored, Father," he said diplomatically. Despite his tone, there was no denying the glee in his voice and the twinkle in his eyes.

I knew this couldn't be allowed. Not only would Z's other mates, my brothers, not stand for it, but Z herself would fight tooth and nail if she was forced into the presence of this scumbag. She may not have realized the extent of the damage he'd caused not only me but others as well, but she knew enough to stay clear of him.

"Father...rethink this. Please," I said stiffly. My tone brooked no room for argument.

When Father blinked at me rapidly, I realized it was the first time I'd ever stood up to him before. Ever spoke back. Now that he knew, or at least suspected, the truth of my relationship with Z, I had no qualms about standing up to him to protect her. Standing, being the ironic term.

Forever confined to my chair, minus the few brief minutes of relief before, once again, my legs were stripped from me. Phantom pain resonated through every pore of my body at the memory, but I pushed it down.

"Yes, my son?" He wiped his mouth on a napkin.

"Z is..." I trailed off, unsure how to articulate my excuse.

"A psychotic sexy bitch?" Tavvy taunted, and my fingers curled into a fist. Hearing him call her both a bitch and sexy made me want to kill him. Painfully. With a variety of very sharp weapons.

Maybe Z was rubbing off on me already.

"Shut your mouth!" I screamed before I could stop myself. Anger thrummed through my veins, alighting me. The white-hot explosion churned like molten lava just beneath the surface, a hair's breadth away from exploding.

Father slammed his fist on the table, cutting off whatever retort Tavvy had. Tavvy turned his glare on our father before bowing his hand submissively.

"Dair, come. Now." His tone was the no-nonsense one he reserved for only me. The tone that meant it was either my life...or my mother's.

Or Z's.

Trembling with incandescent fury, I wheeled myself towards where my father was now standing, near the door to the dining hall. This building was specifically built for mermaid royalty. I knew, from experience, that the door opposite would lead to the bedrooms and the lake. The door behind Father led to the sitting room and the king's office.

As I passed Marcella, she dropped her hand onto my crotch, palming me. I hissed, throwing her disgusting hand off me.

"Don't ever touch me again or else I'll kill you," I said darkly. Her face paled at my tone, and she sank further back in her seat. My threat on her, at least, had worked.

Father let out a boisterous laugh.

"Don't be threatening my wife, son," he said jovially. Marcella's face paled even more, and I almost felt bad for her. Almost. We all knew what type of punishments Father dished out when he felt he had been slighted. His preferred wife showing attention to his bastard son? The retribution for that particular act promised pain. Lots and lots of pain.

Tavvy stood as well, moving to stand behind my chair. The twins, surprisingly, remained at the table, eating.

Maybe not surprising, if the looks they threw Marcella were any indication.

Tavvy pushed my chair forward, down the hallway and into Father's office.

The room was as sophisticated and elegant as the man itself, a modern, mahogany desk freshly polished in the very center. A bookshelf devoid of any books took up one wall, and the window was open. The smell of salt wafted to me, and I knew that this room overlooked the immense saltwater lake.

Rummaging through his desk drawer, Father procured a small bottle housing a tawny brown liquid that shifts to green, then blue, then yellow, and then back to brown again.

"Drink," he instructed stiffly. My body screamed at me to rebel, to fight, but my mind warned me against it. Not only was I practically useless against two grown, powerful men who could walk, I also had more to lose than they did. I had no doubt that one act of disobedience would cause harm to the people I loved.

The concoction I drank was created by the mage king, designed to regrow limbs, tissue, and skin.

The second the warm liquid touched my throat, fire flared in my veins. The burning feeling wasn't entirely unpleasant, but pinpricks of phantom pain erupted where my legs should've been. That was soon replaced by *real* pain, so intense that my back arched and tears welled in my ears.

I could feel my skin growing, my bones expanding, my muscles constricting. I didn't even have to open my eyes to see that where there were once stubs were now two golden legs. My legs.

Gifted to me by my father.

I heard rather than saw a blade being sharpened. I didn't want to open my eyes and see their mocking stares and condescending smiles. However, that didn't mean I couldn't hear.

Couldn't feel.

The first cut of the knife sliced through skin only, and I cried out at the initial stab of pain. I knew it would only get worse.

My father's rancid breath entered my nostrils as he leaned over me, and I gagged.

"We gave you these legs..." A knife cut down once more just below my knees. "And we can take them away just as easily. Remember that when you think to disobey or talk back to me."

And so, with bated breath, I fell into a cycle of endless torment.

As always, my cries and pleas fell on deaf ears.

THIRTEEN

Z

The dress was beautiful.

The type of ethereal beauty that you would glance at once and then find yourself unable to look away from.

Staring in the mirror, I felt like a princess. It was something I'd never felt before, and something I hadn't even known I *wanted* to feel before.

The bodice was ornately tailored, modestly clutching my breasts and revealing very little cleavage. Long sleeves, a darker blue than the rest of the dress, were similarly adorned with light blue flowers. From there, the skirt cascaded around me like pure silk and swished around my legs as I walked.

I kept my blonde hair down but decided to straighten it. The golden hair still retained some wave to it, but it was no longer a mess of curls. I wore minimal makeup, enough to bring color to my cheeks and enhance my eyes, but what really completed the outfit was the pair of earrings I'd found left on my bed.

I couldn't be certain which one of my mates had given me such a gift, but the female in me cooed. They were long, crafted from pure gold, and led to an intricate combination of circles that touched my neck with each shake of my head.

I normally hated dresses, despised dressing up, but I couldn't deny how beautiful I felt as I looked in the mirror. I looked like a female who was actually worthy of her seven princely mates.

Of course, I kept two daggers on my thighs and a razor blade beneath my dress sleeve. Some things would never change.

"You look beautiful," a soft, familiar voice said from behind me. I spun, skirt billowing around me, and met Atta's dark eyes. She smiled conspiratorially, flashing me a wink. "Those guys of yours aren't going to know what hit them."

She spoke as if we were old friends, best friends, and a part of me hated her for it. The other part of me yearned for the companionship she was freely offering. I wouldn't admit it to anyone, but loneliness constantly threatened to drown me. Consume me. It was eating away at me ever so slowly.

I missed Diego so badly that it hurt. And I missed Mali, despite everything she'd done. My loneliness was a bottomless pit of pure darkness, threatening to chew me up and spit me out. I wouldn't survive such a fall, and I didn't even know if I wanted to.

"What are you doing here?" I asked stiffly, turning back towards the mirror in my room.

I heard Atta's heavy sigh from behind me.

"I just want to be your friend, Z. I don't have any evil intentions. I need a friend, and I know you do too. You're my brother's mate, for fuck's sake. Why wouldn't I want to get to know you? Befriend you?" She spoke with such conviction, pulling the words deep from her heart, that I wanted to believe her. I wanted to believe her so badly that I nearly started crying.

I didn't, of course, but I wanted to.

Frowning, I fiddled with the sleeves of my dress.

"You don't have to answer me," Atta continued. "And you don't have to forgive Mali. She made a huge mistake, and we both know that. It took me a while to forgive her myself, and I didn't even know Diego—"

"You're right," I snapped, spinning once more on my heel. "You didn't know him, so you couldn't possibly understand what I'm going through. The grief I feel. The pain. The fucking betrayal."

Each word was hissed through clenched teeth. Atta watched me, face impassive except for the slightest, imperceptible tick of her jaw.

"I'm not here to argue with you," she said primly. Her hands folded on her lap. "And I'm sorry for implying that you should forgive Mali. It's your decision, I know that, but I also know that she loves you fiercely. She misses you, and I hate seeing my mate so distressed."

My breaths sawed in and out, and I worked on calming my racing heart. Each breath physically hurt me. No matter how hard I tried, I couldn't release or take in enough air.

"You look beautiful as well," I whispered at last. It was an apology...and it wasn't. It was the sort of muddled, middle ground I often found myself in with the people I cared about. A gray landscape that wasn't quite dark enough to be considered black and not light enough for it to be white.

Still, Atta took the bone I threw her with a grateful smile.

"Thank you."

I wasn't lying. Atta *did* look beautiful. She wore a pink dress that accentuated each one of her curves. Her red hair was piled into an elaborate bun at the top of her head, twin braids twining the hair away from either side of her face.

"I need to go meet up with my date," Atta said, jumping to her feet. She flashed me another tentative smile, and my lips reluctantly tilted up to match her own. I was afraid my smile resembled more of a grimace, but I was trying.

"Your date?" I parroted, following her to the door. Was Mali coming to the ball?

Fear and exhilaration warred for dominance within me before both emotions were swept away by anger, white-hot.

Atta's smile turned apologetic. "No...Jax. My fiancé."

The smile left my face instantly, a bucket of cold water being thrown over my head. My eyes narrowed into thin slits as jealousy reared and bucked within me. They told me that green was the color of jealousy, but that was a blatant lie. All I saw was red as I stared at the beautiful woman preparing to meet up with *my* mate.

I couldn't quite understand the extent of my possessiveness.

Atta held up her hands placatingly.

"It's just for appearances," she said soothingly. "I know he's yours."

When I continued to glare at her, my emotions running rampant within me, she took another step closer. Her tiny hands rested on my shoulders.

"I promise you, Z. You have nothing to worry about. I much prefer the P over the D, if you know what I mean." As if to further emphasize her point, her gaze flickered to my heaving breasts. A delicate flush raced up her neck, and she glanced up quickly. "Jax loves you...well, as much as someone as fucked up as him can. Please trust me. And if you don't trust me, trust him. There's nothing to be jealous of." She laughed heartily, throwing her head back and releasing my shoulders. "If anything, those guys should be jealous of the time I spend with you."

When I raised a brow at her in confusion, she flashed me a sultry wink.

"You have good tits," she said unashamedly. At that, I began to laugh as well. Atta was beginning to grow on me. Like a fungus.

My laughter diminished as I mentally reeled in my jealousy. It didn't completely abate, but I no longer wanted to claw her eyes out. I may not have trusted her completely, but I trusted Jax. I trusted all my guys, actually. Even Bash.

That asshole could talk a big game, but I knew innately that he would never cheat on me or do something stupid.

Flicking her fingers in a makeshift wave, Atta ducked out the door. I wasn't even able to close it before a dark boot appeared in the doorway. The boot led to skin-tight black pants, a white dress shirt, and black suit jacket, and then finally to a mane of golden hair. It took me a moment to place where I knew him from, and fear raced down my veins in icy waves.

Tavvy. Dair's old brother.

I didn't know a lot about him, only that he'd hurt my mate. In a fit of jealousy, he and his father had cut off his legs in order to make him less desirable. Dair tried to hide his pain, tried to bury it in the sand, but there was only so much he could do. For that reason alone, I hated Tavvy. The hate stemmed from deep within my stomach, this baked fire burning red-hot, before spreading upwards. Every nerve in my body was seconds away from exploding just by being in his presence.

I could only describe his smile as predatory as he did a careful perusal of my body. His tongue snaked out to lick his lips, and I shivered in disgust.

"What are you doing here...Your Highness?" I tacked on the honorific at the end, just barely keeping my aversion in check. He chuckled, the sound teetering the edge between annoying and malevolent, before leaning forward. His hand tightened around a strand of my blonde hair, and I resisted the urge to cut that hand off.

Considerable restraint, if I did say so myself.

"I'm your date," he murmured. His face turned into my neck, inhaling deeply. That disgust turned into anger and that anger contorted into fear. The way he touched me...

It was almost as if he believed he had absolute control over me and my body.

That mentality could get someone killed. Me or him —the verdict was still out on that one.

"I'm your date," he repeated huskily. His nose brushed my sensitive skin, and I shivered in revulsion. He mistook my tremble for one of desire, and his hand tightened on my waist. "You're so fucking beautiful. Sexy."

"I don't think this is a good idea, Your Highness," I said diplomatically, stealthily attempting to move away from his wandering hands. My attempted escape found me pressed further against the door, his lean body towering over mine. Fear once more cemented me to the ground, but I pushed it away.

I'd dealt with handsy nightmares before, but this was a prince. My usual method of cutting off his dick wouldn't work in this scenario.

"Why isn't it a good idea?" He breathed deeply, and I felt something slimy against my neck. Was that his...? Was that his tongue?

"Because you're a prince and I'm the assassin," I reasoned. I was pleased when my voice didn't quiver with the desperation that I felt.

Please, please, please, don't make me cut off his dick. I'm not sure that's an offense I could come back from with my life.

But I would, cut off his dick that was, if the situation called for it. Anything, including death, would be better than the alternative.

"Brother."

The glacial voice had Tavvy spinning around, finally releasing me. I slumped against the wall, heart racing, and nearly cried in relief when I spotted Dair wheeling himself forward.

I'd never seen such anger on his face before. It burned, blistering hot, and made his handsome face look ironically colder. More like his brother's.

His body was held tautly, and he leveled his brother with a glare that should've been able to level an entire city.

"Father changed his mind," Dair said icily. He wheeled himself towards me, hands clasping my own.

Tavvy raised his eyebrow at that.

"Father changed his mind?" he repeated in disbelief.

"I will escort Z to the ball now," my mate said smoothly. His hand tightened around mine to the point of pain. A good pain, I noted somewhat dizzily. "You are excused."

Tavvy opened and closed his mouth, gaping at me like a fish plucked from the water. The demented part of me wanted to chuckle at the comparison, but I kept my expression apathetic.

"You can ask Father if you so wish to," Dair continued with a lazy shrug.

Tavvy's glare was just as scathing as Dair's, but he conceded with a sharp nod of his head. His eyes, though, promised retaliation. Pain. Agony. Torment.

That one stare eloquently spoke words he would never need to say. It allowed me to see past his front and into his very fucking soul. His soul that was as dark as night. Twisted and depraved.

With a huff, Tavvy spun on his heel and stomped down the hall. His attitude reminded me of a misbehaving child not receiving the toy he wanted. As soon as he disappeared, Dair turned towards me, eyes desperate. His hands grabbed at my body, my hands, reaching futilely for my neck as if checking me for injuries.

"Are you okay? Did he hurt you?" he bit out. I knelt down so he could touch me easier, and his arms tightened around my middle. Before I could reply, he lifted me up and put me on his lap. His arms remained tight around me, and his face nestled against my neck. Unlike with his brother, this felt right, like a piece of a puzzle clicking into place.

"I'm fine," I assured Dair softly. I lifted his face up, tracing the planes of his handsome face with my fingers. His golden hair glinted in the artificial lighting, and his blue eyes hypnotized me. He was so beautiful, so perfect, that I wanted to skip the ball and memorize every line of his face. "He didn't do anything."

That was technically a lie, but I could see how precarious Dair's grip on his control was. I didn't know what would happen once he realized the truth—that his brother had been seconds away from attempting to rape me.

I knew I'd made the right decision to hide the truth when Dair's body physically deflated. The next second, Dair's hands were cupping the back of my head and his lips were desperately attacking my own. I leaned into the kiss, tangling my tongue with his. Desire set every nerve alive as I leaned further into his bruising kiss. His hands moved to my hips before lowering, curving around the shape of my ass. He gave my cheeks a squeeze, and I moaned into his mouth.

Finally, he broke away, planting sweet kisses to each corner of my lips, down to my jaw, and then across my neck.

"You look beautiful," he whispered huskily. He bucked against me, and I felt something hard brush my sensitive mound. "So fucking beautiful."

Those hands of his continued to knead my ass, and that desire and lust transformed into something else. I couldn't discern what it was exactly, but my entire body went up in flames. And my heart? It threatened to break free of its cage.

"And," Dair continued in a rasp, "you're wearing my color."

"You like it, don't you?" I whispered. I didn't know if it was the dress or Dair himself that made me feel brave. Maybe it was the incident with Tavvy that made me see things differently. I felt...sexy. Powerful. Every inch the badass assassin and mate to seven princes.

A fucking queen.

I removed myself off of Dair's lap, straightening my dress and patting down my disheveled hair. Dair let out a painful gasp, reaching for me.

"You like it when I wear your color," I whispered, barely recognizing the seductive lilt to my voice.

Dropping to my knees, I touched his bulge.

Like his brother, he was dressed in a black suit and white shirt. His golden blond hair was slicked back, showcasing his lightly tanned face and cerulean blue eyes. Eyes that reminded me of long nights on the beach.

With a quick glance down the hallway, assuring no one was in sight, I unzipped his pants.

Dair let out a harsh breath.

"Someone could walk down and see us," he whispered hoarsely. His chest heaved with each of his breaths. Despite his words, his hands settled on my waist, pulling me even closer.

"Then let them see."

I released his cock from its confines, groaning at the sight of it. It was long and thick, the same tawny gold color of his skin. Pre-cum beaded at the tip, and I lowered my head to taste it. Taste him.

His hands left my waist to tangle in my hair. His breathing was erratic, unhinged, and I smiled at being the cause of seeing him so unkempt.

I reached further into his pants to cup his balls, testing the weight with my hand before giving it a light squeeze. He hissed, eyes flashing with heat, before he tilted his head back with a groan.

I licked the tip slowly, using my saliva and his own cum as lubricant. His labored breathing reached my ears, eliciting my own goosebumps of desire. There was something immensely attractive, sexy, desirable, about knowing you were the one tearing a man apart. Making him succumb to desire.

I used one hand to lift his thick girth as I licked the salty underside. His cock twitched with each lick, suck, and kiss. My other hand continued to fondle his balls.

"Please," he whispered breathily. I wrapped my mouth around his length, taking him in as far as I could. The tip of his cock touched the back of my throat, but I knew I could take him even farther.

"Fuck!" he screamed. He grabbed at my hair and

began to fuck my mouth in earnest. I allowed him to, staying still as his cock entered and exited me erratically. When my hand squeezed his balls tightly, he exploded. He tried to pull away, but I held him in place, swallowing everything he had to offer. His body shook as he released his seed inside my mouth.

Finally, I pulled away, smiling in satisfaction. Dair's eyes were dazed, hooded with desire, as they rested on my face. That desire and lust turned into something else, something that caused my breath to leave me in a swooping exhale.

Because the expression on his face looked an awful lot like love.

Love.

For me.

As he continued staring at me, I ducked back into my room, grabbed a washcloth, and returned. His dopey expression didn't leave as I cleaned him up and gently placed his half-erect cock back into his pants.

"Z..." he whispered hoarsely, and I just knew what confession would leave his lips.

"We need to get to the ball," I said, cutting it off, staring everywhere but at him. I managed a humorless laugh. "I am the guest of honor, after all."

"Z." This was said with a heavy, resigned sigh.

Ignoring it, I grabbed his chair handles and pushed it down the hall.

We passed a few elegantly dressed nightmares, all of which stuck up their noses when they caught sight of me. A human. With a Prince of Mermaids.

The chair-bound Prince of Mermaids.

We reached the large, ornately carved wooden doors that would lead to the ballroom. From the other side, I heard music playing and people chatting with one another.

I stepped away from Dair to open up the door, but he grabbed my hand and pulled me back.

His eyes were somehow able to see through every flaw I had, every mistake I'd ever made, every layer of doubt and self-loathing. I felt stripped bare beneath his penetrating gaze. Naked and vulnerable.

"Z, I love you," he whispered. Before I could reply, the ballroom doors were thrown open to reveal the shifter king smiling down at me.

"Z!" he said jovially. "We've been waiting for you."

FOURTEEN

Z

The shifter king leaned over, taking my hand in his large paw. With a bow of his head, he pressed his lips to my knuckles.

"We're happy you could join us," he said, smiling. I didn't trust that smile for a damn minute. This was the same man who avidly supported human work camps and stricter laws for human disobedience. He was evil personified—no number of smiles could curb the malicious glint in his eyes.

"I didn't know I had a choice," I said lightly, feigning a laugh. His own smile thinned, eyes darkening. He pulled his attention off of me to face Dair. He extended a hand, and my mermaid mate shook it. With great reluctance, I noted somewhat amusedly.

"Dair! How are you faring today?" he asked. I wished I could see Dair's face, discern his emotions through his facial features. Instead, I placed my hands on his shoulders, unsurprised to feel them stiff.

"I'm doing good, Your Majesty."

Awkward silence descended. The shifter king remained standing in the doorway, a glass of what looked like wine in his hand. Behind him, I could see a sea of color as people twirled, danced, and chatted. Each of the ladies was bedecked in a dress that put mine to shame. For the first time that evening, self-consciousness crippled me.

I fucking hated that feeling—the feeling that no matter what you did, you would never be good enough. Was that normal? Did females normally feel like that?

Huffing, I smoothed my hands down the silk skirt. I prayed that my hair wasn't still mussed from my rendezvous with Dair a few minutes earlier.

Or that the evidence of my arousal wasn't particularly pungent with all the enhanced senses around me.

"If you don't mind, Your Majesty, I really should get to the party," I said. The shifter king's eyes widened in surprise, but I couldn't decide if it was shock that I'd somewhat spoken back to him or realization that he was blocking the doorway. Either way, his lips curved up cruelly, and he stepped aside with an elaborate, sardonic wave of his hands.

"By all means..." he said curtly. I prepared to wheel Dair in, but a hand on my shoulder stopped me.

"There are stairs here, dear." He said "dear" as if it were a curse word, not an endearment. Unease prickled beneath my skin, but I kept my smile pleasant. "Dair is going to have to enter through the side entrance."

"Then I'll go with him," I said resolutely, already turning his chair around. Dair's hands were white where they gripped the seat handles, but he didn't interrupt our conversation. Trusting me. Allowing me to take the lead in this fucked-up game with a fucked-up king.

Said king chuckled darkly.

"But you're the honored guest! Of course you have to make a grand entrance." He roughly shoved my hands off of Dair's chair, ignoring my yelp of protest, before linking his arm with mine. "He'll meet you there."

I glanced helplessly at Dair, but he begged me with his eyes to play along. Be the good little assassin that everyone expected me to be. And good little assassins didn't castrate kings. No matter how tempting it might've been.

Flashing a smile I'd perfected in the mirror, I allowed the shifter king to guide me to the top of the stairs. It was a Cinderella moment...only I had seven princes instead of one.

And a murderous, sadistic king leading me down the stairs.

The ballroom was beautiful, I noticed immediately. It was a different room than the one we'd held the feast in so many weeks ago—the feast that had resulted in hundreds of deaths and my position as the kings' assassin. A powerful mage had performed a spell that killed everyone in the room, including the young ladies partici-pating in the Matching.

The Matching was a competition for the princes, my mates, to find their wives.

My jealousy, once more, prickled into awareness, but I pushed it aside. They were mine now. Any woman they might've been with in the past was only that—a part of their past. Heaven knew I hadn't arrived into this relationship a virgin.

Shaking my head, I focused once more on the spacious room. A seven-tiered chandelier hung directly in the center of the room, providing the only light visible. The ceiling was an well crafted combination of gold and wood. Tiny angels were intermingled with carved flowers and swooping vines. The walls, too, were made of wood, various pillars protruding outwards.

The entire space felt elegant, as if I had stepped back in time thousands of years ago.

The second thing I noticed was the people. Hundreds of them, all elaborately dressed. The women wore puffy dresses in a variety of colors, and the men wore suits similar to Dair's. Hair was coiffed, slicked back, curled. Everyone was the epitome of beauty and perfection.

And all eyes were on me as I descended the staircase. Shock, curiosity, horror, desire...they all blended together as the nightmares looked, for the first time, at their new assassin. I wondered who these people were.

High-ranking officials? Nobles?

I tried to keep my anxiousness in check as I met each person's gaze. Men and women alike were staring at me, enthralled. Why wouldn't they be? I was an enigma. A woman and a human who'd won the Damning.

I wondered how many of these people knew the truth of who I was, and how many thought I was a normal noble.

Devlin's violet eyes peered up at me from the back of the crowd. His mouth was parted slightly, wonder and awe emanating from him in palpable waves. Beside him stood Killian and Bash. The two of them had similar expressions on their faces, though Bash looked pissed too. Probably because he felt desire towards me at all.

I scanned the crowd with a newfound eagerness now that I knew my mates were lurking nearby.

I spotted Jax next, arm linked with Atta's. I normally would've been jealous, but his gaze wasn't on the beautiful woman beside him. It was on me. Only me. As if I were the only girl in the entire world.

It took me another moment to find Lupe. His large, burly body was leaning against a wall. His eyes roamed me from head to toe, lust darkening his features. He took a step closer, as if he intended to grab me from his father, before releasing a pent-up breath and stepping back into his corner.

A shadow stood beside him, clothed in darkness.

For a brief moment, those shadows departed to reveal the face of my mate I'd only ever seen once. Just for me, Ryland released the shadows. Just for me, he showed me his face. I gaped, stunned, as he smiled cheekily at me. Just as quickly, the shadows reappeared, once more obscuring his face from view. I was momentarily struck speechless, and I couldn't help but wonder if I'd imagined the exchange.

"We have some people we want you to meet," the shifter king said coyly. A sinister smile lit up his face.

He led me to the center of the room, where the mermaid king and incubus king were laughing. Both men stopped when they saw me, and their eyes flashed with something akin to hunger. It made the previous prickle of unease turn into full-blown wariness.

"Z! As lovely as ever!" The incubus king took a step towards me, planting kisses on both of my cheeks. I held perfectly still until he finally pulled away. His power briefly caressed me, causing my nipples to harden. His smirk told me he knew exactly what he'd done.

Asshole.

"Z." The mermaid king nodded in greeting, but his eyes were hooded as they made a slow perusal of my form. I was modestly dressed, but I felt as if I'd walked into the ballroom naked.

"I should wait for my date, Your Majesties," I said, once more scanning the crowd for my mates. I could see Devlin, Bash, and Killian lunging forward on one side, and Lupe parting the crowd on the other. I didn't see Ryland, but that didn't necessarily surprise me. For all I knew, he was already beside me, invisible to the naked eye.

"Date?" The mermaid king straightened with interest. "Is Tavvy treating you well?"

"Tavvy?" I blinked once. "No, Dair is my date."

The king's face puckered and pursed as if he'd eaten something sour. A vein in his forehead throbbed angrily.

I realized then that I'd said something I wasn't supposed to. It became abundantly clear that Dair had been lying when he stole me away from Tavvy.

Shit.

Feigning nonchalance, I shrugged. "Nobody came to pick me up, so I had to walk to the ball by myself. I met up with Dair near the entrance. He agreed to escort me."

I shrugged once more, infusing as much sincerity into my words as possible. If there was one thing being an assassin had taught me, it was how to lie expertly. How to twist words to fit my own needs.

I was an expert liar, able to spin my webs until every helpless fly was captured.

The skin around the mermaid king's eyes smoothed over, and he nodded once, accepting my story.

"Z," the incubus king cut in. A new man had joined the group, and I took stock of his muscular form, cropped black hair, and piercing eyes. "This is Axel. He was our previous assassin before his retirement this year."

He looked young, a few years older than myself, and definitely not old enough to retire. However, I knew things worked differently here. A new assassin was chosen every five years through the Damning. He must've been my predecessor.

"Axel," I said with a respectful bow of my head. He held himself still, coiled tightly, and his muscles flexed with each movement he made. Despite that, I knew he wasn't a shifter. No, the way he held himself, the agile way he moved, the flashing of his eyes, I deduced he was a shadow.

"Z." He brushed his lips over my hand, and behind me, I heard a low growl.

Lupe.

The shifter king's smile widened.

"Here's my boy!" He almost sounded like a proud, loving father. Almost. I turned just in time to see the shifter king slap Lupe on the back. Lupe, however, was focused entirely on Axel, eyes predatory.

Axel released my hand quickly, eyes flickering between me and Lupe with something akin to understanding.

"Lupe, I was just introducing Z to Axel. You remember Axel, correct? Don't you think they would make a good team?" There was no missing the sexual innuendo behind that last word—*team*.

Lupe's growl grew louder.

"Father!" Killian said easily, finally arriving with Devlin and Bash at his heels. "This party is wonderful."

His stutter, I noticed, was more pronounced than usual. I wondered if it was the presence of so many people or one in particular. One that wore a golden crown and wielded his sex appeal like a weapon.

I flickered my gaze from face to face. My mates now surrounding me, vibrating with unconcealed tension. The mocking grins on the kings' faces.

They knew, I realized in numb disbelief. The kings knew about the mate bonds between me and their sons.

And they were fucking playing with us.

They were turning this into a game, a game none of us understood nor knew how to play. Expertly, they were moving us over the board, and we were dumb enough to play right into their hands.

My eyes narrowed at the realization.

To them, we were nothing more than pawns in a game of chess. Each move had a reason. The goal? To checkmate.

If I was the pawn, I would completely demolish their game board.

I would play their game, at least for now, until I could

figure out what they would win from all of this. Would they use me as a pawn to control their sons? Kill me to cripple them?

Or something else entirely?

I kept a smile in place when the genie king appeared with a wine glass, handing it to me with a fake smile.

Yes, I would play their game.

And I would win.

I always fucking won.

FIFTEEN

BASH

She looked...so fucking perfect and beautiful that I wanted to both hate her and fuck her. The contradicting emotions were giving me a headache.

The dress clung to her chest like liquid silk, a light blue color that made her blonde hair shine like molten gold.

And I hated it. I hated that she made me think in terms of "molten gold" and "liquid silk."

My cock was already hard in my trousers, almost to the point of pain, as I watched her descend the staircase like some motherfucking angel of the past. Yup. Hard. I couldn't get hard to save my life, but the second my mate showed up, I was ready to squirt a gasket. So un-fucking-fair. I would rather be hard all my life, like Killian, instead of the limp noodle I currently was most of the time because of her.

"She's beautiful," Killian whispered in a daze from beside me. I merely muttered something indecipherable in response. She *was* beautiful, even I could admit that. She looked like something plucked straight out of a fairy-tale book, something carved into stained-glass windows, someone to be revered and worshiped.

My heart picked up speed, slamming against my ribcage. All I wanted to do was grab her, kiss those chiseled cheekbones of hers, lick every pale swath of skin visible in her dress, tangle my hand in her blonde hair...

And who the fuck was that kissing her hand?

Before I could stop myself, I was charging forward, body thrumming with an almost incandescent fury. Anger burned in my veins, a flame seconds from turning into a full-blown fire.

Dimly, I was aware of Devlin and Killian following behind me. I wondered if they saw the same red sheen that I did? Killian smoothly stepped in front of me, flashing a smile at his father. Anyone who didn't know him as well as I did would've thought he was the epitome of calm. Serene. Only we could see the tension in his shoulders, the pronounced stutter, the way his eyes flickered from his father to the asshat named Axel who dared put his lips on our mate.

...and why the fuck was I bothered so much?

I didn't like the woman, I reminded myself. I didn't like anyone besides my family. I tried to put on a mask of indifference, as if I didn't want to conjure up a spell that would permanently castrate the last assassin, while watching the scene.

My eyes, unbidden, flickered towards Z once more. They seemed to always go to her, like she was a magnet or something I couldn't ignore. She propelled me towards her. A moth to her flame.

Motherfucking shit.

I was whipped, wasn't I?

"Excuse me, Your Majesties," Z said in her musical voice, effectively pulling my attention back towards the conversation at hand. She curtseyed to the three kings present before flashing a singularly beautiful smile at Axel. Lupe, on the other side of the semicircle we'd created, growled low in his throat. The damn mate bond was even making him turn into a Neanderthal. She reverted us back to our basic, primal instincts, where everything was either fuck, kill, or eat. And with her? We wanted to fuck. It was a sort of carnal hunger, a predatory hunger, that left me speechless.

I'd had my fair share of females, but never anyone like her. Never any female that I wanted to cuddle with afterwards, wanted to hear laugh, wanted to know every damn thing she was willing to give me.

Shit. Shit. Shit.

I hated the direction of my thoughts, hated the way they always seemed to lead back to her. I wasn't purposely trying to be stubborn, but there was no secret that the mate bond was preordained by fate itself. What happened to free will? What happened to choice?

And I wanted my relationship with Z to be a choice— both hers and mine.

"I promised Bash here a dance," Z continued lightly. I blinked stupidly at her.

Dance?

Did she get dropped on her gorgeous head or something? Because there was no motherfucking way I was going to dance...

She proffered a creamy white hand, and my heart thudded in my chest. Before I could stop myself, before I could think things through, I placed my hand in hers.

Her smile was smug as I led her to the dance floor, away from the kings' curious, amused gazes and the wistful ones of my brothers.

"I don't fucking dance, blondie," I said, pulling her body towards me. She placed her hands on my shoulders as I settled my own on her waist. Around us, the party-goers were participating in an elaborate dance that included dips, twirls, and some random guy doing the splits. I would rather chop my own balls off than do any of that.

Oh wait. I had no balls. The female before me had taken them.

"Suck it up, Bash-hole," she retorted, and my lips quirked instinctively at the nickname. That was new, I'd give her that.

"So why dance with me? I'm sure any other guy—not just including your mates—would love to dance with you." I couldn't hide the slight bitterness in my voice, but I kept my face impassive. Still, she saw right through me, smile widening.

"Are you jealous?" she asked lightly.

I snorted out a laugh.

"Never. Take all the guys for all the shits I give," I said with feigned nonchalance.

That smirk remained firmly etched in place, the damn temptress.

"So I'm allowed to dance with Axel?" She batted her eyelashes at me innocently, but his name had my hands tightening slightly, almost imperceptibly, around her thin waist. I took a deep breath and closed my eyes.

"Do what you want to do," I replied.

She immediately removed her hands from my shoulders, but I tugged her back to me.

"Oh hell no," I muttered before I could stop myself.

She laughed, a pure, jovial sound that made my cock twitch. It was the first time I'd ever heard her laugh, I realized. Genuinely laugh. A full-on belly laugh.

And god, did I like that sound.

It was music, spun gold, and elicited goosebumps up and down my arms.

"Why are you laughing?" I asked hoarsely. I didn't want her to know what effect she had on me. Hopefully, she attributed my raspy voice to irritation, not lust.

"Because you're so transparent, Bash, no matter how hard you try not to be."

I quirked a brow at her, confused by those words, but she continued on before I could question her further. "Anyway, I picked you for a reason. I need to talk to you."

"About?" I asked. The live orchestra was playing a chilling melody that spoke of love and loss. I didn't know why music spoke to me the way it did, but I could get lost in the noise. It reverberated through every pore in my body, intricate stories being woven together with each slash of the bow against string. Each pluck of the guitar. Each pound on the keyboard.

What we were doing couldn't be considered dancing, more like awkwardly swaying, but it felt right. It felt like us. Her tiny body melted against my own as if she was made for me, and I, her.

Did I hate it?

Or did I love it?

Her warm breath puffed against my neck as she spoke, and each turn of her head had her silky blonde hair brushing against my sensitive, pebbled skin.

Fucking hell. Love and hate were so close together. I couldn't tell the difference between the two terms anymore.

"They know," she said breathlessly. Those words caused her lips to brush the hollow of my throat, and my breath hitched.

Don't come in your pants, Bash. Don't you dare fucking come in your pants.

That was a mantra I never thought I would use in my life.

The mate bond made it so I couldn't get hard around anyone but my mate. Not that I would ever dream of sleeping with anyone that wasn't Z, but it could get damn irritating when I was trying to jerk one off. Instead, I had to fall asleep and allow my dreams to assault me until I was rock-hard and desperate to sheath myself in her delicious cunt.

Because apparently, I had dreams of the future.

And in those dreams, I was always with Z.

Happy. In love.

But was it real? Or was it the mate bond forcing us to feel that way about one another?

I couldn't discern, and I didn't want to look at it too closely.

"Bash," Z hissed in irritation, oblivious to the direction my thoughts had headed. "Did you hear me? They know."

"Who knows?" I asked. Driven purely by instinct, I brought my nose to the crown of her head and inhaled deeply. Her newest shampoo—a gift from Lupe—smelled sweet, which was an ironic feat, considering who the smell was coming from. I couldn't pinpoint the exact scent, only that it did things to me. Things that shouldn't be possible through a mere smell.

"Your parents. They know about the mate bond."

Her words smothered me like an avalanche I couldn't escape from. The rocks settled heavily on my chest, pressing down and cutting off my breathing. I pulled away from her slightly so I could see her face. Surely she was playing some cruel, practical joke on me.

They couldn't know. Not them. My brothers and I had survived this long because we had no attachments besides each other. There was nothing we cared about, no one we loved, that could be used as bait. And the kings weren't stupid enough to use the other princes as leverage, in fear of starting a full-on war.

"You're wrong," I said snidely before realizing how much like an ass I sounded. I blanched when her eyes narrowed, hands leaving my shoulders to rest on her waist. She canted her head to the side.

"I'm wrong?"

Okay, when a woman repeated your words back to you as a question, you knew you were in deep shit.

Scrambling to think of something to say, something that wouldn't bring about Z's wrath, I tacked on, "My father doesn't notice anything besides where his bed is in the room. I doubt he would've noticed."

Her puffy lips parted, a rush of air escaping.

"That may be true, but the rest know. Of that, I'm certain."

"Did they say something?" I asked anxiously.

The kings knowing...

That was the equivalent of standing in a battlefield, a double-edged sword hanging over all of our heads. We were just waiting for the sword to drop and kill us all.

"That's where you come in," Z continued. Her voice was still icy, but she'd once more placed her hands on my shoulders. Progress, though small.

"Me?"

I couldn't stop thinking of the implications behind the kings knowing. If what she said was true, the seven most powerful men in the kingdoms now had something they could use against us, the princes destined to either save the world or destroy it.

And if Z's life was hanging in the balance?

Well...we were sins for a reason, after all. Not one of us would hesitate to watch the world burn to ensure her safety. The kings would know this and would use it to their advantage.

"I remember Diego..." Her voice choked over his name before she continued on. "I remember that he created a spell that could latch onto a mundane object, such as a flowerpot or a teacup, and you could hear everything from the room that item was in. Could you make something like that? Or more than one of something like that?"

I eyed the crazy girl warily.

"You want us to spy on the kings?" The disbelief was evident in my voice. And the fear. Because what she was suggesting...it went beyond crazy. It was fucking suicidal.

"That's the only way to know what they're up to," she insisted. From the determined set to her chin and the steel glint in her eyes, I knew there was no talking her out of this. She would either do this with or without my help.

As much as it pained me, I knew what my answer would be. I'd follow her through the fire if that was what she so desired. I'd been burned before, after all. What was one more inferno?

"You stupid, crazy, reckless girl," I muttered beneath my breath. I rapidly shook my head from side to side, almost as if I could unhear all the crazy nonsense she'd just spouted. At this point, I wondered if she was trying to get herself killed.

Was it to teach me a lesson?

To show me how shitty of a mate I was?

"Will you help me?" she asked.

"Fucking hell," I cursed, piercing her with a glare. "You're crazy and psychotic, you know that, right?"

Her smile was luminous, splitting her face in half.

"And I think you're crazy too. Maybe that's why the universe made us mates?"

God help me, the world was going to burn because of this damn girl.

Z

There were two things that the ladies of the ball liked to do—gossip and drink wine. While I wasn't the biggest fan of the former, I was a huge proponent of the latter.

Smiling coyly at the women before me, I took a tentative sip from the glass. It had a strange, bitter tang to it, but it wasn't horrible. The bitterness was immediately soothed away by something sweet—berries, if I remembered correctly.

Devlin had given me the drink himself, so I knew it hadn't been poisoned.

Poisoned. I scoffed at the word. Zack had claimed to have poisoned me at the fatal dinner, but I was beginning to believe it was the ramblings of an insane man. At the beginning, I'd felt slightly lightheaded and had coughed up blood, but the pain had long since diminished. I felt fine.

Poisoned. Zack had been full of shit all the way to his death.

Or had he?

Denial was a funny thing. You could bury the truth beneath layers upon layers of sand, but like with any treasure, it would always be uncovered. I, however, chose to stick my head in the sand, ignoring anything and everything that might have been contrary to what I believed.

I didn't want to think about Zack or poisons, choosing instead to take another sip of the sweet liquid.

I wouldn't have put it past the kings to attempt to off me during this grand ball in my honor. Poetic justice. Even as I chatted, I kept one eye on the seven men converged in the center of the room. The mermaid king had his arms wrapped around two petite females. One, I recognized as his wife, or at least one of them, but the second I knew to only be a noble lady. At least for the time being. There was no question that the mermaid king coveted her. The incubus king was sucking face with an unknown man, and the shifter, vampire, and genie kings were deep in conversation. I recognized the thick cloak of shadows as belonging to the shadow king, and he stood directly beside the mage one.

Bash's father's eyes were heavily lidded, head lolling against his chest. He looked as if he was seconds away from falling into a deep slumber.

I couldn't help but snort, a rather unladylike sound, at the scandal that would cause.

"So, Zara...I haven't seen you around." The lady who spoke had orange tinted hair cascading just to her waist. Her violet eyes indicated her to be a genie. She'd introduced herself as Cassie, the daughter of one of the nobles.

At my mates' urging, I'd introduced myself as Zara.

The world knew Z as the assassin. It was for my own safety, and my mates', that I kept my true identity as a secret. That wasn't to mean that the world wouldn't ever know, since nothing stayed a secret for long in this fucked-up game of cat and mouse, but it was vital that I didn't paint an even bigger target on my back.

For the time being, I was Zara, a rich heiress. The only people who knew differently were the kings, their sons, and Axel, the old assassin to the kingdom.

"That's probably because I haven't been here before," I stated dryly. Cassie pursed her lips further. At this point, I was afraid they'd get stuck in a perpetual pout.

"I saw you dancing with Bash earlier," another female piped up. She had the glacial beauty and features that could only be mean she was a vampire. Her dark skin was unblemished, and her cheekbones looked as if they could carve ice. She was beautiful, they all were, and I felt insignificant standing beside them.

For only a brief moment.

Then I remembered I could kill them in a variety of ways using only a butter knife as a weapon. Any and all self-consciousness diminished at the thought. Call me a sadist or a psychopath, but I felt myself preen at the mere thought.

That *preen* turned into actual fantasies of murder when the vampire added, "He was a rather attentive lover. God, his cock was so long. And his hands..."

The ladies erupted into damn titters as my breathing sawed in and out.

Out of my peripheral, I spotted Bash standing against the wall, his arms crossed over his chest. He looked handsome, no surprise, with his blond hair slicked back and his suit accentuating each and every muscle. I yearned to memorize every inch of his body through feel alone. Every dip and crevice. Every bone and muscle. Every hair.

I also knew, without a doubt in mind, that he wished to do the same to me.

There were hundreds of beautiful women in the room, and nearly half of them were vying for his attention, yet his eyes were only ever trained on me. I watched, unbeknownst to him, as a simpering female put a hand on his arm and batted her abnormally long lashes at him in what she probably thought was a seductive manner. Before, he might've talked to her. Flirted. Flashed her a sultry smile that would have any woman throwing their panties at him. And then, he would've had no problem with taking her up to his room and lavishing her with all of his attention. Come morning, he would forget her name and dismiss her like yesterday's trash.

Now, Bash glared at the woman's offending hand, shrugging it off. She pouted prettily, said something inaudible to me from where I stood, and he responded with another incandescent glare. With what looked like a huff of indignation, she stomped in the opposite direction.

Towards Killian.

I didn't even bother looking at my incubus prince. I knew that both he and Lupe, who was standing beside him, would dismiss the female. It wasn't them that I was worried about. It wasn't them that I was focused on with rapt interest.

I knew in my heart that Bash would never do anything to hurt me. He may not have known it yet, but he was mine as surely as I was his. He may fight it till the very end, but there was no faking it for me. I could see it in his eyes when we danced.

With Bash...it was complicated. He was a sword that repeatedly threatened to ram straight into my heart. He wanted to hurt me, but only because he cared for me. A man like him wasn't used to having those types of feelings, so he hid them away. Brick after brick, impenetrable wall after wall, he hid himself from the world. Buried his head so far in the sand, it was impossible to reach him.

Until now.

I didn't have weapons, but what little I did have was forged from steel of my own making. I was determined to break down his defenses as the other princes had done mine. Maybe, together, we could learn how to love.

I hated the direction of my thoughts. How cheesy they'd become. How cliché. If anyone was to hear me, they'd think I was a hopeless romantic, constantly spouting sappy love poems.

Fucking Bash.

"Zara," Cassie asked coldly. "Are you listening?"

That was all said with feigned nicety. I had no doubt in my mind that she would say one thing and then do the opposite. Two-faced bitch didn't even begin to describe that woman.

"I'm sorry," I said, mimicking her tone. "I must've zoned out. What did you say?"

I knew that I'd infuriated her. It wasn't often, I imagined, that people didn't listen to her. If she hadn't had the signature violet eyes of a genie, I would've suspected her to be an incubus. That term could be used interchangeably with males and females, just as a mermaid could be used for both a man and a woman. And Cassie fit the requirements of an incubus to a T.

"I was telling Odessa that I plan to...I suppose you could say *seduce* one of the princes."

This time, I didn't see red. There was no jealousy in my heart, only grim amusement. Taking another sip of my drink to hide my smile, I batted my lashes innocently at the genie female.

"Why would you do that?"

"Because the Matching was a fuck up," Cassie retorted, as if it was obvious. "They didn't find their mates, and all of their prospective wives ended up dead." This was said crassly, carelessly, with no respect at all given to the innocent females who'd died. Females who Cassie might've even known and befriended. It made me hate the bitch more. "They're probably so lonely, so sad, so scared. Especially since they haven't taken a lover in months."

"Oh really?" I asked, quirking a brow. Cassie nodded seriously, seemingly pleased that I was showing interest in what she deemed as important.

"Really. Bash over there used to have a new girl or two every night. Sometimes a man. He hasn't even looked at a female since the incident. Rumor has it, Bash was in love with one of the contestants that died and now is unable to be with anyone else."

I nodded my head decisively, but my mind had latched onto the thought of Bash with a *man*. Why did that thought make me feel so hot and bothered? My nipples were beaded nubs, straining against my dress.

Clearing my throat, I nodded again. And again. I was practically a bobblehead at this point.

"That's very strange," I agreed, but internally, I was squealing. I knew Bash hadn't taken a lover in a while, but hearing it confirmed made me warm and tingly. He may have claimed that he hated me, but behind that hate was desire too. Desire and kinship, two broken souls desperately reaching for one another in the dissonant chaos that was our reality.

"And same with Lupe and Ryland. Not a lover in months," the vampire, Odessa, added.

"So which one will you try for?" I asked Cassie, just barely keeping my laughter in check.

"Obviously Bash," she sneered. Giving me a dismissive once-over, she nodded towards the far wall. "Go stand over there. I don't want to be seen with a human. I don't think even Bash would stoop that low."

I bristled, hands clenching into fists, but flashed her a singularly beautiful smile.

"You're right," I said softly. I wiped beneath my eyes with the pad of my finger, sniffing. "None of the princes would ever look at a pathetic human like me. I'm no one. Just a girl who happened to inherit a lot of money. Just a girl who wants to support her kingdom."

Sniffle. Sniffle.

"I'll just hide my face in the corner of the room, away from sight. Bash only danced with me because he pitied me. He doesn't care about me."

I turned away and marched towards the far corner of

the ballroom. Only when I was out of sight did I release a tinkling laugh.

Just who did that girl think she was?

Insulting me, when I had walked in on the arm of the shifter king?

Wanting to seduce my mates?

She was going to get what was coming to her, and I would have a front row seat to the show.

A masculine chuckle greeted me, warm breath coasting over my earlobe. That breath was replaced by teeth nibbling lightly, and I gasped, goosebumps erupting on my skin.

"If you choose to retire from killing people, you'll have a career in acting," Ryland whispered, amusement ringing his voice.

I snorted. "I don't kill people. Well...I don't kill people who don't deserve it."

I watched Cassie sashay up to where Bash was standing. He glanced over at her with distaste before turning his attention once more towards where I was standing.

"Do you want to get into an ethical discussion about killing?" Ryland asked teasingly. "When is killing justified? Does war justify killing? Does revenge?"

"Let's not," I suggested brightly, spinning in his direction. As always, there was nothing but shadow, misting over the floor and vaguely resembling the shape of a person. I reached a hand forward and was surprised when my fingers touched solid flesh. For some inexplicable reason, I'd assumed my hand would go right through, that touching Ryland in this form would be like trying to touch gas.

His breath hitched, heart hammering.

"Why do you always hide?" I asked softly. My hand crept up his shoulder, curving around the length of his neck. I knew his skin would be dark, nearly as dark as the shadows themselves. It felt like silk beneath my fingers, and I carefully moved my hand farther up, until it reached his jawline. "You don't have to hide from me, you know that, right?"

"You saw my face," Ryland stated. There was no bitterness in his voice. It was merely a recitation of the facts. "You saw what I look like."

"So why do you still hide?"

His body tensed beneath mine as I moved my hand even farther up, resting the tips of my fingers on his cheekbones. I paused there with bated breath, searching his face. If he wanted me to stop, I would, but the diminutive seed of trust growing between us would stop as well. Trust went both ways, after all. He wanted me to trust him, and it was completely rational of me to want the same in return.

I waited, heart beating against my ribcage, as he took a shuddering breath. It fanned against my skin.

"I want—" He broke off suddenly. And then, louder, "What the hell is he doing?"

I jumped. Out of everything he could've said, I hadn't expected it to be that. I blinked up at him rapidly.

"What do you mean?"

He placed a shadowy hand on my shoulder and spun me around. The move, so sudden, nearly propelled me off my feet, but I held firm.

"What the hell are you talking about, Ryland?" I

hissed. Were the kings up to something? Were they finally moving the last pawn into place?

But he wasn't talking about the kings.

No, he was talking about Bash, my mage mate.

My mate who currently had his hand clasped with Cassie's as he led her out of the ballroom.

SEVENTEEN

Z

The floor opened up and swallowed me.

I'd once been pushed out a window by an enraged shifter. This feeling was somewhat similar. My stomach was bottomless, perverse fear sinking its claws into my heart and refusing to release its grip.

Suddenly, the world didn't make sense. It was just a blur of faces and names, of species and genders, of good and bad. The facets of nature, of mankind, blurred together until everything was indecipherable. I could barely breathe, barely think, barely hear anything over the sound of my heart beating.

Breaking.

I think the asshole just broke my heart.

My chest grew as taut as the strings on a violin.

"What the fuck is he thinking?" Ryland muttered irately.

All I could do was stare at the door they'd disappeared through. Stare. As if that would somehow compel them to come back.

My hands were shaking, horror and rage the predominant emotions. They settled heavily in my stomach, curdling like spoiled cheese.

The silence stretched until it became almost unbearable. Ryland's eyes remained on me. Even through the shadowy cloak, I could feel their gentle caress.

"It doesn't matter." My voice was soft, devoid of emotion. "He can do what he wants."

"Z...it's not what you're thinking."

"Do you know for sure?" I spun around to face him, hands clenching into fists. "You're with me, not them. How do you know? How do you fucking know?" A humorless laugh escaped me, followed immediately by a snort. "I wonder how she'll react when she discovers he can't get hard."

"I think you're blowing things out of proportion," he cajoled soothingly. The shadows moved as he stepped closer, hand extending as if he meant to put it on my shoulder and comfort me.

I took an automatic step backwards, bristling. I imagined that if I were a cat, my fur would be standing on end and I'd be hissing. My emotions were running rampant within me, a hurricane that threatened to flood my mind. I tried to calm them, tried to reel them in, but they assaulted me repeatedly.

"Says the coward who hides his face," I spat and then immediately regretted it. "Ryland..."

But he was already gone. The shadows had dimin-

ished as if a giant spotlight had come, effectively elimi-
nating them. I was now alone.

Alone.

Alone.

That thought echoed in my head.

Before I could second-guess myself, I walked briskly
to the backdoor. It led to a magnificent garden, currently
sheathed in moonlight. I could distantly decipher the
shape of a marble fountain, emitting a soft blue glow.
Whether that was from a spell or electricity, I couldn't
decide.

A few people gave me strange looks as I stepped
outside, but none of those people were my mates.

I imagined they would be furious with me, but at that
moment, I didn't care. I didn't care about anything.

My rage had ebbed, leaving behind an icy numbness.
It sprang from the tips of my fingers, up my neck, and
then down my body, encasing me in a slate of ice.

Suffocating me.

The air was crisp, a slight wind blowing my hair back.
It smelled like scented pine, despite the fact that there
was no pine tree in sight. A facet of magic, I imagined.

Steps brisk, I walked farther into the garden.

A stone statue caught my attention. The artist had
outdone himself. Each detail was intricate, carved with
precision. It was a man dressed in finery, mouth opened
in a scream. The artist had captured the horror
emanating from his eyes.

Rubbing my hand over the statue's cold shoulders, I
thought back to what I'd seen.

Bash's treachery was still too raw, a wound that

hadn't quite scabbed yet. The child in me, the insecure girl, wanted to pick repeatedly at the skin until it bled.

Why had he done it? I'd thought, perhaps misguidedly, that we were making headway. When we'd danced, he hadn't been looking at me like the enemy. He hadn't looked at me as if he hated me.

Stupid. Stupid. Stupid.

I should've listened to myself the first time. I should've listened to the warning voice in my head steering me away from these seven deadly men.

And because of my own stupidity, my heart had broken.

I'd offered it up to him, and he'd watched it crumble. I had no one to blame but myself.

Never again, I vowed, pulling up my dress and grabbing the diamond encrusted dagger. A gift from Devlin.

Spinning it in my hand, I finally released the scream I'd been holding in. The dagger flew from my hand, flying through the air and bouncing off another statue a few feet away.

Why hadn't my mates followed me into the garden?

Why did that even matter?

And why the fuck was I so emotional?

Realization settled over me like a heavy cloak.

The asshole kings.

They'd done something to me.

I knew, from both research and experience, that incubi were able to manipulate emotions if they were powerful enough. All it took was skin to skin contact.

My mind flittered back to when the king kissed my hand.

Since then, everything had felt enhanced, as if I were seeing the world through a new lens. Shinier. Brighter.

Those fucking assholes!

The despair turned to anger, white-hot. It threatened to burn me from the inside out. Burn me alive.

Through the hazy cloud of fury, I realized that I was playing directly into their hands. They wanted a strong emotion from me, planned on it, and no doubt were waiting for me back in the ballroom.

Did they want my fury?

Because they could fucking have it.

Mentally, I planned using my dagger to carve off their skin. The incubus king would go first, of course. I would pay extra attention to his nutsack. I wondered how appealing he would be with a castrated penis.

Fuming, I marched towards my dagger and picked it up. I was so focused on my mission that I almost missed the statue mere inches from me. Almost.

But I saw it.

A scream threatened to burst out, even as I took a step backwards, eyes widening in horror.

Killian.

Even in stone, his handsome, chiseled face was impossible to miss. His lips were pursed into a perfect O. Unlike the other statue, he didn't seem scared, only confused. He was wearing the same outfit I'd seen on him in the ball, including the incubus crest on his jacket lapel.

Horror filled me.

What the hell was this? Had someone been commissioned to carve a statue of Killian? Or...

Dread curled in my stomach.

Or was that Killian?

I stumbled backwards, tripping over my own two feet, and hit something hard.

Another statue.

His broad shoulders, extended canines, and hate filled eyes were impossible to miss, though that hate had never been directed at me.

Lupe.

He, too, was dressed exactly as I'd seen him previously.

"They were looking for you," a soft voice said from the shadows. There, flowers and hedges rose from the ground in a sort of makeshift maze. With the darkness blanketing the garden and only a thin shaft of moonlight, it was impossible to make out the figure.

I held the dagger steady, pushing my emotions to the side. It was surprisingly difficult to do so with the spell heightening them.

"Who are you?" I asked darkly.

The voice was a girl's, of that I was certain.

"While you were talking to your shadow, I told them that I saw you leave. They, of course, ran after you like obedient puppies."

Something moved in the distance, and I took another step closer. From this angle, I could see down another pathway.

Three statues glinted in the moonlight, one of which was sitting. Dair, Jax, and Devlin.

Anger hummed through my veins. There were no words adequate enough to describe it. It was the sort of anger people started wars for. Fear, simultaneously, twisted my gut.

These were my men, my mates, and this bitch had harmed them, maybe forever.

What if I could never free them from their stone prison?

"Release them." I didn't recognize my voice. It was practically a growl.

"All we want is you, sweet girl," she cooed. "Come with me, and I'll release your loves."

"Who the fuck are you?"

I realized that the correct question should've been 'what the fuck are you,' but I was too pissed off to care.

Finally, she took a step closer. The light caught first on her pretty face—plump lips, white eyelashes, and a button nose. Something hissed as the rest of her came into view. No, not something.

Her hair.

Her hair hissed.

Dozens of snakes slithered around her head. Green, a ruby red, and a few still were as yellow as aspen leaves. Each snake hissed, beady eyes fixated on me.

The girl laughed, a surprisingly jovial sound.

"My sweet child," she said. The snakes rose from her head, their hissing a cacophony of noise. She smiled with feigned sweetness. "Have you ever heard of a gorgon?"

EIGHTEEN

Z

A gorgon.

My mind rapidly attempted to sift through all the information I'd acquired over the years.

A mythical creature, descended from a demon. Snakes for hair. Female, always. Extinct.

And with the ability to turn people into stone.

I squeezed my eyes shut, heart racing. Her laughter caught in the wind, a twinkling of bells.

"So you heard," she said, and there was no mistaking the cockiness in her tone.

"Your reputation precedes you," I drawled sarcastically. I held the knife handle stiffly as Ryland's training flickered through my mind. He'd prepared me for this, I realized. Prepared me to fight an enemy I wasn't able to see.

The hissing of snakes grew louder as she grew closer.

"I don't want to have to hurt you, Z, but I will."

"Did Aaliyah send you?" I asked, teeth gritted. There

was a change in the air, and suddenly, I felt warm breath on my face.

"Of course," she replied immediately. Casually. Relaxed.

"Why?"

The question haunted me. Why? What did that psycho bitch want from me? Why me? I was afraid I would never get the answers to those questions.

The gorgon giggled, a surprisingly young and innocent sound. Still, I didn't believe it for one second. This woman was not innocent nor young. She was a killer—she may have already killed my mates.

It was that thought that made my hands move. Blindly, they reached out and yanked at her slithering mound of hair. She yelped, even as something sharp pierced my skin.

Cursing, I released her hair—her snakes? —only to immediately punch her in the face. The sickening crunch of bone greeted my throbbing knuckles, and I resisted the urge to smile like an idiot.

"You bitch," she hissed, the noise more snakelike than human.

"You know my name," I began, listening intently to the wisp of fabric. The snakes had quieted down once more, but the gorgon could do little to conceal her footsteps against the dirt. The crinkle of leaves. The scattering of rocks. "I think it's only fair that I know yours."

I spun around and held up an arm a mere second before something slammed into me. I staggered, but my arm shielded my face from the worst of blows.

"Haven," she answered. Her breathing was heavy, as if this fight was taking a lot out of her.

I kicked my feet out, listening to her body clunk as it hit the ground. She muttered a curse.

"Pretty name," I mused. My foot intended to slam on her head, but she moved at the last second.

"Better than Z," she retorted from behind me.

Something hard slammed into my back. The pain was immediate and intense. Pinpricks of fire raced down my spine, tears blurring in my eyes.

"Nah. I'm rather fond of it," I countered, remaining crouched on the ground. Her warm hand tangled in my hair, pulling my head back, but at the last second, I swept my foot out behind me and brought her down as well.

She snarled. Honestly, it was a hideous sound. Grown ass women shouldn't snarl. It just wasn't attractive.

"What does she want with me?" I asked darkly, twisting my body. My hands once more tangled in her snake hair. Ignoring the stab of pain from the snakes' fangs, I brought her head up, only to push it back into the dirt. "Answer me!"

"Fuck off!" Haven hissed.

My head throbbed suddenly. So suddenly, I very nearly released the bitch.

Dizziness and nausea swarmed within me. A strange pain erupted on my arm. It felt like thousands of needles numbing my skin. That was the only description I could think of. It raced from the tips of my fingers, up my arm, and then down my body.

Suddenly, I couldn't move.

I kept my eyes squeezed shut as I was kicked unceremoniously onto the rocky ground. It was the strangest sensation to not know if you had a body. To have your sense of sight ripped away. To not feel your toes wiggle or your fingers grasp at dirt. Only my brain existed in this strange world. I was disembodied, a shell of myself.

"Making eye contact may turn you into stone, but my snakes?" Her lips touched my ear, and I wanted to shiver in revulsion. "They paralyze you."

Well.

Fuck.

I finally dared to open up my eyes.

Haven stood over me, smirking, and as I watched in rapt horror, she bent down to pick me up. I may have been skinny, but I wasn't a short damsel. Still, the gorgon didn't struggle as she dumped me over her shoulder.

"You know, I might've liked you, Z. We could've even been friends."

Somehow, my lips were able to move. They were the only thing besides my eyelids that were able to.

"Please don't."

Haven released a heavy sigh.

"I wish I could," she said softly. I almost wanted to believe the sincerity in her voice, but I wasn't stupid. "Aaliyah gave me life in exchange for this one task."

"Me?"

"I'm not ready to die," she said earnestly. "Between you and me, I choose me."

Hatred did not begin to encapsulate what I felt for this motherfucker.

I opened my mouth to retort something snarky, probably along the lines of, "But I choose me, cocksucking bitch," when I realized I couldn't get my lips open. Panic settled heavily in my chest with the strength of a tsunami, drowning me.

Would my breathing go next? I wondered if it would be horribly painful to choke from lack of air.

Stomach sinking, all I could do was focus on the twinkling stars blinking in and out of existence. I would be like those stars if Haven had her way with me.

"It's not like you're going to live much longer anyway," she continued. "I know denial when I see it. I can sense death—" Her voice broke off abruptly.

In a span of seconds, I was dropped to the ground, but no pain registered. I moved my eyes rapidly to the side, just in time to see Haven's blank gaze and pretty head.

Disconnected from the rest of her body.

The snakes were dead as well, cascading around her in a kaleidoscope of color. A figure dressed in black stood over her, a katana sword held in his or her hand.

Terror blinded me, momentarily overcoming the paralyzing effect from the snake bites. This motherfucker had just killed a gorgon with an ease that left me baffled. He, or she, knew exactly how to stop the bitch.

I was jostled as I was grabbed once more, head nestled beneath someone's chin. I couldn't see who was holding me, and my body thrummed with pent-up tension.

As we walked, we passed the statues of my mates. I was relieved to see the stone chipping away to reveal skin and vibrant colored hair. I nearly sobbed with relief. They were alive.

The unknown figure gently set me down on a stone bench, and I felt fingers brush my hair out of my face—the only part of my body that wasn't completely numb. There was so much tenderness in that one gesture that my heart caught in my throat. I willed my head to move, to look at the figure, but it remained stubbornly frozen.

There was a ruffle of fabric, and I knew my savior was gone.

Just like the stars.

NINETEEN

Z

The next couple hours were chaos.

If you could call it that. Chaos didn't even begin to encapsulate all that occurred. Someone, probably a noble girl and her lover, were dallying in the garden when they came across my prone body. My prone, unmoving body.

Well...

Screaming at the top of their lungs that they found Zara dead did not bode well for them.

In a span of seconds, I felt tantalizingly light fingers brush my hair, the palm of his hand curving around my cheek. He let out a broken sob, burrowing his face into my neck. I wanted to tell Ryland that I was still alive, still breathing, but the words got stuck in my throat. I couldn't even blink anymore, my eyes trapped in a perpetual state of awkward staring.

"Give her to me!" a different voice growled. I recognized it, but I'd never heard it like that before. Raspy, almost. Distorted with a guttural growl. Ryland hissed something indecipherable before I felt my body being lifted.

Felt. The irony of that term.

Bash stroked my hair rapidly, repeatedly, his hand trembling with each desperate movement. I wanted to yell at him to stop. My body, if I had been in control of it, would've tensed.

It was all fine and dandy to act like you actually gave a shit about somebody when you thought they were dead. Despite the whispers of love, I couldn't stop thinking about his hand in Cassie's as she pulled him away. What had they done? Where had they gone? I knew I wouldn't like the answers to either of those questions.

Still, I allowed myself to be held by him. To pretend that he actually cared about me, maybe even loved me. But with any fairy tale, there was always a catch. The clock striking twelve or turning the prince into a frog or however that story went.

"She's still alive!" The new voice sent tremors of relief down my spine.

Killian.

My body hummed as he approached, and soon, his face was leaning over mine. Red garnet strands of hair interwoven with dark brown and gold brushed my face. There were still tiny pieces of stone clinging to his body and hair, but he was whole. He was alive.

Cheeks flushed, he smiled down at me.

"You hear me, sweetheart?" he questioned. I didn't know what he expected me to do. Blink twice for yes?

Oh wait. I couldn't fucking blink.

"It's venom from the snake bites," added Lupe,

jogging to stand beside us. I couldn't see him, but I could feel his presence seeping into my bones.

"What can we do?" Bash asked desperately. His hand continued to trace my features—across my nose, the seams that connected my lips, my eyebrows. I imagined it would feel very good, comforting and relaxing, if I could actually feel his touch.

"Just wait," Lupe said. "When I was researching fae and revenants, I came across a whole list of extinct supernatural creatures. I remember reading about gorgons. Their venom paralyzes a human, but only for twenty-four hours."

Twenty-four hours! He better have been fucking joking.

"When the she-bitch died, it released us from our stone prisons," he added.

"Back up a second. A gorgon?" Bash asked in alarm.

"She was sent by Aaliyah apparently." Dair. "I couldn't hear the entire conversation, but I got the gist of it. Aaliyah gave the gorgon life in exchange for Z."

"Fuck!" That exclamation came from Ryland.

Fuck was a vast understatement.

My vision was jostled as I was carried through a door —a separate entrance than the one that led back into the ballroom. All I was aware of was the ceiling. A rather pretty ceiling, if you asked me, with golden trim, intricately carved designs, and wooden panes.

A door opened and closed, and I was dropped onto something. A bed, more than likely. My bed.

I could hear my men settling around me. A few curled up by my feet, one went above my head, and one went on either side. With the way my head was facing, I could clearly see Bash crawling into bed directly beside me. His face was worshipful as he stared at me, eyes grazing my features with a reverence that made my throat close. He curled up against me, hand wrapping around my waist.

With a quick glance in both directions, as if assuring no one was watching, Bash leaned forward and kissed the tip of my nose. The chaste gesture made my heart stop before restarting with a vengeance.

And so I began the long, excruciating wait.

MY TOES WIGGLED FIRST.

Then my hands.

Pinpricks raced up and down my arms, thousands of needles grazing the skin. The feeling wasn't entirely unpleasant. It reminded me that I could feel. That I was alive.

And then my head could move. My lips opening and closing, my eyes blinking rapidly, my neck craning from side to side.

My mates had fallen asleep around me, and I took the moment to survey them. Bash still slept beside me, but in sleep, he looked like an entirely different man. Peaceful. The stress of his position as a prince and a powerful mage diminished when he slept. His face appeared as if it were carved from marble, and his lashes feathered against his high cheekbones like twigs of ebony. His breathing was steady, sawing in and out.

Turning, being careful not to remove the arm around my waist, I stared down at my feet. Lupe was clutching one of my feet in his sleep desperately, as if he were afraid that removing his hand would be letting me go.

Silly boy. Didn't he know that I wasn't going anywhere?

That realization took me by surprise. I didn't know how to deal with it, so I did what I did best. Bury it in the sand to uncover at a later time.

Devlin and Killian were on the opposite side of my feet. Devlin was clutching my foot as if it was his favorite stuffed animal, and Killian was curled around Devlin. Aww. Killian was a cuddler. It was too adorable.

I wished I could take a picture or something to remember that moment.

Jax was draped over my head, face inside my hair. I canted my head backwards, smiling softly when Jax muttered something indecipherable, inhaling deeply. I could've been mistaken, but it almost sounded like my name.

Finally, I turned in my bed, meeting Dair's bright blue gaze.

"You're awake," I whispered accusingly. He smiled, blinding me with his white teeth.

"I've been awake for a while," he replied. He scooted closer to me so we were nose to nose in the large bed. His golden skin was peppered with freckles from all the time he spent out in the sun. Irrationally, I wanted to stay in bed and count each and every one of them. I wondered if he had more on his body, and the thought sent a thrill straight between my thighs.

"Why haven't you moved?" I asked softly. As if it had a mind of its own, my hand lifted and began to lightly trace his features. His skin was smooth, velvety, beneath my hand.

"I like watching you sleep," he replied unashamedly.

"Creeper." My hand caught on a shard of stone, and I tugged it out of his hair distastefully. "How do you feel?"

He chuckled. "Shouldn't I be asking you that? *You* were the one who was paralyzed."

"Yes, but you were the one who was turned into stone." I laughed, quickly smothering it with the back of my hand before the sound could carry. "Are we going to start comparing tragedies? Declaring winners?"

He laughed as well. "I would rather not."

"Good. Me neither." My breathing hitched as his eyes lowered to my lips. We were so close, so painfully close, that all it would take was one inch of movement and we would be kissing. I wanted to taste him, to decide whether or not his lips tasted as salty as his skin. "And in answer to your question, I'm fine."

"Me too," he whispered.

And then our lips met, and we were exchanging the lightest, most innocent kisses imaginable. Our lips moved over one another's as if they were meant to do exactly that. It was the sweetest kiss I'd ever experienced before in my life.

He pulled away with a simple peck to the corner of my mouth. His eyes were alive, brightening with exhilaration and awe.

"I love you," he whispered. Another kiss was planted on my cheek. "I love you." His lips touched my jawline before moving lower. Tiny kisses were trailed down my neck, each one accompanied by a declaration of love. I raised my chin to grant him better access. "I love you."

"Dair," I whispered breathlessly. "I—"

Before I could finish my sentence, a startled yelp came from by my feet. I turned, amused, just in time to see Devlin jumping up as if his ass were on fire. He was throwing daggers with his eyes at Killian, who looked sheepish.

"Sorry," Killian murmured.

"Your fucking cock was against my asshole!" Devlin yelled in horror. His hands reached for his butt as if he were protecting it from phantom cock. "I felt it. Why the fuck are you that hard?"

"I'm always hard," my incubus protested indignantly.

"Awww, Devlin, do you not want a dick in your ass? There goes my plan for pegging," I teased lightly, and his violet eyes snapped to mine. Relief shuttered over his expression as he practically climbed over Lupe to get to me. He peppered my face with kisses, seemingly oblivious or choosing to ignore Dair still kissing my neck.

"You damn, stupid girl. Don't you ever fucking scare me like that again."

"Us," a soft voice corrected. I stared over Devlin's shoulder at Ryland, who was standing in the corner of the room. The shadows obscured his face from view once more. "Don't ever scare *us* like that again."

Why the fuck was he all the way over there?

"Us. Me. Whatever. Don't do that shit again." Devlin accentuated the final statement with a bruising kiss to my lips. There was no doubt that they were becoming swollen.

"Yes, sir," I whispered, and his eyes darkened. Oh yes. Devlin liked that.

"I thought you were fucking dead," Bash croaked out from beside me. His hair was sleep mussed, bags still evident beneath his eyes, but his smile was luminous. He interlocked his fingers with mine, but I immediately pulled away. Hurt flashed in his eyes, briefly, before that was replaced by icy indifference. Without a word, he pushed back the blankets and stormed out of bed. My traitorous eyes automatically latched onto his ass looking especially delectable in his boxer briefs.

Damn eyes.

And damn heart crying for him to come back.

"I'm sorry," Killian blurted, drawing my attention back to him. He was now standing at the foot of my bed, eyes trained intently on me. He was shaking, I realized somewhat distantly. His body shook with tremors, and tears filled his eyes. "I'm sorry I couldn't protect you, Z. I'm a horrible, shitty mate. I stupidly thought... I just don't... I'm sorry. I'm so fucking sorry."

I moved my eyes away from Killian's briefly, to meet Devlin's stare. He gave me a small nod to show me he understood.

"Why don't we give them a moment?" he suggested, and my other mates reluctantly moved out of my bed. Lupe, Dair, and Devlin each gave me a final kiss. Jax merely sniffed my chest, no surprise, but Ryland refused to even acknowledge me as he glided out of the door.

What the hell was that about?

Ryland was momentarily forgotten when Lupe picked up Dair and held him like he was a baby.

"This is humiliating," Dair murmured beneath his breath. Of course, that seemed to be permission for Lupe to baby talk Dair as they exited the room. I heard statements like "Do you need your diaper wiper changed?" and "Does little Dairy need a nappy wappy?"

I snorted out a laugh, but that laughter died in my throat when I took stock of Killian. Shirtless. His tattoos and muscles on display, so delectable that I had to restrain myself from licking a pathway across his glorious skin.

For the first time that I could remember, I was locked in a room with my incubus prince.

KILLIAN

I watched her crawl to her knees on the bed, her glorious blonde hair trailing behind her like liquid gold. In her formfitting blue dress, she was a sight to behold—something ethereal that I sought to worship and love until the end of time.

Anxiously, I pulled my lower lip between my teeth. Why did it make me so nervous to be around Z, my mate? It wasn't just because she was beautiful, though that could've been one of the many reasons, but because she was able to see *me*. Not the me the rest of the world saw and revered, but the me I reserved solely for my brothers.

And it scared the shit out of me.

That transparency...it shouldn't have been normal. I'd never felt more vulnerable than I did in her eyes, stripped bare of all masks.

"What's wrong, Kill?" she asked, nibbling on her lower lip. I couldn't help but smirk at the nervous gesture she displayed—a mirror image of my own. She realized it at the same time I did and released her lip, smiling. "Oops."

I forked my trembling fingers through my tousled red hair, my agitation physically manifesting itself. All I could see, repeatedly, was Z's body falling to the ground. The gorgon carelessly tossing her over its shoulder. The fight draining from her eyes, bleeding dry...

I shuddered at the images, the feelings they evoked within me. I never wanted to feel that helpless again. Being able to see and hear everything, unable to step in, was torture.

"I want you to train me," I blurted. She paused, mouth partially opened as if she was going to say something. At my words, her mouth slammed shut and her eyes widened.

"Train?"

"Yes." I nodded my head. The more I thought about it, the more sure I was. Never again did I want to sit on the sidelines. To be a mere witness in our fucked-up world of predators and prey. "To fight."

When she continued to stare at me blankly, I hurried to explain. To some, my decision may have come across as impulsive, but I knew Z would understand. She had to. "When we were...frozen..." My voice wobbled over that one word. Frozen. Entrapped. I could still feel my body weighed down by cement. Clearing my throat, I continued doggedly. Z didn't laugh as my stutter became more pronounced, something that always occurred when I felt a strong emotion.

"When we were frozen," I repeated, "we were able to

see everything. We watched you come into the garden, but we were helpless to warn you."

My jaw clenched almost painfully at the memory. I'd tried to scream at her, but the words became lost. All I could do was watch...

"The others, at least, were faced away. They didn't have to see you...they didn't see you get attacked. They didn't see your body..."

I began to pace as if that could somehow quell the tension reverberating through me. My fingernails dug into my biceps, and I impatiently scratched at the skin.

"Kill," she said softly. Sweetly. It was a tone of voice I imagined she wouldn't use with anyone else, only me. At first, I felt a rush of exhilaration and a strange sense of giddiness. That dissipated just as quickly.

She had to treat me with kid gloves because she thought I was weaker.

Still, I couldn't resist grabbing the hand she proffered. Immediately, I fell face first onto the bed, and her small body wrapped around mine. I ended up with my head beneath her chin, and her hand lightly stroking my arm.

God, I could die in her embrace.

I loved her.

I loved her so damn much that it sometimes hurt to breathe.

It wasn't a surprise for me, this revelation. Not really. A part of me had always known it, had known it from the very first time she'd protected me, when I compared her hair to food.

I twirled a piece of her hair around my finger, smiling gently. Definitely spaghetti hair.

"So you want to fight?" Z asked, breaking the silence we'd grown accustomed to. I tensed immediately in her arms before willing my body to relax. She wasn't like my father. She wouldn't laugh at me or reprimand me or talk down to me.

"I want to protect you," I admitted earnestly.

Snorting, she tapped her finger against my chin, tilting my head up. I lost myself in her gaze, the heat and love emanating from her. Her pink lips twitched slightly, but it wasn't in laughter. It almost seemed to be...approval.

"I can take care of myself," she said. "But I agree—I think you all should learn how to fight...but not to take care of me." This time, her sigh was resigned. "There's more to the world than me, Killian. I want you guys to protect yourselves, to live life to its fullest, you know?"

I was silent for a long moment, but not because I was ignoring her. Instead, I processed her words.

She seemed to severely underestimate how much she meant to my brothers and me. The second we'd discovered the mate bond between us, she became our entire world. I knew for certain that I could never go back to the shy, timid boy I was before I met her.

"I don't know who I am without you," I admitted, and I could feel her body stiffen beneath mine. I cut her off before she could protest. "I said that wrong. I've changed since I met you. We all have. You make us better versions of ourselves, you could say. Not one of us wants to go back to the person we were before. Z, you may hate to know this, but you're our world now. I didn't know the mate bond could feel like this...feel this right. I want to love you. And hold you. And fuck you senseless. And—"

"You want to fuck me senseless?" Z murmured, and I stilled. That was what she focused on?

And then I realized what I'd said, what I'd admitted to, and panic raced down my veins.

Abort mission! Abort!

"'Fuck' is such a crude term," I stuttered out.

She propped herself on an elbow, the gesture knocking me onto my back. Her golden hair provided a shield between us and the outside world.

"So you don't want to fuck me?" she asked innocently, batting those damn eyelashes of hers.

I immediately began to backtrack.

"Of course I want to fuck you! I want to do a lot of things to you. Why would you think that I don't want to? And—" I broke off when I saw the mirth dancing in her eyes. "You're teasing me, aren't you?"

She pinched her thumb and pointer finger together. "Just a bit."

"Just a bit?" My hands flexed on her sides, tightening before releasing. "That's not nice."

"Haven't you heard?" She sprawled onto her back, and I crawled over her. The move found my legs on either side of her thighs and my hands near her head. "I'm not a nice person."

Her chest rose and fell, lust coloring her cheeks.

And we almost lost her today. I almost lost her. The mere thought had me wrapping her spaghetti hair around my finger once more.

"You scared the shit out of me today, you know that?"

She nodded wordlessly.

"I can't..." I took a deep breath to rein in my emotions. "I can't imagine a world without you in it. I don't want to live in one like that. Do you understand?"

Again, she gifted me with a small nod. I wondered if she was paying any attention to my words. Her gaze flitted from my shoulder blades, to my stomach, and then back to my eyes.

Suddenly, so suddenly that I gasped in shock, her hands grabbed my ass, pulling me even closer.

Her neck strained as her pink lips clasped around my nipple. The heady sensation sent lightning bolts of desire straight to my perpetually hard cock. I groaned, squeezing my eyelids shut as her tongue swirled around my aching nub.

"Fuck," I muttered through clenched teeth. She pulled her mouth away with a satisfied slurp, and I dared a glance down. Her breathing was heavy, and her eyes were hooded. So fucking gorgeous.

"You've never done this before?" she asked softly. Her hands kneaded my ass.

"I've been saving myself. For you," I whispered. As an incubus, I needed lust to live, just like a human needed food and a vampire needed blood. However, that didn't mean I had to partake in sexual activities myself. The pheromones that permeated the air in most brothels were substantial enough. Hell, I would sometimes sit in front of my brothers' rooms and get fed.

And of course, after I met Z, I would touch myself. A lot. But before that? I hadn't ever felt the need.

"So you haven't...done anything?"

"Not with a female," I replied, my body still thrumming from her touch. The hands on my ass paused.

"But with a male?" she asked. She didn't sound disgusted, only curious and a little turned on. Still, my face flamed in embarrassment when I realized how my words could be construed.

Chuckling nervously, I said, "No, not with a male either. Well, technically a male, since I do touch myself a lot."

Shit, Killian! Stop!

"I meant...um..." My face was an inferno. God damn my mouth.

She chuckled, her hands once more resuming their ministrations on my ass. I practically mewled like a cat in heat.

"Don't worry." She leaned up once more, teeth finding my earlobe. She bit down once before suckling the skin. Nibbling on it. This time, I couldn't contain my groan. "I touch myself too."

My cock was painfully hard, throbbing almost, inside my pants. There was a fine line between pleasure and pain, and the damn thing was dead smack in the center. I pictured Z lying in bed, her hand between her slick folds.

I was going to come in my pants.

Her fingers fisted in my hair, and she eagerly brought my lips down to hers. I swallowed the appreciative moan she made in the back of her throat, prodding her lips with my tongue and demanding entrance. Everything felt instinctual to me, as if I'd done it a thousand times before. There was no hesitation as my tongue tangled with hers in a choreographed dance. She still tasted sweet, despite being paralyzed for hours. Delicious.

She salaciously grabbed my bottom lip between her teeth, tugging. Her eyes remained fixed on me. Gauging my reaction, perhaps?

When I nodded once, encouraging her to continue, she reached for my boxer briefs and tugged them down. I froze, briefly, but any self-consciousness I might've felt disappeared when she ran her eyes over me.

"God, you're so fucking big," she whispered.

"Thank you."

Was that a thing people said? It felt appropriate. After all, she was complimenting my cock.

And I had a rather great one, if I was being honest. Not that I had a lot to compare it to. Nobody would let me look at theirs and see—

My thought cut off when her hand pulled at my balls. I whimpered, the feeling unlike anything I'd ever felt before. It was ten times better than when I'd touched myself there.

"Wait," I breathed, and her hand immediately released me. For the first time since I knew her, Z's face turned a delicate shade of red, and she hid her face.

"I'm so sorry, Kill. I just got carried away—"

I cut off her ramblings with a searing, claiming kiss.

"Don't ever apologize," I whispered harshly. I gently grabbed her hand and brought it back to my aching cock. "I want you to touch me."

I kissed her again, hoping she was able to feel all that I felt for her through the clash of our lips.

"I don't want to have sex tonight," I stuttered, and if I

expected judgement or anger, I was sorely mistaken. I shouldn't have expected anything else, though. This was Z. She understood me better than anyone. "And it's not because I'm not ready, because I am. I'm so fucking ready, you have no idea."

I leaned down to breathe her in before planting a kiss to her shoulder, directly where her dress was sliding down.

"I want you, Z. I want to love you and fuck you and do so many other things to you. But I don't want our first time to be like this." My face heated. "I had it planned. I would make it romantic and shit, with rose petals and candles and chocolates. I just...I want it to be perfect. I want—"

She cut me off with a quick kiss. Her eyes were glittering with a suppressed emotion, and my heart hammered at what I suspected I'd just seen.

"It's okay, Killian. You don't have to explain yourself. We can go as far as you want."

As far as I wanted...

"Take your dress off," I whispered darkly. Huskily. I barely recognized my own voice.

Eyes heated, Z made quick work of sliding the dress over her shoulders and shimmying out of it. My tongue turned to cotton in my throat when I took in, devoured, her scantily clad form.

She wore only a white, strapless bra and matching panties—panties that were currently soaked through.

"You're already wet for me," I murmured in observation, and she let out a whimper. Huh. She liked when I said that.

I grabbed the tip of my cock, using the pre-cum as lubrication. Slowly, I began to rub myself from tip to balls. My cock had always fascinated me. The velvety softness of the skin contradicting the hardness underneath.

"You need to get naked, sweetheart," I said softly. Because really, at that point, it just wasn't fair. "Be a good girl and remove those clothes."

Once more, a needy whimper escaped her.

Huh. Interesting.

With a blistering speed, she unsnapped her bra and kicked off her panties. I made a mental note to undress her myself when we finally did make love. To take my time removing each article of clothing, showing her my love with each kiss to her soft skin.

Worship her, the way she deserved.

Breathing heavily, she glanced up at me. Waiting.

For what?

Instead of answering her silent plea, I took a moment to take in her perfect body.

Her skin was porcelain in appearance, the occasional scar marring the perfect smoothness. Her breasts were large, quite easily a handful, and her pink nipples screamed at me, demanding me to put each one in my mouth as she had done with mine.

Patience, I told myself firmly. The last thing I wanted to do was explode before we even started.

I lowered my gaze, taking in her dripping pussy. Her legs were spread wide, offering herself to me. My own personal feast.

I continued to rub my cock, eyes alternating between her nipples, lips, and pussy.

"Touch yourself," I pleaded and was shocked when my voice came out sounding authoritative. I was even more shocked when Z released a breathy moan.

"Where?"

"Touch those perfect tits," I instructed. I fondled my balls, once, before moving my hand back down to the tip. Z's eyes were fixated on my cock, even as her own hands moved up her sides and to her breasts. Two fingers from each hand pulled and tugged at her nipples.

"Shit, Z," I whispered, awed. She was beautiful and perfect and mine. I'd never been overly religious before, but I thanked God that I'd gotten her.

"Keep touching your breasts, but I also want to see a hand in those pretty pink lips," I said. I figured if she'd listened to me the first time, she'd be willing to listen to me a second time.

If the gasp of pleasure was any indication, she liked what I'd said. A lot.

One hand continued to fondle her breasts, her thumb circling around her nipple but never quite touching, while the other spread her pussy apart for my viewing pleasure. I groaned low in my throat, utterly transfixed as she jabbed a finger inside of herself.

I erratically stroked the length of my cock in tandem to her own finger entering and exiting her liquid heat. She began to fuck herself in earnest, jabbing a second and then a third inside.

Her fingers pinched her nipple before moving to her neglected breast. She tested the weight before pulling her nipple out and releasing it. The momentum caused her boob to bounce, and she moaned.

"Look at me," I whispered harshly. "I want to see you come."

Her eyes lifted from my cock to my eyes and held them as she played her body like a violin. She knew which string to pluck and when to pluck it, each moan that reverberated from her body a symphony of music.

I could feel myself reaching the precipice of pleasure. One more tug, and I would be tumbling head over heels off a cliff.

"Come for me, sweetheart. My love."

I exploded the same time she did. Our cries echoed in the large bedroom. My balls clenched painfully as I released the last of my seed onto the bedspread.

"Fucking hell," Z breathed, panting. She glanced up at me with doe-like eyes. "I didn't know you fucking had it in you." She sounded awed.

"I don't know what you're talking about," I admitted, standing up from the bed and moving to the adjacent bathroom. Turning on the faucet, I wetted two towels before moving back to the bed. I gently cleaned Z off before rubbing the cum off my own dick. Our mixed seed still darkened the bedspread, but I was too lazy to send up servants to change the bedding.

Instead, I grabbed a blanket from a chest near the foot of the bed and laid it over the sex drenched one. Z waited until it was spread out before climbing back on the bed, still naked. I curled around her, tucking my head beneath her chin.

This was heaven. Bliss.

It was unlike anything I'd ever felt before.

"Kill?" Z mumbled sleepily. Her fingers were idly stroking patterns on the skin of my arm.

"Yes, my love?" I asked, tentatively pressing a kiss to her neck.

"You don't have to be a fighter or a protector for me to love you. You just have to be you." The last words were nearly unintelligible, but I heard them as if they were screamed.

Did she...?

Did she just confess...?

I didn't want to hope, but my heart began pounding against my rib cage. All I could do was hold her closer against me, surrounding her in my love. I languidly lowered my head and nuzzled her perky nipple with the tip of my nose.

Before I could ponder her unintentional confession, I felt darkness encroaching at the edges of my vision. Sleep claimed me like a thief in the night, stealing away the last of my coherent thoughts.

I fell asleep holding the love of my life in my arms, her confession of love hanging palpably in the air.

Z

The kings loved to hear themselves talk.

I imagined they spent hours in the mirror, practicing their speeches and animated facial expressions.

The send-off was small, with only the kings and their sons present. I stood in the center of the throne room dressed in tight, leather pants and a black shirt that clung to me like a second skin. Over my shoulder, I had a bow and arrow set and a sword sheathed. On my wrists, I kept two throwing daggers hidden beneath my shirt.

I felt powerful, exuding danger that no number of haughty smirks from the kings could replicate.

A part of me missed the badass outfit—my ninja costume, as Mali had called it—that Diego had made me. One push on the magical pendant allowed me to completely transform into Z the assassin, not Zara the simpering maid. Complete with a black cloak, white mask, and a variety of invisible weapons.

Unfortunately, the kings had procured the pendant

after the Damning ended. Too much power, they'd insisted.

Too much, my fucking ass.

As the mermaid king droned on and on and the incubus king released tiny sparks of his power straight to my core, I focused on the men present. Namely, my mates.

Dair sat behind me, muscles taut and knuckles white where they gripped the wheels of his chair. He looked strikingly handsome today in his fighting leathers and with his golden hair slicked back. Beside him stood his three brothers. Tavvy and the twins, whose names I couldn't recall. I'd have to ask Dair at a later time.

Lupe and Devlin stood behind their fathers, eyes intently trained on me. Killian stood off to the side, not next to his father but still close enough for the king to flaunt his ownership.

My core tightened when I met Killian's eyes, memories assaulting me of our time together only last night. The way he'd taken control. The domineering voice. The lust emanating from his eyes. Who knew my sweet incubus was an accidental Dom?

He offered me a salacious grin, completely unlike the timid man I'd grown to care for, and I felt my own lips curving in response. Just as quickly, I shut that shit down.

Now was not the time to lust over my sexy, seductive mate.

Bash was leaning against the wall, arms crossed, eyes flickering from his sleeping father to me. His expression was unreadable whenever he met my gaze. Seeing Bash brought back the aches and pains that had all but diminished after my time with Killian. It rubbed repeatedly at the wound until blood spurt out, draining me.

I wrenched my eyes away from Bash's. Did he notice the pain and betrayal in my eyes?

Did he care?

Did I care?

It was the latter question that bounced around in my head. It brought about implications that I'd accepted the mate bond and everything that went with it. Accepted Bash as one of my mates.

The man barely tolerated me, keeping me at arm's length, as I did him. Still, my mind traveled backwards to when we'd danced together, carefree and laughing. He'd held me so tenderly, so reverently, as if he were afraid I would dematerialize as quickly as I'd arrived.

That was one road I couldn't travel down until I was sure of where we stood. Sure of what we both wanted.

Jax and Ryland were both missing, and their absence slammed into me like a sledgehammer. I wasn't necessarily surprised about Jax, but Ryland? Where the hell was he?

I hadn't seen him all day, not after the awkward stare off in my bedroom. I would've believed him to be mad at me if I hadn't known him better than that.

Everybody began walking towards the door at once, and I realized I'd missed the dismissal. Oops.

Frowning, I once more removed the map the king had given me when announcing my first task. My eyes traced the sloping lines adorning the crinkled page. No particular landmarks stood out.

And then the description of the man I had to find and kill...or lack of one.

I sighed heavily. This wasn't a mission that they expected me to complete. It was a game designed for failure.

"Dair," the mermaid king called, waving his hand. Dair's jaw clenched, but he obediently wheeled himself towards his father. I remained standing near the entry-way, watching their exchange with narrowed, suspicious eyes. The rest of my mates and their fathers had already been ushered out, leaving only me, Tavvy, the mermaid king, and Dair.

Tavvy's smile was smug, almost sardonic, when his eyes met mine. He offered me a wink that he probably thought was attractive but came across as constipated.

The king said something to Dair, and I watched my mate lower his head minutely. Reaching into his pocket, the king handed Dair a small bottle, the liquid continually changing colors in the artificial lighting. A potion, I realized dumbly.

As Dair put the liquid to his lips, my fascination turned to horror when he keeled over, falling out of his chair.

I ran towards him, ignoring Tavvy's dark chuckle and the king's expectant grin. Dropping to my knees, I pressed the palm of my hand against Dair's forehead. His skin had taken on a ruddy tint, sweat plastering his hair to his forehead.

"What's happening?" I asked, fear tightening my stomach until it was a mesh of tangled nerves. I glared at the older man towering over us. King or not, if he'd hurt my mate, I would end him. Painfully.

Dair's breathing evened out, but his eyes were pained.

"Z..." he whispered helplessly, and it was only then that I got a good look at him. Where his stubs had once been, two legs sprouted out, the skin as golden as the rest of him. His toes flexed, wiggling, before he slowly stumbled to his feet.

In my dazed state, I couldn't help but think he reminded me of the Little Mermaid learning to walk for the first time. A laugh bubbled up, threatening to break free at the accurate comparison.

"It's...it's a miracle!" I gasped, covering my mouth with my hand. Tears burned in my eyes, and I wasn't ashamed to admit that more than one escaped.

Dair's smile was sheepish when he looked at me, eyes haunted. Why wasn't he more excited about this? He could walk!

Before I could stop myself, I threw myself into Dair's arms and peppered him with kisses. He kissed me back instinctively, arms tightening around my waist before releasing me.

The mermaid king released a feigned gasp of shock, and I threw him a glare. "I know you already know. Don't act so fucking surprised."

That expression of shock morphed into one of pseudo sweetness. His eyes were bright, illuminating. It always struck me to see my mate's blue eyes—a color like the clearest shade of water—reflecting back at me from such a cold man's face.

"I had my suspicions," he hedged, that same damn amusement dancing in his eyes.

"Not suspicions," I said without hesitation. "You knew."

Shrugging a broad shoulder, he amended, "Does it matter what I knew? You should be grateful, little girl, that I gave him his legs back. It took years to find all of these ingredients and convince Justin to create the potion."

Justin. It took me a second to realize that was the mage king's name. Bash's father's name.

Dair had gone rigid in my arms, his muscles flexing and tensing. I rubbed his back, attempting to soothe the tension away.

"Show your gratitude," Tavvy said stiffly. He moved to stand beside me, and I felt his finger caress a pathway down my arm. I shivered, but not in pleasure. Disgust curdled in my stomach at having a hand on me that wasn't one of my mates'.

"We figured today would be an opportune time to test this potion," the mermaid king continued, a wicked glint to his eyes. I couldn't quite understand the reason behind that emotion. "Since Dair and my sons will be accompanying you."

"They will?" I blurted before I could stop myself. I'd known Dair was coming with me, but I hadn't expected the others to come as well.

Tavvy's smile was predatory—a nightmare out for the kill.

"Of course," he answered. The tips of his fingers brushed the sides of my breasts, and both Dair and I stiffened. I immediately pressed myself further against Dair, willing him to calm down. This, his legs, was a gift I had no doubt would be ripped away the second the king felt like it.

Fighting his brother would just fuel his already vindictive fire.

"Thank you, my king, for your gift," I managed to spit out through gritted teeth. Those were words I never wanted to say to such a despicable man, but if they gave Dair his legs back, I would say them repeatedly.

When Dair continued to stare blankly over my head at his father, I nudged his stomach. A muttered "Thanks," left his lips.

What was going on with him?

I'd thought he would be happy, overjoyed, to have his legs back. Why was he looking as if he'd been punched repeatedly in the face?

As we moved to exit the room, I grabbed his hand and pulled him to a stop, waiting for the others to pass us. Both Tavvy and the king met my eyes when they passed. The king's expression was smug, while Tavvy's was...lustful.

"You okay?" I asked Dair in a whisper as soon as his family was out of earshot. He refused to meet my inquiring gaze, despite the fact I knew he could feel it probing his forehead.

"I'm fine." His voice was resigned. Tired. Weak.

"Dair...you're walking," I stated, awed. With him on two feet, I realized that he was tall, nearly a foot taller than me. I wanted nothing more than to climb him like a tree, claim those pouty lips of his, wrap my legs around him...

"I'm walking," he agreed, subdued. With a heavy sigh, he finally glanced down at me, meeting my eyes. Whatever he saw in my face had his own expression softening. His hand snatched a blonde curl, wrapping it around his finger. Another sigh. "Z..."

"Don't," I warned. "This is something to be happy over. Something to celebrate." My throat closed with emotion, and I stood on my tiptoes to press my lips to his skin. I couldn't quite reach his lips, so I brushed them against the hollow of his throat instead. He shuddered delicately, arms wrapping around my stomach. "You're walking. You're fucking walking."

I wanted to scream it to the world. From the highest rooftops and mountains, from the lowest oceans and valleys. Happiness bubbled up inside of me, unlike anything I'd ever felt before.

Dair met my excitement with a smile of his own. That smile turned from tentative to luminous as his hands tugged me even closer, my body molding against his.

"I'm walking." His voice was dazed. "I'm walking."

His lips crushed mine in a bruising kiss. Possessiveness exuded from his body in waves as he held me to him. One hand cupped the back of my head, while the other snagged my ass, kneading it.

Pulling back, we were both breathing heavily. I knew my face was as flushed as his.

"Go," he urged me, swatting my butt. "Go say goodbye to your mates."

"They're not coming?" I asked, the amusement instantly waning. I didn't know why I was surprised, but a part of me had expected them to join us. Join me. Their absence was going to kill me if just the mere thought of it pierced my heart.

"Some of them are," he assured me, noting my rising panic. "But not all of them can sneak away." When I opened my mouth to ask for more details, he held up his hands in a placating, universal, *I don't know everything, so don't attack me* gesture.

Pressing a quick kiss to the corner of his lips, I allowed another smile to break through my apathetic façade. "I'm really happy right now."

It took him a second to answer. His eyes were trained on something on the ceiling, but they lowered after a moment, meeting my gaze. A tiny smile flicked his lips up. "Me too."

With one last kiss, I glanced at the clock hanging overhead. One hour to find my mates.

And I knew which one I was starting with.

TWENTY-TWO

I knocked once on the plain white door. Silence greeted my announcement of arrival before a warm voiced carried.

"Come in."

Stuffing my hands into my pockets, I stepped into a room as familiar to me as my own bedroom.

Father's office was cluttered—that was the only word adequate enough. Having spent years traveling when he was a prince, he'd procured quite a collection. Ornately carved wood interwoven with threads hung from the ceiling. Dream catchers, he'd told me. Created by humans and spelled by mages at a time when the two races had worked together. The shelves were adorned with books, all varying in age and wear. Dust coated the spines and permeated the air.

There were a few statues on his desk, along with a framed picture, something that was called a yo-yo, and a coffee cup that said 'Taste the Rainbow.'

The shadows were pulled away from my father's face

to reveal his dark skin, the color of burnt porcelain, and golden eyes. His buzzed black hair only accentuated his square jaw and arresting features.

"Father," I said by way of greeting. I rescinded my own hold on the shadows, allowing my face to peer through. Dad looked up from where he was bent over a stack of papers, muttering.

Over his shoulder, an immense map of the territories hung. The capital was directly in the middle, with smaller human communities scattered around it. These communities weren't recognized by the powers that be, but I knew for a fact that Z had lived in one of them, just between the capital and the Incubus Kingdom.

In a circle around the capital, the seven kingdoms sat. There was no rhyme or reason for their placement, except for the fact that it had been decreed by the original Sins. Or something like that.

I'd never been a particular fan of history or geography. Still, my eyes zeroed in on the Mermaid Kingdom, nestled between the Shifter Kingdom and Vampire Kingdom. It was nothing more than a splattering of islands inside a large, saltwater ocean. It, by far, had the least amount of land compared to the others.

"What are you working on?" I asked, finally directing my attention back to my father. His head was still bent over his latest project, indistinguishable muttering escaping his parted lips. At my words, he snapped his head up and widened his eyes.

"I didn't see you there, boy."

"You invited me inside," I pointed out, amusedly.

He waved a hand in the air as if to say let bygones be bygones.

"What do you need?" He finally looked away from his stack of papers, leaning back in his chair and folding his hands over his stomach. He was muscular from long days in the gym...and my mother's consistent harping about his weight. The one time he'd grown a beer belly, my mom never let him hear the end of it.

"Any new information?" I asked. I hated how desperate that one question was. How pleading.

Father's eyes dimmed slightly, a curtain being drawn closed. He shook his head once, and it felt as if he'd punched me in the face.

"Only what I told you before. They're up to something. This task isn't what it appears to be." His lip curled up distastefully. "Your mate is going to have to be extra careful."

I gave him a decisive head bob, but my mind was already wandering. If what my dad said was true, and I thoroughly believed it was, Z was in danger. The task the mermaid king had chosen for her was designed for her to fail.

Designed for her to die.

The thought had me clenching my fists and grinding my jaw against the onslaught of emotion.

With a heavy sigh, Father glanced back at his desk. He looked tired, disheveled, and unlike the impeccably dressed and put together man I knew.

"I don't know what else to say," he admitted tersely. "I don't know exactly what they have planned...but I would keep an eye on her, son." There was a short pause as he grabbed a pen, scribbling something on a ledger before glancing back up. His eyes were soft in what most would've considered a hard, glacial face. "Does she make you happy?"

The question took me by surprise, a physical blow that had me staggering back a step. My hand steadily unclenched, and my muscles relaxed. Thoughts of Z no longer aggravated me, worried me, but instead brought about a long forgotten sense of peace. I tried to keep the dopey smile to a minimum, though, and instead gave my father a brisk nod, face solemn.

"Yes."

"Good. That's good. You need some happiness..." Father trailed off as his eyes narrowed on the slip of paper. "That doesn't make any sense. It should be less than that..."

As he began his usual mutterings, I realized I was excused. When I was younger, I'd found his constant chatter embarrassing and confusing. Now I only found it endearing to see the old man talk to himself as he sorted through a particularly hard problem.

I waited a moment longer, to see if he would once again acknowledge me, before slipping out of his office.

My thoughts traveled to what he'd told me...or the lack of what he'd said. I tried not to feel irritated, but it bled through anyway. How was I supposed to protect Z when I knew nothing about the threat?

Fuming, lost in my own thoughts, I pulled the shadows back around me and slid into my bedroom.

The room would give Z a run for her money. Weapons lined the walls, some of them dated to the before time, while others were brand new. Swords, knives, spears, and even a couple of axes. Smirking at the collection that would make my girl orgasm, I grabbed twin swords off the wall and slung them over my back. They were my preferred choice of weapon, and I could wield them like an extension of my limbs.

There was a soft knock on my door.

Even with a wall separating us, I could feel her presence as if she were standing beside me. I fortified the shadows around me, making sure there wasn't a crack in my barrier, before taking a deep breath.

I knew she would come for me, but I was hoping to delay the inevitable.

"I know you're in there!" Her irate voice shattered the last of my resolve, and before I realized what I was doing, I had the door pulled open.

Z stood there, hands on her hips and a frown on her beautiful face. Like me, her body was adorned in weapons—a bow and arrow, a sword, and if I had to wager a guess, throwing knives up her sleeves and on her thighs.

Her brow was furrowed, but I watched as it smoothed over, eyes widening in wonder.

"What the fuck is this? And why am I only just seeing it?" She took a dazed step into the room, eyes latching on each and every weapon. She looked like a kid in a candy shop.

Or a Bash in a sex shop, that kinky shit.

She spun around in awe filled wonder before turning an accusatory glare in my direction. A lesser man would've pissed themselves at the fury in her gaze.

I merely prayed to the heavens that the tiny blonde female wouldn't cut off my balls.

"You never asked," I replied easily.

"You never asked," she mocked, lowering her voice in a poor impersonation of my own. Her finger jabbed through the shadows, touching my chest. I jumped at the contact. "Why weren't you in the throne room today?"

"Excuse me?" I asked, undeterred by her anger. I used the shadows to move around her and brought my lips to her ear. Goosebumps pebbled on her skin as I released a deep breath.

"You've been weird since the whole Haven thing," she snapped.

Wait a minute...?

"Who the fuck is Haven?"

"The gorgon," she answered dismissively. Were we apparently giving monsters names now? Fitting, I supposed. I was a monster too. "Is this about our fight in the ballroom?"

Once more, I called on the shadows to carry me to her other side. My hand snaked out and cupped the back of her neck, skin and hair brushing my fingers. Both were soft, like silk, and I never wanted to remove my grip.

"Fight? Was that what we did?"

Another shift, this time landing me right in front of her. I stared at her tiny nose, golden freckles scattered across the bridge. It wasn't something I'd ever noticed before, and for some undefinable reason, it made my cock painfully hard.

"Did we have our first couple fight?" I teased, barely

resisting the urge to lower my head and kiss each individual freckle.

"Couple." She snorted at the word, and I tried not to let her dismissal and rejection gut me the way it did. "We're mates, Ryland. We should be better than this petty shit."

Mates.

The leaden, miserable feeling lifted until I felt lighter, buoyant. If she were to see my face, she would know I was smiling like an idiot.

Mates.

I loved how easily she'd claimed me as hers.

Mates.

And then the rest of her words washed over me, dousing me in an icy wave.

"Petty? You're right—*mates* shouldn't have petty fights." I twisted the word, made it ugly.

Z remained in front of me, hands balled into fists and eyes capable of penetrating skin.

"What the hell are you even going on about?"

"Because of—as you correctly named it—a petty fight, I left you alone! You were nearly taken! Killed!" I agitatedly ran a hand through my black hair. It wasn't as short as my father's, but it wasn't long by any means.

My breathing was heavy as I faced Z down. There. That was the root of my issues.

Because I'd childishly left her, she'd nearly been taken. I didn't know if I could forgive myself for that, and I didn't think she should forgive me either.

Her chest heaved, eyes narrowing, before a shocked laugh escaped her. The sound was melodious but out of place in the tension filled room. I gaped at her and quirked a single brow, a gesture I knew was lost on her.

"You guys all have big fucking heads if you blame yourselves for what Haven did." She shook her head. "Why would you blame yourselves?" She paused suddenly, lifting a single finger into the air as if she just had a grand epiphany. "Did you send her?"

Shock reeled through me, and I staggered. How could she think such a thing?

"No—"

"Did you lure me away from the party, so that I was alone?"

"Of course not!"

"Did you drug me with venom?"

Understanding of what she was trying to do dawned on me, and I pursed my lips. Trying to divert the blame, to remind me that it wasn't my fault. That I hadn't instigated the attack. Blah. Blah. Blah.

"I know what you're doing," I said aloud, and she merely batted her eyelashes innocently. "Trying to alleviate my guilt."

At that, her eyes rolled practically into the back of her head.

"There's nothing to be guilty of," she insisted once more. The earnestness in her voice was nearly impossible to ignore. Still, I remained stubbornly silent. "All of you males have a fucking god complex or some shit! Seriously!" She threw her hands up in the air and began to pace. I watched my mate with rapt interest, my self-loathing steadily turning into amusement. How was she able to do that? To see the parts I hated the most in me and smooth down the jagged edges?

Spinning to face me, she jabbed a finger accurately into the center of my chest.

"You. Are. Not. To. Blame." She released a pent-up breath. "Now stop all this pouting or else I'll cut off your balls."

Now there was the threatening Z I knew and loved.

For her, only her, I allowed my shadows to recede. Unlike the first time I showed her, she didn't recoil in disgust. Instead, fascination lit up her face like a beacon calling me home.

Home.

She was my fucking home.

A small hand reached up to trace the dozens of scars marring my skin, but it didn't shake.

"Why do you hide?" Her voice was soft, as soft as her hand. The wing of a butterfly. A torrent of snowflakes seconds from burning away by my skin's heat.

"Because I'm hideous," I whispered. For some reason, I spoke just as softly as she had. I didn't dare speak any louder and break the tranquility we'd found ourselves in.

I hadn't realized how much self-loathing I felt, how much doubt I felt in our relationship, until she called me out on my bullshit. Since I'd first discovered she was missing to the moment I thought she was...dead...I'd been adrift at sea. Guilt didn't encapsulate what I felt just then. It was something more, something other. It was an aching pain that began just in my heart and clawed its way down my body. In those brief moments, I had to imagine a life without Z in it. A life without the titillating female. Without her snark and laugh.

And...I didn't want to live it.

When I'd discovered she was alive, a life preserver had been tossed to me, and I had to decide if I was going to hold on. The waves would be erratic, I knew that, but the paradise we found would be worth it.

But because of my stubbornness at the ball, she'd nearly...

I shook my head succinctly. She was right—I wasn't to blame for the actions of others, and if I had been with her, it might've ended much differently. Maybe in both of our deaths.

I had to be grateful that she and my brothers were alive.

"Are you ready to get your head out of your ass?" she asked lightly, and I nodded.

"You're welcome to have your head in my ass anytime you desire," I responded.

She snorted.

"You might think that's sexy, but the last thing I want to be privy to is your man farts."

"Man farts?" I brought my hand to my chest in mock horror. "I'll have you know that that's sexist. My farts smell like daisies."

"Why are we talking about farts when I was thinking about kissing you?" she mused, tapping her finger to her chin.

"Wait? Kissing?"

"Not anymore." She laughed, the sound misting away the last of my doubts. "Now, are you coming with us?"

I gestured towards the swords hanging from my back.

"No," I drawled languidly. "I just carry around swords wherever I go."

Her lips tilted up, and she leaned forward to whisper conspiratorially in my ear. "I wouldn't blame you. I do."

Did it make me a psychopath to get slightly turned on by her proclamation?

With a sultry smirk, she pressed a kiss to my cheek and raced out my door.

TWENTY-THREE

JAX

S he was leaving me.
Leaving.
Leaving.
The crisp white walls seemed to be closing in on me, surrounding me, suffocating me. To my horror, the framed pictures adorning the hallway walls changed and contorted. A landscape of flowery hills transformed into gallows, a young woman hanging precariously from the rope around her neck.

Her blonde curls and beautiful face were unmistakable, even in death.

A sob caught in my throat as I stared at the portrait of my beautiful mate. My beautiful, dead mate.

Death.

It followed me around constantly, an ominous cloud hovering just above my head, threatening to release a torrent of heavy rainfall.

Death. Death. Death.

Around the picture, blood cascaded down the pristine white walls in rivulets. They puddled on the wooden floorboards.

Death. Death. Death.

My hand fisted in my hair, pulling to the point of pain. I knew that more than one strand of brown hair broke free each time I pulled.

I took a deep breath, trying to ease the tightness in my chest. It pressed down on me like a weight I couldn't quite carry but wasn't heavy enough to kill me. It just sat there, mildly uncomfortable.

Death.

Death.

Death.

The blood on the floor rose from the ground, as if pulled by an unseen force, and molded itself into the shape of a person. First the small body, then the glasses, then the flowing hair.

Her presence stabbed me, gutted me. I couldn't look away as she took one step closer and then another.

"You did this to me." Her voice was the sweet one I remembered, though I hadn't heard it often. Once or twice, maybe, but my memories of that time were foggy. "Why did you do this?"

"Sasha, I'm sorry," I sobbed. My back hit the wall, and my feet gave out. Crumbling to the ground, I held my head in my hands. Pain slammed into me with the force of a meteor. It burned me on impact.

"You did this," Sasha repeated. Her gaze was accusatory, lips parted in a silent scream. Anguish. It emanated from every pore of her little body. "You did this to me."

My mind staggered back in time, recalling memories I'd tried to keep buried.

A young Sasha looking at me as if I held the moon.

My fangs piercing her neck.

And then...

A cry escaped me, a pathetic, whining sound.

Still, Sasha did not stop her advancements. She stood directly in front of me, her body of blood swishing with each step she took. A bloody hand reached out to caress my cheek, and I knew it would leave a handprint.

"You're going to kill her too," she whispered, eyes flickering towards the painted picture. It had changed once more. Instead of gallows, it showed the blonde-haired female lying on the ground. Her unseeing eyes focused on me.

Me.

Death.

"No," I whispered, unable to tear my gaze away from the bloody wounds on her neck. The product of fangs, *my* fangs. "I wouldn't hurt her."

"You would," Sasha insisted in that same airy voice. "And you're going to."

"No!"

I straightened, shoving at her small body in my attempt to escape. I felt my body tilting, falling, before I hit the ground with a resonating slap. Pain darted down my legs.

"No." I shook my head once. "Never."

I needed to see *her*. I needed to see with my own eyes that she was okay and safe.

Pushing myself back to my feet, I began to move

down the long hallway.

Behind me, Sasha's laugh carried.

Mate. Where was my mate?

I found myself in front of a familiar door, and I pushed it open without preamble.

My desperation ebbed when I noted how empty the room was. I tried to feel her, sense her presence. My skin no longer prickled as it usually did when she was around.

Did that mean...?

Another anguished cry escaped me as I sunk to my knees. Tears ran down my face, but I couldn't find the motivation or even the desire to brush them away.

Loneliness swamped me. It was unlike anything I'd ever felt before, a tsunami that I couldn't escape from.

She'd left me.

She'd left me all alone.

Alone.

I was alone.

There was nothing else to do, nothing else to say.

Around me, the walls began to laugh, the noise taunting. Somewhere in the cacophony, Sasha's laughter echoed.

Alone.

Alone.

The walls whispered it to me.

I curled into a ball, placing my hands over emy ears to block out the onslaught of noise. Too much. Too much.

Death.

Alone.

Always alone.

What was left besides waiting for death to find me?

TWENTY-FOUR

Z

Iblew out an irritated breath, staring through the window of our transport. Dair's knee touched mine as he gently wrapped an arm around me.

"He's fine," he assured me for what felt like the billionth time.

"It just makes me worried."

Before we'd left, I'd searched for and rounded up the majority of my mates. Except for Jax. The vampire had been suspiciously missing, and no matter where I looked, I couldn't find him. Dair had promised me that the eccentric man was no doubt hiding in the walls or beneath a bed, but fear niggled me.

Still, we were out of options. With one last reluctant look at the capital, I'd slid into the car.

Now we were curving up steep roads and hills on our way to the Mermaid Kingdom. The first kingdom I'd ever traveled to.

Living in the human communities, just on the outskirts of the capital, felt like living in a war zone. A sect of land breeding slaves and food. There had been little to no electricity, the houses had been in disarray, and the people had been either cold or crazy.

Despite my mission, I felt myself bounce in my seat, eager to see all this world had to offer.

"You're talking about the vampire, right?" one of the twins asked. I still couldn't recall his name. His hair was slightly darker than Dair's, and his eyes were a blue-green color. Turning towards Dair, he flashed a malicious smirk. "How does it feel to know your mate shares a bed with six other men?" He tittered, his twin joining in. Turning towards me, he asked, "Doesn't that make you a slut?"

When Dair's face flushed red, hands clenching, I put a placating hand on his thigh to calm him. I could handle a bunch of bullies.

Leaning over Dair, I flashed Twin One a sultry smile. "Yes," I answered breezily. "It does."

Twin One and Twin Two sputtered, not expecting me to agree with them, while Dair choked on a laugh. Tightening his arm around my shoulder, he pulled me into his side, lips caressing the top of my head.

It seemed that my presence helped abate the tension constantly thrumming through him.

Tavvy glanced back from where he sat in the passenger seat, beside a driver I wasn't given the name of. His blue eyes were fixated on the sliver of space between my body and Dair's, brows furrowing. When he spotted me looking, his expression smoothed over to be replaced by icy indifference.

Fate really hated me. For some reason, it had chosen

my car buddies to be the princes from hell. At least I'd snagged Dair before the car took off. The last thing I wanted to be was alone with three men who looked at me with predatory, carnal hunger.

Ryland, Lupe, and Bash rode in the car behind us, the latter of which had been sullen and moodier than normal. He'd gifted me with a glare when he arrived, suitcase swung over his shoulder. I'd canted my hip to the side.

"What are you doing here, Bash?" I had asked curtly. His lips had pressed into a thin line, but he didn't automatically respond. He seemed to have been choosing his words carefully.

I'd waited, silence stretching, before he'd turned on his heel and stomped towards the second car.

The whole weird exchange lasted only a few minutes, though it had felt like a year.

Devlin had to stay behind. Something with his father, he'd stated, though the details hadn't been explicitly given. Killian had also stayed behind at the capital after completely devouring my lips and cupping my ass.

His cheeks flushed, though I hadn't been able to discern if it was from embarrassment or lust, he'd made me promise to contact him if I ran into any trouble. Killian didn't feel right leaving Jax alone, and I'd never loved my incubus as much as I had at that moment.

Wait...love? No.

Shaking my head to clear my thoughts, I glanced once more out the window.

The sight was something to behold, something you would've seen in an beautifully rendered painting. There were rocky, russet-colored cliffs falling into a turbulent sea. The water itself was frothy in appearance, white foam cresting the shoreline. From our perch high above the ocean, I could see dozens and dozens of tiny islands. Some were small, barely capable of hosting one house, while others were large and sheathed in green grass.

My mouth dropped open as complete and utter awe filled me. This place...it was stunning.

Dair chuckled as he took in my expression eagerly, devouring it. His arm tightened around my shoulders almost imperceptibly.

"You see that island?" Dair asked softly, pointing towards a particularly small one floating in the violent sea. There was nothing on it besides a single tree and a wooden hut.

"Yes."

"My mom used to live there," he explained. "With her parents and mate. When my father chose her as a bride and my grandparents died, she kept the house. Said it helped her feel connected to what she once had."

It felt odd to be having this intimate conversation in front of an audience, but if Dair wasn't bothered by it, I wasn't going to be either.

I turned fully in his arms, so I could see his expression easier. His blue eyes were wistful, trained on the splotch of green land. There was so much tenderness in his face as he reflected on his family home.

"She used to take me there a lot," he continued. "When I needed an escape. When I was having a bad day. When I—" He broke off, nuzzling my neck with his nose. I thought of younger Dair, then. Wide-eyed and innocent, without the weight of the world pressing down on his shoulders.

"When you lost your legs," I finished for him, and he nodded, the gesture something I felt rather than saw. I ran a gentle hand through his golden blond hair, relishing in the way he shuddered beneath my touch.

Once more, I felt a pair of eyes on me, but when I glanced in Tavvy's direction, he was facing straight ahead. I wondered if I'd imagined it, though my sixth sense warned me I hadn't.

And I always trusted my sixth sense.

Unease unfurled in my gut, but I shoved it away. I would worry about Tavvy at a different time.

"Is your mom there now?" I asked, still stroking Dair's soft hair. It slid through my fingers like fine silk, the texture addicting.

A dopey smile appeared on Dair's face as he glanced up at me through his fringe of lashes.

"Yes, with my sister."

"You have a sister?" I gasped in disbelief. It was times like this when I remembered I didn't know everything about these men. I knew the big stuff, the life-altering stuff, but little details eluded me. With time, I would learn it all.

Start with the big, end with the small.

Dair went rigid beside me, eyes pleading with me to remain quiet. I glanced anxiously from the twins, whispering amongst themselves, to Tavvy.

I nodded to tell Dair I understood while mentally recalling what I knew of his family. His mother had a mate, but she'd been forced to leave him after being coveted by Dair's father. His sister must've been his half-sister.

Filing the information away for later, I glanced once more out the window, just as we parked in front of a magnificent building.

No, not a building. Not even a house.

A castle.

It was a tan color, the sun bleaching it white in more places than one. Tall pinnacles brushed the sky from various locations, each one a swirling point. Seashells bedecked the sides and roof. Somehow, it came across as more elegant than cheesy.

"Shit," I whispered, awe filling me.

Ignoring my outburst, Tavvy swiveled in his seat to face me. "You'll have your base of operations in here. Come."

Without waiting for my response, he slid out of the car and marched towards the front entrance. I exchanged an amused look with Dair at his brother's pissy behavior before following him out.

The front entrance was two large white doors, jewel-studded shells making up the handles. I almost didn't want to touch something so beautiful, afraid that my own darkness would tarnish it.

Fortunately, I didn't need to touch anything. A guard rushed forward—where the fuck did he come from? — and gestured us through with a dramatic swooping motion. I nodded at him in response, stepping into what would serve as my home until I completed the mind-numbing mission assigned by the mermaid king.

The inside was just as beautiful as the outside. The

color combination, no surprise, was azure and white, heightened only by darker blue brush strokes. Numerous paintings of seashells and seahorses, fish and starfish, lined the front entrance, creating a walkway towards a white-trimmed spiral staircase. The opulence of the room was startling but not surprising.

If I had to wager a guess, half of these items didn't initially belong to the royal family.

"There's not as much security as I would've expected," I whispered to Dair, surveying a pair of guards rushing forward to converse with Tavvy. They, too, wore blue clothing with white crests just above their hearts. I would have to ask Dair if that was the symbol of the royal family.

Dair chuckled at my question, grabbing my elbow to steer me towards the staircase. I'd been shamelessly standing in the foyer, gaping at everything like a toddler.

"This isn't our main home," he admitted. "It's...how would you say it? A summer home."

"A summer home," I repeated blandly. Before he could respond, a guard hurried towards him and said a few words in a language I didn't recognize. Dair replied back in the same language. It was a beautiful sound, all soft vowels and smooth consonants. I waited until the guard had disappeared with a brisk nod before raising an inquiring eyebrow at my mermaid prince.

"It's Mer," he explained, hand on the small of my back. He guided me past the staircase and down a long hall. "It's the official language here. We only speak English at the capital."

"Does every race have their own language?" I asked,

peering through each room as we passed. One was what looked like a billiards room. Another, a bathroom. And a... Was that an indoor beach?

Before I could gawk further, Dair led me to a room at the end of the hall. The door was already open to reveal a large bed, easily twice as large as the one back in my room at the capital, with golden trim and a teal canopy overhead. There were at least a dozen drawers separated between three dressers, and a single desk sat in the center of the room, not against the wall as I would expect.

"I instructed the servants to set up this room for us," he admitted, unbuttoning his white shirt. My eyes latched onto the blond chest hair peeking through, and his eyes heated.

There was the sound of glass shattering, followed immediately by, "Motherfucking ass wipe." Moments later, Bash entered the room, suitcase slung over his shoulder and eyes brewing with irritation.

Behind him, Lupe sauntered into the room with a smug, satisfied smile on his handsome face.

"What did you do?" I asked, cocking a brow up.

Ignoring me, Lupe turned towards Dair with a devious smile. "Hopefully, those vases in the hall aren't expensive."

"Oh, they're just gifts from the genie royal family from hundreds of years ago," replied Dair dryly.

Lupe chuckled, the sound sending delightful shivers up and down my body. "Good. You can just ask Dev for a new one."

"You didn't need to throw it at me!" Bash protested.

He tossed his suitcase onto the bed and spun on the shifter with narrowed eyes.

"I was aiming for Tavvy, but he ducked." Shrugging carelessly, Lupe opened up his suitcase and began unpacking his clothes into drawers.

"Why were you aiming for Tavvy?" I questioned. At this point, I felt like I'd missed an entire conversation.

In a dark voice I almost didn't recognize, Lupe replied, "He was looking at your ass."

"Oh."

Thank you for defending my honor?

That didn't sound right.

"Where's Ryland?" I spun in a circle, searching the corners for my shadow. After our blowout earlier, I wanted to check on him. To make sure he was okay.

Both he and Killian felt misguided guilt for what had happened with Haven. Wrongfully placed guilt. I briefly wondered if any of my other mates felt like that.

It was ridiculous. I was more than capable of taking care of myself, and these men weren't gods, just godlike in appearance. They couldn't control or influence other people's actions.

Lupe held up his finger for silence. A second later, an earsplitting, masculine scream echoed from upstairs. Ryland appeared at the doorway, chuckling softly. When he saw me looking, the shadows moved even closer to where I stood, and I knew he was smiling unabashedly.

"The twins were looking at your ass also," he explained casually. I snorted.

Possessive, overprotective, sexy fools.

Lupe moved from his bag to mine and began

unpacking my own clothing. I watched in fascination as the big man's cheeks warmed when he pulled out my bras and panties.

"So do you have the map?" Dair asked, sprawling back on the bed.

Nodding, I reached into my pocket and held up the fading piece of paper. I set it on the desk, and my mates moved to crowd around it.

Ah. That was why the desk was positioned where it was.

"So we know nothing about him besides he's a male and has red hair and was last seen three months ago in the Mermaid Kingdom," Bash murmured, and even his voice sent a wave of irritation through me.

"No shit," I snapped before I could stop myself. His eyes snapped to mine, flaring hotly.

"What the hell is your problem?" he asked tersely.

"You're one to talk—"

"Enough!" Lupe bellowed. He slammed a large hand down at the table. "Now is not the time."

"No petty fights," Ryland reminded me teasingly, and I rolled my eyes.

This wouldn't be a petty fight. This would be an ass-kicking, ball crunching one.

Or a ball sucking...

No! Bad, Z!

"I don't know what the hell this even means," I admitted, refocusing my attention back on the slip of paper. "Do you think your dad just wrote down random gibberish? Am I just supposed to kill a random man?"

The thought made my stomach clench and tighten uncomfortably.

Dair took the paper from the table and began to scan the contents. A single wrinkle formed between his blond brows, and I yearned to smooth it out with my hand.

"Wait," he said suddenly. His finger touched an island on the map. "That doesn't exist."

"Huh?"

"That island doesn't exist."

When I just continued to stare at him blankly, Dair heaved out a breath and hurried out of the room. Not even a full minute had passed before he returned carrying a larger replica of the map the mermaid king had given me.

It resembled what I'd seen when we had first entered the kingdom. Islands, a large landmass that made up the western seaboard, and an endless ocean. Dair held the small map up to the larger map to compare.

Everything was the exact same, except...

The island Dair was pointing to, one of hundreds, didn't exist on the large map.

"How did you know this?" I asked breathlessly. A tiny piece finally fell into place.

Dair blushed delicately.

"I, um..."

"He had a crush on his geography teacher when he was younger," Lupe filled in with a chuckle. Dair's cheeks reddened further, and I couldn't resist teasing him.

"Maybe because you did so well, I could give you a

reward," I whispered in his ear. His eyes widened, hands clenching the desktop.

What the hell had come over me?

I'd turned into a sexual deviant since I found my mates. And I liked it.

"Gross," Bash muttered like a petulant child who'd walked in on his mom and dad kissing. I snorted out a laugh.

"You just wish—"

Once more, our banter was interrupted, but not by Lupe.

Tavvy stood in the open doorway, arms crossed over his muscular chest and eyes trained on me.

"Your task has begun," he said stiffly.

Irritation filled me.

"I know," I snapped. "We're working on—"

"Come." Without another word, he stormed out of my room and down the hall. I remained standing, fuming with fury. He really needed to stop treating me like a dog with basic commands. Come. Stop. Eat.

What was next? Fuck?

I shivered at the thought of fucking Tavvy. Frankly, I would rather eat shit.

"Are you coming or not?" Tavvy bellowed, and the childish part of me wanted to rebel and remain where I was. However, I knew that would be futile in the long run.

A pawn, I reminded myself. I was their pawn until I could destroy the damn game board.

Sharing an irritated look with my mates, I stomped after Tavvy, while they followed behind me. I made sure to take my sweet damn time. The asshole could wait for all the fucks I gave.

By the time we reached him, his face was flushed with anger. Unfortunately, he didn't comment or rise to my bait. Instead, he led us towards a staircase that descended into a basement.

A dungeon.

Gray walls loomed everywhere I looked, and the smell of piss saturated the air. The heat was almost palpable, and sweat was already beginning to coat my skin.

"What is this place?" I whispered to Dair, but he looked as shocked as I felt.

He hadn't known this place existed.

"This door always led to another hallway," he explained to me in a harsh whisper. "It must've been illusion magic."

Bash muttered something indecipherable, and Lupe's nostrils flared as he sniffed the air. The muscles in his back tightened at whatever he uncovered, and I placed my small hand in the middle of his back.

Fortunately, the first few cells were empty.

But my luck could only last for so long.

We stopped in front of the largest cell, one that housed six individuals. Each one had red hair, various shades that ranged from garnet red to a carrot orange. Each was a male. Each was naked.

And each was covered in blood.

"What the hell?" I whispered, eyes tracking each of the men's movements. Their dirty bodies ran towards the bars of their cage, hands extending as they pleaded to be let out. There was a wide range of ages too, I noted. The youngest appeared to be sixteen, and the oldest was in his mid-forties.

"What is this, Tavvy?" Dair's voice was tight with disgust and horror. Lupe had gone still beside me, and I knew he was fighting his beast. He was a gentle soul by nature. It must've been difficult for him to see so many people distressed. I knew it was for me.

"This is her task." Despite addressing Dair, Tavvy's eyes remained fixed on me. "Choose one."

"What?" I breathed, staggering back a step. My movement landed me against Bash's hard chest, and his hands came to wrap around me. I leaned into his embrace, any and all anger I felt for him disappearing at his comfort.

"One's a traitor. The others are innocent." His smile widened, sharklike. Predatory. Malevolent. "Twenty-four hours. Choose one to die."

TWENTY-FIVE

Z

The muscles in my stomach tightened to the point of pain. All I could do was stare at Tavvy —a fucked-up soul wrapped in a pretty face and body.

Ice slithered down my spine, encasing me. It felt as if I were standing in a tundra with wind howling through my hair. Distantly, I could hear the men crying and screaming and begging, but their voices began to blur together.

God...

They were all humans! Powerless and defenseless against the nightmares.

One of them was a child...

I must've said the last thought out loud, as Tavvy's lips twisted into a grin.

"So you would choose to spare him because of his age, even if he was a traitor? Even if you were condemning an innocent man to die in his place?"

The tightening in my stomach reached exponential

levels, threatening to expel the contents of my last meal. I heaved, and Bash hugged me tighter to him.

"This is sick, Tavvy. Even for you," Dair whispered, aghast.

At that, his smile fled to be replaced by something colder. Darker.

"In this world, you have to be sicker. Harsher. Crueler." He spat on the ground, near my feet, and Bash lifted me slightly to move us both backwards. "All I ever wanted was Father's attention, but did he spare me an ounce of the time he gave you? No. You got all his fucking attention. Perfect Dair." He twisted the last words, spittle clumping at the corner of his mouth.

Dair's eyes were comically wide in his face.

"Are you fucking kidding me?" he snapped at last. "The attention...you can fucking have it!"

I didn't understand what was happening, but I knew the confrontation stemmed from years of pent-up aggression. On both ends.

Before I could blink, Dair lunged forward and tackled Tavvy to the ground. For a man who'd just gotten legs, he sure knew how to use them.

Eyes radiating an incandescent fury, he punched at Tavvy's face.

And something inside me broke.

Running forward, I grabbed Dair's shoulder, preparing to pull him back, only to use my free hand and punch him square in the face.

What the hell?

Even as panic settled in my chest, I felt my body move instinctively, protectively, in front of Tavvy's prone form. A gurgled laugh escaped the evil prince as the others looked at me in shock. Blood coated Dair's lips from my fist, and I would forever hate myself for being the cause.

I tried to convey with my eyes how sorry I was, how I had no idea what was happening, how my body's reaction was instinctual.

Understanding dawned on Bash's face first in the slightest widening of his eyes and sharp intake of breath.

Behind me, Tavvy still laughed maniacally.

"It's the spell, dumbass," he said, and I glanced over my shoulder. Tavvy was staring at his brother, eyes slitted. "The bonding one. It makes her incapable of harming anyone in any of the royal families." He staggered to his feet and brushed a hand down my arm. Lupe growled at the contact but did not dare take a step closer. "It makes her first reaction to protect them."

"It doesn't mean I'm going to play along with your sick games," I snapped, pivoting to face him. Instead of the anger I expected, his eyes danced with amusement.

"Then you die." This was all said with an indifferent shrug of his shoulders. "Refuse a task given to you by the kings, and you explode. Another caveat of the little binding spell."

The smug bastard sounded giddy. I wanted to punch him in the face repeatedly.

Huh. At least I could still mentally harm him.

"You son of a bitch," Lupe hissed through clenched teeth. He looked as if he was seconds away from tearing the blond prince's head off his body.

"Twenty-four hours," Tavvy cooed, wiping blood

from his mouth with the back of his hand. Throwing me a wink, he glanced once more at the redheaded prisoners. They screamed at him, but their words ran together. One emotion was painstakingly clear—anguish.

It cleaved my heart in two.

"Find the traitor," Tavvy told me. "And then kill him."

———

I PACED the bedroom that had once felt homey but now resembled a prison.

That was what I was, after all—a prisoner. A piece of clay that the kings could mold and shape until they had their perfect, obedient assassin.

And because of the binding spell, there was nothing I could do.

"Fuck!" I shouted, throwing something at the door. I didn't even bother to see what it was as glass shattered. Hopefully, it was another expensive vase that the mermaid king treasured.

"You need to calm down," Bash snapped, and I rounded on him.

"Don't tell me to calm down! I have twenty-four hours to figure out who the traitor is, so I don't accidentally sentence an innocent man to death." My breathing was heavy, chest rising and falling.

"We have a starting place," Dair whispered. It was the first time he'd spoken since we'd left the dungeons, and his voice was hoarse. Not the hoarse you would get from screaming, but a sort of tired reluctance. Face strained, he nodded towards the map still on the wooden desk. "This is a game to my father. A scavenger hunt."

"Everything with the kings is a game!" Spreading my hands wide, I spun in a circle to encompass all of my mates present. "And we're losing! Don't you see that? The one element of surprise we had—our relationship as mates—is out in the open. They all know. Your brothers even know!" This last statement was directed at Dair, who ducked his head.

"So we change the rules," Lupe cut in. "We change the rules and break the game board on their head."

"How do you suggest we do that?" I hated how desperate I sounded. The uncharacteristic whine in my voice grated on my nerves. But it was true—we were losing this game, this battle, with the kings. Maybe Lupe was right when he said we needed to rewrite the rules.

"I don't know," he admitted. His eyes met mine demurely. "I honestly don't know."

"We finish this game." Bash's strident voice cut through the air like the slash of a whip. "We win this game, and then we step back. Look at their overall goal." Sighing heavily, he brushed a hand through his ash-blond hair. "But, guys, we don't have time for this conversation. We have twenty-four hours to find a traitor and save five innocent lives."

I took a deep breath to abate the mounting tension rising inside me. Still, it seeped through, crashing repeatedly against me like a heavy wave.

"We take a...boat?" I looked towards Dair for confirmation, and he nodded. Straightening with resolve, I faced the three men in the room. "We take a boat and head to this island. Dair can scout the water in his mermaid form. Ryland can…"

I trailed off, glancing desperately around the room devoid of any shadows.

"Where the fuck is Ryland?" The previously dissipated tension came back with a vengeance. He wouldn't have just left. Not after everything we'd been through, what he had confessed.

Lupe and Bash exchanged quick, wide-eyed stares.

"Bash, go look for him—"

"We need him to drive the boat, love," Dair said. My irritation flared white-hot.

"Can't you or Lupe do it?"

"I'll be in my mermaid form, and Lupe doesn't know how to drive it." He sounded almost apologetic, though his eyes were sharp as they flickered from my face to Bash's.

I didn't have time to argue with him. I needed to find the traitor and Ryland. Now.

Trying to tamper down my growing panic, I met Lupe's eyes first. "Lupe, stay at the castle and look for Ryland. Bash, I need you with me. Dair's right—we need you to drive the boat, and your magic might come in handy."

Both men nodded, but Bash's face had tightened like he'd eaten something sour. Still, he didn't complain.

"In twelve hours, we meet back here. Is that understood?" I stared purposely at Lupe. Dair, Bash, and I were staying together, and I hated leaving Lupe to fend for himself. The big man held my gaze, dozens of thoughts swarming in his bright blue eyes, before he bobbed his head in agreement.

"Good. That's good." I wiped my hands and, consequently, my excess sweat on my pants. Now that I'd finished giving orders, my courage had been drained from me. I was suddenly weak and tired and vulnerable—a scared little girl playing big, bad assassin.

"Hey," Lupe said gruffly. He grabbed the back of my head and brought our foreheads together. "Everything is going to be okay."

I desperately brought our lips together, a clash of teeth and tongues. The kiss was over as quickly as it had started.

My voice was shaky when I responded, further confirming that I wasn't as tough as I pretended to be. "I hope so."

TWENTY-SIX

JAX

D ark walls.

Everywhere.

The sickly copper scent of blood permeating the air. Sweat.

And desperation.

One may not think desperation had a scent, but they were mistaken. Sweat glands combined with piss, an entirely unpleasant smell. It clogged my airways.

I curled into a ball, willing the voices away. I tried to repeat the mantra Killian had taught me when I became lost in my head.

This isn't real.

This isn't real.

Somewhere in the distance, a scream reverberated, shaking me to my very core. I huddled in the corner of the dank, gray room with blood staining the walls.

This isn't real.

This isn't real.

This isn't real.

My eyelids fluttered shut. If I didn't see it, it wasn't real. Wasn't that why little boys and girls hid underneath their blankets at night? To hide from the monsters?

My mind had always been a cage. It was ironic that I'd found myself quite literally trapped in one.

"I'm sorry, Sasha," I whimpered, searching the darkness. Walls. Pressing in on me. Blood dripping from the ceiling.

Drip.

Drip.

Drip.

Always dripping. Why did blood have to drip?

Absently, I began to murmur that one word beneath my breath.

Drip.

Drip.

"Sasha!" I cried again. One could get lost in this darkness.

If I didn't have my heightened senses of hearing and smell, I might've gone insane.

Drip.

Drip.

A figure's shadow moved to stand in front of me. While I could vaguely make out shapes and colors directly in front of me, he or she was too far away to see clearly.

I waited with bated breath for the familiar tingling of my skin—a sign of my love's presence.

Nothing.

My skin remained tingle free.

"Tingle. Tingle. Blood. Itches. Doesn't itch." I scrubbed a hand agitatedly down my face. I needed her to stop the constant tingling, the constant drowning sensation, as if I were sucking up too much water and not enough air.

"Jax," a soft voice cooed, and I froze. Could it be...?

"Sasha?" I whispered.

But no. Sasha was dead.

Dead.

Drip. Drip. Drip.

Blood continued to splatter around me. The ominous sound was almost addicting, breaking apart the monotony of silence I'd grown accustomed to.

"I can be Sasha if you want," the female who wasn't Sasha said.

"Where is she?" My skin felt too tight, and I desperately wanted to rip it off. Undress myself from my skin. Free myself of the burden.

"She?" Not-Sasha released a lilting laugh. "You're not talking about your dead school friend, are you?" She moved to crouch in front of me. "She left you. All alone. She knows what type of person you are, what type of monster. She knows what you did to Sasha."

"No. No. No." I shook my head vehemently in denial. I refused to believe that. She promised she wouldn't leave me. Maybe not in words, but it had been clear in her eyes...

Eyes gorged from her head.

Blood.

Drip.

"She left you, Jax. She left you. They all did. Your

brothers chose her over you. They don't care about you. None of them do."

I continued to shake my head, as if that could somehow dispel her words from my mind.

"You're not real," I whispered harshly. Taking a deep breath, I closed my eyes and willed the images away. The illusion, as my brothers repeatedly told me. I willed away the bleeding walls, the mysterious woman, and the smell of sweat.

Drip. Drip. Drip.

When I opened my eyes, minutes later, I was alone once more.

Alone. In darkness.

With the walls that dripped blood.

TWENTY-SEVEN

DEVLIN

I drummed my fingers against the thin oak table, my father's words going in one ear and out the other.

He stood haughtily in the front of the board-room dressed in a pristine black suit with his hair slicked back. The similarities between him and me were eerie. Curly brown hair, olive-toned skin, and rich violet eyes. But his eyes...

Glacial didn't even begin to describe them. They were devoid of warmth and affection, of feeling. Looking into them was what I imagined looking into dark, purple abysses would feel like.

The meeting dragged on and on, and by the time we were dismissed, I was practically running out the door. I moved briskly down the hallway before stopping in a tiny crook between two doors. There, I leaned against the wall and folded my arms over my chest.

Waiting. The tension in the air could be cut with a butter knife.

After a moment, Laurel appeared with a slight sway

to her hips. The female genie was immensely powerful, though not more powerful than me.

As a descendant of Greed, genies relied religiously on deals and wishes. Contracts magically crafted with numerous stipulations to ensure obedience.

Fail to hold up your end of the bargain, and your soul became the genie's. That was the purpose of our lamps. A cage, one would say, of souls.

And the reason I was meeting Laurel in the dark hallway away from prying eyes.

"You found it?" I asked tersely, kicking myself off the wall. In answer, she thrust a purple bag into my proffered hand, and I checked the contents.

My heart, which was beating steadily, picked up speed. I could feel it reverberating in my chest, the sound deafening. I released a breath I hadn't realized I'd been holding.

"I granted your wish," Laurel said bitterly, hand extending. I fumbled in my pocket for her golden lamp and passed it to her. She held it reverently in both her hands, stroking her fingers down the sides.

I knew it was taboo to steal another genie's lamp and ask for three wishes, but I was desperate. That desperation clung to me like a sickly poison.

Laurel finally looked up from her ogling of the lamp, and her eyes narrowed into thin slits. No doubt, I'd made an enemy out of the petite genie.

Still maintaining eye contact, she snapped her fingers and a scroll appeared, unraveling. I knew the words printed on the contract by heart. Every phrase and clause. Every condition. My name was signed in blood at the bottom, glaring back at me.

"I remember," I told Laurel curtly, peeling my gaze from the dreaded paper. How could something so insignificant be so damning? "I'll hold up my end of the deal."

"You better." She took a step forward and jabbed an accusatory finger into my stomach. "I hate being fucking used."

Her finger lowered, trailing down my chest, and I stepped away from her touch as if it were toxic. I imagined my eyes were glowing vividly like a flame lit beneath the surface. She must've seen something in my gaze, felt my power whipping through both of us, as she took an automatic step back.

"Don't. Touch. Me." My words were a growl, nearly inarticulate. For the first time since I'd known her, true fear flittered across her face. It was there and gone too quickly for me to be certain.

"You better hold up your end of the deal, Devlin," she whispered icily. "Or else your soul is mine."

In response, I flipped her the finger. Childish, yes. Effective, also yes.

Cuddling my new treasure, I sidestepped the very pissed off genie and moved purposely down the twisting hallways. I must've given off a vibe that said *don't fuck with me* because everybody did just that.

I passed my own room, stopping in front of Z's. Her absence hung like a sword above my head, seconds from dropping. It was all I could do not to follow her to the

Mermaid Kingdom and ensure with my own eyes that she was safe and well.

Pushing open the door, I took stock of the empty room. It was exactly as she'd left it, the bedroom door wide open to reveal the bed still unmade from her night with Killian.

As I stared at the crumpled bed sheets, I waited for jealousy to hit me. If it was any other guy besides my brothers, I would've gone insane. Instead, all I felt was...relief.

I sifted through my thoughts to get a better understanding of my emotions.

Relief and acceptance were the predominant ones.

Killian needed someone in his life to take care of him, to love him, to protect him from himself. Z was capable and willing to do just that. I couldn't fault my brother for being happy, just like I couldn't fault my mate for making him happy. She was good for him, and he, her. He brought out a tenderness that was absent normally, even when she was with me.

I could see the way she looked at him, like he was something to be cherished and protected at all cost.

So no, as I stared at the bed, I felt no jealousy. No animosity for two people I cared about more than anyone else in this godforsaken world.

Diverting my attention from the fluffy white bed, I walked to the couch and collapsed down. My fingers were white from how tightly I gripped the package Laurel had given me.

I could scarcely believe I held it. I kept expecting to

blink and have it disappear in a cloud of smoke. To dematerialize, as if it had never existed at all.

Hand shaking, I grabbed the golden hued lamp from inside the purple bag. It was small, smaller than even Laurel's, with a color that wasn't quite gold but wasn't yellow either. Umber and amber blended together, a dark shade of black at the bottom. There were no jewels encrusted on the sides like my father's.

Simple. Relatively unremarkable. It gave no indication of the power it had wielded, the power it continued to wield.

I felt as if I were going to pass out. My entire attention was fixated on the lamp in my hand. The lamp that had been missing for years now.

When you made a wish with a genie, you had to be specific. There could be no loopholes. It sometimes took weeks, months, to articulate a wish. If you fucked up...

Well...

It wasn't unheard of for things to become dire for you.

Unfortunately, I hadn't thought of wishing for my lamp until Z had come back into my life. That would've saved me years of fruitless searching.

With bated breath, I rubbed my hands down the smooth sides. Cliché, most definitely. It was a stupid practice implemented at the beginning of time.

Unlike Laurel, I didn't revel in collecting souls. I didn't like granting wishes to unsuspecting people, despite my entire survival depending on it.

I took clients that wanted little. A new dog, for example. Or a roof over their heads. Unlike the other assholes,

I tried to keep the wishes straight to the point. No loop-holes. No stipulations.

It didn't change the fact that the universal cost for not holding up your end of the contract was your soul. There was quite literally nothing I could do about it, no matter how hard I tried.

I only had one soul in my lamp. One soul trapped in a cage for all of eternity. One soul that had failed to uphold his end of the deal.

My hands scrubbed the sides erratically, waiting for the soul to appear.

Nothing.

Not even a wisp of smoke.

Fear strangled me, and I once more rubbed a shaky hand up and down, up and down.

I couldn't seem to take in enough air. It wasn't grief, not yet, but a strangling type of fear. It closed off my airways and made me lightheaded.

It shouldn't be possible. No, from what I gathered, it was *im*possible.

A soul didn't magically disappear from a genie's lamp.

After one more ineffectual scrub down the ice-cold sides, I pulled at my magic. Violet tendrils escaped me, snaking to the lamp and encompassing it in a soft embrace. My magic sputtered once before dying out.

It, too, didn't sense anything or anyone inside of my lamp.

But that was...

I took a breath meant to calm me, but it did little to slow down my rapidly beating heart.

The soul was gone. Disappeared.

If that was the case...

I shook my head, as if fending off dizziness.

If that was the case, Z was going to hate me.

There was no doubt about that. She would hate me once she discovered the truth, once she discovered what I'd kept from her.

And the rest of us?

We would be fucked.

Z

There was a certain sound the water made as the boat was steered cleanly out of the basin. I wouldn't call the boisterous sound soothing. Loud, would be a better description. Almost comforting and hypnotic, a noise that could lull you to sleep. The slightest swoosh of water brushing the edge of the boat.

Why they had boats when the majority of the population could breathe underwater, and were required to for at least half a day, I had no idea. But I wasn't willing to look a gift horse in the mouth...or however that saying went.

The castle and summer home—as Dair called it— were located on the mainland, a couple hundred miles away from the capital. From there, it led to an immense body of water, Leapon Ocean. Hundreds of islands freckled the ocean water, all varying in size and wildlife according to Dair.

Bash expertly steered the boat through a narrow

canal, the only sound the rippling of water and puttering of the engine.

"I don't like this," I whispered tersely. My eyes constantly scanned the horizon. What I was searching for, I couldn't discern. Something didn't feel right. The unease prickled the skin on my arms, snaking to my throat and choking me.

I didn't like being separated from my mates, not so soon after I'd met them.

Not so soon after I'd claimed them.

I didn't want to think about that, about them, and I once more looked out into the distance.

A tapestry of green surrounded either side of the narrow canal. Tiny dots of yellow adorned the majority of the leaves. The only trees I recognized were palms, spaced intermittently along the waterway. Another one looked like a palm tree but held the needles of a pine. Another was teetering against a trunk, seconds from toppling.

Despite the copious wildlife, there were no mermaids present. I'd expected to see at least one on my journey to the boat, and then more once we set off. However, the only mermaid nearby was Dair.

"It's too quiet," Dair agreed. He leaned against the railing of the small sailboat. His father's, he'd told me, before sheepishly adding, "He stole it from a rich genie."

Typical.

He was right. Normally, I would be grateful for the tranquility and silence, but I was too wound up. Too suspicious. Any second now, the serenity could shatter like a rock being thrown at glass.

Movement captured and ensnared my attention. Dair was slowly undressing, and despite the direness of the situation, I found myself taking in his golden expanse of skin. He had delectable back muscles, and two dimples leading down to his ass. I never knew that would turn me on so much.

When he shucked his pants, bending down to pull his feet out, I got a good view of his ass and balls. Pleasure swirled in my lower stomach, and I bit my lower lip.

"Stop fucking gawking," Bash bit out. He turned his glare onto Dair. "And stop giving her a show."

Dair smiled cheekily at me over his shoulder, winking once, before he dived into the water. Once he was gone, the mood instantly turned somber, and I spun on Bash.

"Why are you such a fucking prick?" I asked, and his eyes narrowed.

"Because this is serious, Z. Or don't you understand that?"

"Of course I understand! I understand that better than anyone. It's my life on the line, Bash. Not yours. Not Dair's. Mine. And it's the lives of all those men in that dungeon. And maybe even Ryland's! But we don't fucking know anything." I threw my hands up into the air in agitation. "Excuse me for enjoying one moment of normalcy. One moment with my mate before shit hits the fan."

Bash's hand tightened over the steering wheel. He looked as if he wanted to run to me, but I couldn't tell if it was to strangle me or kiss me.

"You still don't get it," he settled on at last, dismissing

me with a slow shake of his head. I narrowed my eyes at the pompous asshole.

"What don't I get? Why don't you fucking speak in words instead of these cryptic statements?"

I balled my hand into a fist, seconds from decking him. I could learn to drive a damn boat if the need arose, and I was sure Bash would be quite tasty fish food.

Bash turned abruptly, face red.

"If you die, we die," he seethed. "It's that simple. Maybe not literally, but mentally. You saw what happened when the shifter king lost his mate. He went fucking insane! Did you know that he begged for death?"

His question took me by surprise. For some reason, it was almost a physical blow to my stomach. I staggered back a step until my thighs were resting against the teal leather seats at the back of the boat.

"What?"

I tried to visualize what he'd said. The shifter king may have been evil, an asshole of massive proportions, but he was the epitome of strong, alpha male. He practically exuded raw masculinity from his gruff voice and burly appearance to his condescending remarks. The picture Bash painted was impossible to imagine.

"Even he couldn't survive the death of his mate, and he didn't like her very much," Bash continued. His voice had lost its initial heat and now sounded subdued. Tired. Weary.

"Like us?" I mused, and heat once more flared to life in Bash's eyes.

"They're nothing like us," he protested vehemently. The fire in his eyes grew to an inferno.

"You hate me." My voice was weak, even to my own ears.

"I don't fucking hate you," he snapped.

"What about Cassie?"

"Who the fuck is Cassie?" He looked genuinely confused, and I couldn't help but snort.

"The girl you left the ball with." I mentally winced at how jealous I sounded, like a pathetic, needy girlfriend. What had these men done to me?

Understanding flickered in his eyes followed immediately by horror.

"Is that why you've been such an icy bitch to me?" he asked, mouth agape. My hair rose on the back of my neck.

"Wow. Thanks."

"Guys!" Dair's voice floated to us from down below, and I risked a glance over the railing. His golden hair was spun with darker shades of umber as he bobbed in the water. Waves rippled over his chiseled, nicely defined chest. As he moved, I caught sight of his tail.

It was a deep, cerulean blue, and two times the size of his torso. I knew from experience that the tail was a rather sensitive area for the male mermaid.

"You leading the way?" I asked Dair, turning my back on a fuming Bash. He was right—the conversation, and maiming, could wait until we were done with this ridiculous task.

"Yeah," he called back, swimming in front of the boat. His muscles flexed with each swipe of the water, and once more, I had to remind myself not to drool.

But my damn vagina wanted to pee on him and claim him as my own. Shameless hussy, that one.

Bash sullenly moved back to the wheel.

"Can we go faster?" I asked after a few minutes of uncomfortable silence. We'd barely made a dent in the long strip of canal, slowly puttering along.

Bash glared at me like my question was the stupidest thing he'd ever heard.

"It's shallow here," he snapped. "Unless you want the boat to get stuck in sand and break."

"It's not my fault I've never ridden a fucking boat before," I retorted. He muttered something in irritation, but thankfully, did not respond. I wasn't sure I could take another comment from him without ripping his dick off his body.

The silence stretched, thickening.

"I didn't do anything with Cassie," Bash bit out. He sounded...frustrated. Frustrated and appalled. From where I sat behind him, I couldn't see his face.

"You left with her," I pointed out. There was no bitterness in my voice. Instead, it was a statement of fact. He'd left with her, so he couldn't deny that. Maybe he didn't sleep with her or even kiss her, but he'd left.

I closed my eyes and took a steadying breath.

The sun was bright and blinding today. Behind my closed eyelids, it painted a picture of dark red and black. I knew that my skin was burning, unaccustomed to the blistering heat.

I kept my eyes closed as Bash released a sigh.

"She told me she had information about you," he admitted at last.

"Me?"

That wasn't at all what I was expecting.

"I went, of course. I thought maybe she had some information about Aaliyah or some shit like that." Another intake of air followed by a heavy exhale. "Maybe it was a diversion. Maybe she was actually working with Haven. I was stupid and believed her when she said she had information about the new noble, Zara."

There was another long pause, and I pictured him forking his fingers through his blond hair, a few shades lighter than Dair's. It was an anxious gesture that a lot of my mates had. A product, I was sure, of their life growing up together. I knew I picked up habits from the assassins in the Alphabet Resistance.

S and T used to always bite their nails down to nubs until B, our leader, poured syrup over their heads. I didn't know how that helped them, only that it did. The bad habit stopped instantaneously. T still joked that he could feel phantom remnants of syrup in his butt crack.

"Anyway...I'm not going to lie to you. She tried to kiss me."

I remained immobile, expression stoic, as I processed what he'd confessed. She had tried to kiss him. I wasn't surprised, especially after her spiel about snagging one of the princes, but it still left a hollow hole in my stomach.

"You didn't kiss her back." It wasn't a question, despite my need for confirmation.

"Of course not!" He sounded aghast. "I would never do that to you, no matter how much you annoy the fuck out of me."

Silence. Water rippled, smashing against the side of the boat.

"Why does fate hate us?" I whispered. "Is it just some

cosmic joke? To be the mates of the men you were supposed to kill? To be the assassin for a kingdom you hate? To be the mate of a man who hates you?"

Those questions were ones I asked repeatedly. In the dead of night. Huddled in Killian and Devlin's arms after making love. Walking through the halls of a capital I despised. Bowing to kings who would never earn my respect or devotion.

"I don't hate you," said Bash adamantly. "How many times do I have to tell you that?"

"You don't like me," I pointed out.

"I don't know you! All I know is that you're this beautiful, kickass assassin who loves knives and has my brothers and me wrapped around your finger. I don't know you, Z. I don't know what your favorite color is or what you like to eat. I don't even know anything about your family."

"Black," I answered immediately. "My favorite color is black."

Finally, I peeled open my eyelids. Bash was staring straight ahead at the open expanse of water. We were reaching the end of the canal, which hopefully meant we would be able to speed up.

"Why black?" he asked, not bothering to turn around. I shrugged.

"It's made up of all the colors."

"Black is not a fucking color," he protested with an indignant huff.

Fucking Bash. Always had to argue with me.

"It's every color," I insisted. "Red and blue and green and pink and purple and every color you could think of.

Have you ever painted before, Bash? Have you ever combined every single color together? What does it get you?"

Bash was silent. Usually, he was only silent when I was right.

"And for what I like to eat... Hmm...I like steak." I shrugged, a gesture I knew he couldn't see. "What can I say? I'm a carnivore."

Once more, Bash snorted.

"What?" I asked. "Don't tell me you're a vegetarian?"

"Vegan, actually," he said. I could hear the smirk in his voice. "All mages are. It's part of our evolution, I guess. Years ago, the mages were too fucking lazy to go hunting for their own animals, so they lived on the greens genies provided. It must've stuck."

"Diego wasn't a vegan," I mused, tapping my chin. "The things that man did with a hot dog..."

At that, Bash spun around to face me.

"Why the fuck are you talking about Diego's hot dog?"

And...I smiled. I heard Diego's name, and I didn't completely fall apart. It still hurt, the softest of pinches, but it no longer overwhelmed me. I could hold the hurt in two hands and know that I was stronger because of it. My mates had helped me understand that, had walked with me through my grief.

I hadn't even realized it.

My mourning would've gone differently if it hadn't been for them.

"Guys!" Dair barked, and I immediately went on alert. The copper handle fit perfectly in the palm of my hand as I unsheathed my knife, searching. The water rippled, bubbles appearing, but that could've been from the boat itself.

Up ahead, Dair continued to swim, golden hair clearly visible in the blighted sun. He paused suddenly, back muscles tensing, before beginning again, this time slower.

"Be careful," Bash warned. He stood, still holding the wheel, and searched the nearby land. I kept my focus on the water.

Waiting.

Waiting.

Something pushed through, and I staggered backwards, heart hammering. Just as quickly, I caught my bearings and rushed at the offender.

A dolphin.

A fucking dolphin.

It rode alongside the boat, its fin the lightest shade of gray.

"It's just a dolphin!" I called to Dair, my muscles minutely relaxing. Dair, however, stopped abruptly. He swiveled around to face me, and even from this distance, I could see the panic in his eyes.

"There shouldn't be fucking dolphins in water this shallow!" he called back.

The boat had finally reached the end of the canal and was now floating haphazardly in the open ocean. Waves rocked the boat, but Bash didn't seem inclined to go any faster. We all waited with bated breath, eyes flickering from the dolphin to the canal and then to the endless sea of water.

Finally, the dolphin swam away with a cheerful mewling noise, and I released a breath I hadn't realized I'd been holding.

"We should be good," Dair said. His voice was nearly lost in the cacophony of the ocean—waves and seagulls and roaring wind. "I'll—"

Dair was cut off by a whining noise, and we both turned our attention towards the dolphin once more. It was a dozen or so feet ahead of us.

As I watched, in utter horror, a gaping mouth closed around the dolphin and swallowed it whole.

Revulsion churned in my belly, but that disgust quickly transformed into fear.

The creature that ate the dolphin rose from the water...all five stories of pure muscle.

My mind flickered back to the book I'd read in the library with Lupe. An extinct supernatural creature.

"Motherfucker..." I cursed. "Guys, that's a kraken."

Z

Reading about a kraken and seeing a kraken were two entirely different things.

The book had said it was big, but that word failed to encapsulate how mammoth the creature actually was. It rose from the water like some unholy being, a ruddy gray color. Dozens of tentacles snaked from its immense body, and its single eye blinked rapidly, fixated on the boat.

On me.

"Shit," Bash breathed, and I wanted to snort at his use of the word. "Shit" was a vast understatement. "Dair, get out of there!"

My mermaid prince was already swimming back towards the boat, muscles rippling and tail flipping erratically.

"What the hell do we do?" Dair asked the second he got near the side of the boat. I reached a hand down to help him up, but he brushed it away dismissively.

"We fight," I whispered. I'd meant for the statement to sound badass, but my voice trembled. I could handle a lot of things, like fucked-up assassins and fucked-up kings, but what I couldn't handle was a sea creature larger than the mansion we'd come from.

I was going to have nightmares for years.

Still, I tightened my grip on the dagger...before realizing I was going to need something bigger. Deciding quickly, I dropped the dagger into a cup holder and grabbed my bow and arrow. Distance would be key for this monster, at least for the time being.

"Fucking hell," Bash muttered beneath his breath. Despite his trepidation, he lifted his hands and began to chant softly beneath his breath. I didn't know what type of spell he was incanting, but I knew whatever he did had to be done fast.

"Give me your sword, Z!" Dair called up to me. I hesitated, only a second, before releasing the sword from the strap on my back and tossing it into the water. Dair caught it expertly before taking a deep, shuddering breath.

And then his body cleaved in half. Before I could even scream, those halves turned into fourths and the fourths turned into eighths. Soon, there were dozens of fish in the place of my mate, all swimming in separate directions to surround the kraken. I had no idea what had happened to my sword, but I trusted Dair had a plan.

The kraken opened its mouth and released a roar. Row after row of teeth in various shades of brown sat crookedly in its gaping mouth, and air from the roar blew my hair back. It smelled of decaying fish and blood, permeating the air in a sickly perfume.

That one eye remained trained on me. All it needed to do was reach out a tentacle...

I hooked the arrow into the bow and leveled it at the monster. Pulling the taut string back, I waited until that one eye was in my direct line of vision. Then I released the arrow.

It flew through the air with a blistering speed, landing directly in the kraken's eye. Its cry this time was anguished, pained, and the sea creature withered. The arrow protruded from the milky, sunken eyeball, black blood drizzling down the creature's face.

With a newfound vengeance, the kraken wrapped its tentacles around the boat, shaking it. I let out a squeal as I was roughly thrown against the siding, my head hitting metal and black spots forming in my vision.

"You okay, Bash?" I asked, staggering back to my feet.

He ignored me, eyes still squeezed shut and lips moving rapidly, even though he was on the ground.

The tentacles crushed the side of the boat, and water gushed through the many holes now adorning the side.

"Shit. Shit. Shit." Apparently, I was borrowing Bash's use of language. There wasn't a word in the dictionary that could encompass the epic clusterfuck we'd found ourselves in.

I turned my attention back towards the kraken's head, just in time to see two dozen fish lunging from the water. One of the tentacles retreated from the boat to swat at the onslaught of fish, and panic tightened my stomach.

Dair...

The man in question materialized on the top of the kraken's meaty body, sword in hand. Without preamble, he jabbed the sword into the creature's head.

Once more, the kraken bellowed and bucked its body. Dair held the hilt of the sword, but the movements of the kraken were getting more and more volatile. With a cry, Dair was brutally tossed off its body and landed with a deafening splash into the water.

"Dair!" I screamed, but I didn't have time to worry about my mermaid mate. The kraken had already turned its attention back to me, a tangible incandescent fury burning in his one bloody eye.

Bash's voice grew to a scream as he finished his incantation, and he smiled in smug satisfaction.

Only to have the smile change to horror as the kraken grew. And grew. And grew.

His form continued to expand until it blocked out the sun, coating the water and surrounding landscapes in darkness.

"What the fuck, Bash?" I screamed, not daring to pull my attention away from the hideous monster.

"Shit!" My mage scrambled to his feet, eyes wide. "That wasn't supposed to happen!"

"No shit!"

I grabbed a second arrow and placed it in my bow, pulling the string back. The second I would've let it loose, I felt something slimy wrap around my feet. I only had a second to scream before I was dragged off the edge of the boat and into the water.

My ears rang, head reverberating with pain from where it had bounced off the railing.

Then I was submerged completely in water.

The change was so sudden, so abrupt, that I didn't have time to inhale before I was pulled beneath the freezing water. Panic clawed up my chest as I desperately twisted my body. The kraken's tentacle still held my leg in an iron vise.

I was going to die, I realized with a vivid clarity. And my death wouldn't be from assassins or the kings.

But a damn sea creature.

I was going to drown.

Black spots penetrated my vision, and I desperately wanted to gasp for air. The need was so strong, and my lungs were burning. One tiny inhale...

I was yanked from the water abruptly. Coughing, I only had a second to see that I was dozens of feet away from the boat and still clutched in the kraken's grasp before I was pulled back under.

Like the others, the kraken didn't seem to want me dead. Instead, he was taking me somewhere.

No, not somewhere, but to someone.

Aaliyah.

The she-bitch had some explaining to do.

Strong hands wrapped around my arm, tugging. I didn't even have to open my eyes to know that it was Dair, and relief filled me instantly.

I wished I could open my eyes, could see, but I had to rely on sound and touch instead. The guttural roar of the kraken. The release of the tentacle around my leg.

The sweet, sweet air as I was pulled out of the water.

I gasped, coughing wildly, and Dair patted my back.

The kraken continued to roar, and it was only then that I noticed one of his tentacles was shorter than the others. Dair must've cut it off to save me.

"Are you okay?" Dair yelled. Even treading water inches from me, he was difficult to hear over the kraken's bellow and the rippling waves.

I nodded to tell him I was, though my throat burned and my body felt leaden. Still, I couldn't focus on the many aches and pains vibrating down my body.

He cupped the back of my head and brought me into a quick, desperate kiss. His hands rested on the back of my thighs as he lifted me.

And then I was flying, flying, flying through the air, landing sharply on the nearest landmass. I screamed as pain radiated up my now broken leg.

"Fuck," I cried. Unbidden, my eyes traveled to my skin. From the kraken's tentacles, black and blue bruises covered the pasty skin of my leg. Red welts, like ones you would get from too tight rope, intermingled. And from Dair's throw...

My leg was twisted backwards, the brittle bone peeking through.

The pain was immediate and intense, unlike anything I'd ever felt before. A strangled sob got caught in my throat.

Still, I tried to get to my feet, using a nearby tree as leverage. The shooting pain clambered up my leg, and I immediately fell back down with a cry and curse.

In the water, Dair still fought the kraken. Or at the

very least, attempted to fight. It was apparent to me that it was a losing battle.

He dodged and parried, sword stabbing any expanse of skin it could find. The kraken cried, obviously in pain, but didn't relent its ruthless assault.

I watched in horror as the kraken batted Dair away as if he were nothing more than a pesky bug. My mermaid mate went flying, blond hair disappearing into the thicket of trees.

He didn't return.

I waited, breath held.

Please, Dair. Please. Please be okay.

Slowly, ever so slowly, the kraken turned his face towards me. I didn't know how he knew where I was, how he sensed me, but the single eye in his head seemed to narrow into a thin slit. I remained frozen on the ground, shivering.

Dair, please. Please.

The kraken, oblivious to my desperate pleas, unfurled another long tentacle. It slithered through the water and onto the grassy shoreline I was lying on.

The monster suddenly released a wailing sound, head canting backwards, before it began to shrink.

And shrink.

And shrink.

Soon, it was the size of a large fish bobbing on the water, single eye wide and fearful.

I whipped my head in the direction of the now sinking boat. Bash stood on the railing, one hand tightly gripping the white sail and the other raised.

"That," Bash called, breathing heavily, "was what I meant to do the first time."

All I managed to do was release a giddy, dazed sound that was a mixture of a laugh and a cry before darkness consumed me.

DAIR

I shook my head rapidly from side to side, but it did little to clear the fogginess in my brain.

My body ached, pain radiating down my sides and to my legs.

I tried to recall what had happened, how I'd ended up here, but the memory eluded me. I squeezed my eyelids shut, waiting.

Something had happened...

Water...

Monster...

Z...

I scrambled upright, wincing at the initial stab of pain in my stomach, before running through the trees.

Memories bombarded me with a dizzying clarity. The kraken. Z. The fight. The asshole monster tossing me through a forest and into a tree.

Z.

Her name echoed in my head, giving me the strength to run through the pain. After what felt like hours later, but was probably nothing more than a few minutes, I broke through the tree line and landed waist deep in water.

Immediately, I felt my body change. The stretching sensation wasn't uncomfortable, just strange. My tail emerged, and I kicked it out wildly, splashing up water.

Holding my breath, I surveyed my surroundings.

The ship was completely submerged in water, only the side railing visible. It must've tipped at some point, water greedily swallowing it whole. There was no kraken that I could see, and the sea was almost calm. It was a direct contrast to what we'd just experienced.

On the shoreline, Bash knelt over Z. It was there that I headed, pushing the water aside with each breast stroke.

"Is she okay?" I asked roughly, pulling myself out of the water. My tail was instantly replaced by two long legs.

Bash ignored me, perspiration beading on his forehead. His eyes were closed as his hands hovered over Z's form, a golden glow emitting from his hands.

Healing magic.

Most mages didn't have that type of powerful magic, the magic capable of defying death itself. From all I knew about my mage brother, Bash didn't have it either.

So how the hell was he healing her?

As I watched, transfixed, the skin on her leg knitted back together, taking on a light pink pallor. My stomach twisted when I thought about how she'd obtained those bruises and red welts.

How she'd broken her leg.

Disgust filled me, disgust directed at myself, but I

pushed it aside. I'd been trying to protect her. Who was better to take on a sea creature than a sea prince?

Bash finally removed his hands from above Z. His breathing was ragged, but his eyes, when he opened them, were clear. They flickered to my naked stomach, the skin between his brows crinkling.

"You're hurt," he said stiffly, and I followed his gaze. I must've bruised myself when I landed. The skin was already taking on an onyx black and light blue color. I knew that cuts marred the length of my body, both from the tentacles and my fall through sharp branches, but it was nothing serious. I would live.

"I'm fine," I said, pushing his hands away when he moved to heal me. Healing magic took a lot out of a person, and the last thing we needed was Bash incapacitated. Speaking of healing magic... "What the hell was that?" I blurted, nodding towards the mended flesh on Z's legs. Her chest was rising and falling steadily, and I couldn't help but inch closer to her, peering down at her beautiful face. She looked so peaceful asleep. Younger. Vulnerable. Her golden hair, matted with blood and dried seawater, was splayed around her.

Keeping my gaze on Z, I addressed Bash. "And what happened back on the boat with the kraken? Why the hell did you help him grow?"

Bash made a nonsensical noise in the back of his throat.

"I don't fucking know," he admitted harshly. "I don't know how I was able to heal Z when I've never had healing magic before. I don't know why my spell misfired and made the kraken grow instead of shrink. I. Don't. Know."

I glanced up then, only to see Bash's eyes fixed on Z. There was a tenderness in his gaze I'd never seen before. A warmth. His hand absently reached out to stroke the smooth skin of her inner wrist.

"My magic," Bash continued softly before breaking off. He swallowed hard. "My magic is acting...wonky. It's not listening to me. It's not behaving the way it should."

"Do you think it's because of the tension?" I asked, stroking Z's hair out of her face.

"Tension?" Bash glanced up in alarm.

I nodded towards our sleeping mate. "Between you guys. It's not normal."

He bit down on his lip, expression contemplative. He didn't seem angry by my observation, only a little sad. I knew that he cared for her more than he'd ever cared for anyone before...and I also knew that it terrified him. He had these feelings for her that he didn't know how to deal with, because he was afraid of getting hurt. Afraid of the consequences of falling in love.

It was tearing a wedge between the two of them—a chasm that one of them would have to jump before they could be a whole.

"Maybe," Bash agreed after a long moment.

A splashing sound had us both turning. Immediately, Bash jumped to his feet, swaying slightly from his depletion of magic, and held Z's dagger out in front of him. I must've lost her sword in the woods, but I begged the water to heed my call. Instantly, the water rose from behind the creature, an impenetrable barrier trapping it with us.

The kraken pulled its small body onto land and crawled over to Z, long tentacles digging into the grass. Bash lowered his dagger, preparing to stab the ugly fucker, before he paused.

The kraken was cuddling against Z's prone body, desperate sobs escaping it.

"What the hell?" Bash asked.

Friend, the water whispered to me. *Don't kill friend.*

"Friend?" I asked in disbelief, and Bash turned to look at me as if I were crazy. Ignoring him, I stared out into the ocean. "How the fuck is this asshole my friend?"

Friend, the water insisted.

The kraken slipped underneath Z's arm, curling around her body like some damn spider monkey. My poor mate moaned, and I immediately dropped to my knees beside her.

She moaned again before she flickered her beautiful eyes open, and I was lost in her fiery gaze.

"Z?" I whispered. Bash moved to kneel on her other side. His hand was desperately gripping at her wrist, releasing it, only to grab it once more. "How are you feeling?"

"Like I had my leg broken by an asshole mermaid who thought I couldn't protect him and myself," she said dryly, and I winced, smiling sheepishly.

Yup. She was pissed about that.

She blinked rapidly, no doubt blinking away the fatigue, before her gaze rested on the tiny asshole still curled around her side releasing pitiful cries. Z glanced back up at me.

"Why the hell is the kraken cuddled up to me?" she asked. Her eyes roamed over my body, and my cock hardened when heat rose to her gaze. "And why the fuck are you naked?"

THIRTY-ONE

Z

I named him Slippy.

Why? Because the damn bastard constantly slipped through my fingers. Trying to hold him was like trying to push back a wave. And yes, it was a he. I made a very reluctant and pissed off Bash look.

Now, the two of us sat huddled on the dock where we'd gotten the boat from while Slippy swam in the water. One of Bash's palms was pressed down on the ground behind my back, and I used his position to lean against his shoulder.

The water rippled against the shoreline, an endless abyss of blue green and glimmering pseudo diamonds.

After two excruciating hours, Dair returned. We'd unanimously decided that he would swim to the spot the map had indicated. Not only was he faster than an average boat, but he knew the area better than anyone. Whatever the king wanted us to find, he would find.

Only...

"There was nothing there," Dair said, climbing out of

the water. Dair's clothes were destroyed in the boat, so Bash handed the mermaid his shirt. Dair immediately wrapped it around his waist. His golden skin was covered with bruises and red welts, but if he felt any pain, he didn't show it.

"What do you mean?" I asked, moving to my feet. I held out a hand for Bash to take and pulled him up as well. "There wasn't supposed to be anything there. That's the point."

Dair was already shaking his head before I'd even finished speaking. "You don't understand. I searched everywhere. Bottom of the ocean. Miles in either direction. There was nothing there. No clues. No hints. Nothing to indicate who the traitor is. Z, it was a dead end."

I heard him, I did, but I couldn't quite process the words. They went through one ear and out the other, circulating in my mind constantly like a whirlpool. I couldn't quite grasp a coherent thought.

"So it was a diversion?" I asked numbly. "A trap?"

"Do you think your father knew about the kraken?" Bash seethed. "Is that why he sent us here?"

Dair shrugged his shoulders, reaching up a hand to push dark golden hair out of his eyes. It only flopped back down, refusing to be tamed. "I don't know. It could be a coincidence, but the map led to nothing. Dad must've known that I would recognize the extra island. He was trying to confuse us and lead us in the wrong direction."

The numbness iced over, turning into a tundra of snow. Anger thrummed through my veins. The king had led us on...what was the saying? A wild goose chase. He knew we would find nothing, yet he sent us there anyway. He might've been behind the kraken attack as well.

My eyes flickered to Slippy splashing in the water, a strange cooing sound emanating from its—his, I had to remember—little mouth. I wanted to say that the little, murderous guy was cute, but that was a lie. Even not trying to kill me, the monster was butt ugly.

"How much time do we have?" I asked, swiveling my head to face Bash. His expression was tight, answering my question without words. We had no time. It had taken us more than six hours to get here and would take us just as much time to get back. The fight with the kraken. Dair's quest. Both had taken time—time we didn't have. We had to get back to the castle, to the dungeons, before at least five men, maybe all six, were wrongly sentenced to death.

And we still didn't know who the traitor was.

My heart beating, hammering, breaking my rib cage, I glared up at the sky. "Fuck!"

***

LUPE MET me the second I stepped into the mansion's foyer. His large, muscular arms wrapped around me, pulling me to him. I allowed myself to relax in his embrace only for a moment before I pulled away and met his gaze.

"Ry?" I asked, voice terse.

Lupe shook his head sullenly, and my stomach dropped through the floor.

"I'm sorry, love. I couldn't find him."

"It's okay," I whispered, though it was anything but. I secretly wished that Ryland had left me, left the mate bond, left his brothers, though I knew that wasn't the case. I would rather have him hate me than be dead or harmed. The mere thought nearly sent me into hysterics.

I was doing fine before these men came into my life. Maybe I wasn't happy, but I was alive. Or at least a version of it. Now, I couldn't help but wonder if I'd spent my whole life holding my breath, my lungs screaming for air. Drowning, almost, in too deep water. With them, it felt like I could breathe. Could finally reach the pocket of fresh air that had constantly been just out of reach.

Quite ironic, if you asked me, because they constantly took my breath away and made me scared shitless.

"You're back!" Tavvy glided down the staircase, arms extending as if he meant to give me a hug. He was freshly showered and wore a formfitting black suit. "I didn't think you were going to make the deadline."

"Bring me to the dungeons," I demanded coldly. Tavvy's grin widened further, but he elaborately gestured towards the doorway.

"Ladies first."

"Then go," I retorted oh so maturely. His eyes flared briefly, though I couldn't tell if it was in anger or arousal. I really, really hoped it was the former.

Without another word, Tavvy peeled the door open and stepped down into the dungeons. Piss, mildew, mold, and blood blended together, and I wanted to gag at the pungent scent. Lupe kept his hands on my shoulders, steering me through the darkness. Candle flames flickered intermittently, something I hadn't noticed during my first trip down.

Bash and Dair moved to stand in front of me, shoulder to shoulder, a wall of muscle Tavvy would have to go through to get to me.

The little psychopath chuckled.

"Z! Z! Z!" he called in a singsong voice. "Do you know who the traitor is?"

Shouldering past Bash and Dair, I faced Tavvy with a defiant set to my chin. He stood in front of the now opened cage, hands sweeping wildly as he gestured.

Seven men were kneeling inside the cell, hands bound in front of them and brown bags over their heads.

"How the fuck am I going to identify the traitor if I can't see their faces?" I asked harshly.

Traitor.

Whom I still didn't know.

Nausea churned in my lower stomach.

"That's the second part of your test, my sweet Z." He dared to venture a step forward, hand raised as if he wanted to brush my hair, but Lupe's threatening growl stopped him mid stride. He glanced at the large shifter with only mild annoyance before turning back to me. "You have five minutes."

"Five minutes?" I asked in disbelief. "I have at least a few hours until my timeframe is over."

Tavvy clicked his tongue, shaking his head. "Rules change. Timelines change. You now have five minutes. If you don't choose by the end of the allotted time, the chains around their necks will tighten and kill them."

I was shaking so hard that I thought I would pass out. Not even Lupe's hands on my shoulders could provide me comfort.

The seven men...

Wait? Seven?

I narrowed my eyes, and my gaze immediately latched on a pair of dark hands, directly in the middle.

Horror filled me.

"Ryland..."

Tavvy laughed maniacally, throwing his head back. In the next second, he was behind the seven prisoners and removing their hoods.

The first three were the redheads I'd noted before, including the young teenager, but the fourth was my shadow mate. His eyes burned with a ferocious anger, blood coating the edges of his lips. Around his neck, a silver chain dug into his skin.

His scars were more pronounced now that he couldn't hide behind his shadows. They covered every inch of his dark face. His cheeks, his forehead, his lips, through his eye. There wasn't an expanse of skin on his face that wasn't mutilated.

He turned towards me, and the anger ebbed immediately, replaced with relief.

"Z, you're okay," he whispered.

"What the hell?" I took a trembling step forward. My fingers went to my bottom lip. "How did this happen?"

"The damn twins," Ryland said, venom spewing. "They ganged up on me. Put this collar around my neck that prohibits the use of my powers."

I'd never heard of a collar like that. With that

weapon... It was a game changer. The Alphabet Resistance would love to get their hands on it.

It was no wonder only the royal families had access to it.

"Enough!" Tavvy moved to the end of the line and removed the hood off the last man. "Choose who to kill before the five minutes are up, or else they'll all die, including your mate."

"Just pick one," Lupe whispered into my ear.

But what if I accidentally chose an innocent man? How could I live with myself? What type of person would I be if I chose myself and my mates over innocent people? It wasn't a person I wanted to be.

"Four minutes," Tavvy said cheerfully.

My eyes flickered over the men present, absorbing every detail. The scatter of freckles on Man One's arms. The abnormally long hair that might've made me believe he was a shifter if I hadn't known he was a human on Man Two. The missing finger on Man Three. The tattoo on Man Four. The unblemished skin on Man Five, and the scars zigzagging Man Six.

Something niggled at the edges of my mind, a memory. I reached for it desperately only to have it slip through my fingers.

"Three minutes."

"Shut the fuck up, Tavvy," Lupe growled out.

Six men. One traitor.

Nine fingers.

The random thought came to me suddenly, Jax's ramblings echoing through my head.

"I have five fingers on one hand. Four on the other.

Five plus four equals nine. And nine is the number. I heard the devils talking. Five plus four equals nine. Nine fingers. We need nine fingers."

It was the senseless ramblings of a mad man, wasn't it?

I gazed harder at the man missing a finger. He had garnet colored hair with streaks of black in it. His hair was longer than the others, and his face was unremarkable. Nothing about him screamed traitor, yet I knew. I knew it as surely as I knew my name was Z and I had seven mates.

"He's the traitor," I whispered, lifting a trembling finger in the man's direction. His eyes widened in horror even as the other men collapsed in relief. One of the older men began to sob.

"That's quite the accusation," Tavvy said, tsking at me. "Do you have proof to back it up?"

"Do I need proof?" I responded harshly.

I had to rely on myself, my sixth sense. It had never led me wrong before, and I knew it hadn't this time.

"I suppose not." He shrugged like he didn't care either way.

"Now let my mate go." My hands were clenched tightly into fists, nails digging into the palm of my hand.

"Isn't it funny," Tavvy drawled, "that the magical binding spell placed on you to protect us doesn't work on Ryland like it does me? I wonder why that is?" When I merely quirked a brow at him, he met my gaze with a malicious smirk. "The spell the mage king put on you would've you running to his rescue at this very moment, not strategically playing my game. It just confirms what I've always suspected."

"What did you suspect?" I asked, though his words caused a chill to brush through me.

"That the seven perfect princes aren't actually related to the royal families." Behind me, Lupe's breathing hitched. Ryland had gone rigid where he sat, still in my peripheral vision. I didn't dare pull my gaze away from Tavvy's to read the expressions on my other two mates' faces.

"Enough of that." Tavvy waved a hand dismissively and stepped behind the man I'd deemed a traitor. He pulled on his red hair sharply, and the man let out a cry. "Why don't you tell the beautiful Z here what you did to betray the crown."

The man began to cry in earnest, large, fat tears cascading down his sunken face.

"Please," he sobbed helplessly, and my heart lurched.

"Tell her," Tavvy instructed darkly, and his hand tightened on the red strands.

The man opened his eyes and turned to meet my gaze. Begging me. Pleading with me. I instinctively stumbled further into Lupe's warm embrace.

"Please," he cried again, this time directing his plea at me.

Once more, Tavvy pulled at the red chunks of hair, and more than one handful broke free. The man whimpered in pain.

"I fell in love!" he choked out at last. Tavvy released his grip, and the man's head swung forward, lolling against his chest. "I fell in love with a mermaid."

"And?" Tavvy asked darkly.

"And she loved me back. We planned to run away together." He finally looked up, meeting my gaze. I hated the anguish in his eyes, the pain. It stabbed me repeatedly in the chest until I was nothing more than a puddle of blood. "She was the wife of the mermaid king." This confession was said around an exhale of air. His head dropped as if he wasn't able to hold it up any longer. "Not his mate, but one of his wives. She told me I was her mate. Me. A human.

"Her name was Ali, and she was beautiful. Smart. Funny. Kind. I loved her with my entire heart. Until she died."

When the man paused in his story, I swung my gaze over to Dair. This woman had been one of his many step-moms. Had he known her? Been close to her? Cared for her? However, his impassive face and slightly pursed lips gave nothing away.

"When the king discovered our affair, he killed Ali. It wasn't a quick death. He wanted her to suffer. He cut off her legs and made her crawl across the floor. And then, in front of me, he cut off her head." He choked on a sob. "I did the only thing I could think to do—I tried to kill the sick bastard."

"So you admit you're a traitor," Tavvy said lightly. He flashed a smile at me. "Good job."

"Good job?" I whispered. I couldn't get in enough air. I was gasping, choking, vomiting on my own breath. Tears burned my eyes.

What had been this man's crime? Falling in love? Defending her from a crazed madman?

I stared into the man's bright green eyes. I didn't even know his name, and the powers that be wanted me to kill him. Wanted me to snuff the light out of those eyes that were looking at me with such hope.

Those eyes suddenly widened. His brows had been furrowed, but as I watched, they smoothed over.

And then his head toppled from his body.

A scream lodged in my throat, and I desperately grasped at Lupe's arms. I'd seen death thousands of times before. Hell, I'd even been the one to kill.

But this was different. I didn't know how. Innocent people died all the time. It was just the way life worked. Maybe it was because he'd been staring at me with such hope. The man, whose name I still didn't know, had truly believed I would save him. Me. A savior.

It might've been laughable if I didn't feel like crying.

Tavvy stood over the man's body, a bloody sword held loosely in his hands. A manic grin twisted his blood red lips.

"You're a kind soul, Z. It's going to be your downfall. But don't worry. I'll look after you."

Somebody touched my arm and I jumped, but the dark skin and calluses were familiar. Bash or Dair must've released Ryland when I was focused on Tavvy. I immediately jumped into my mate's warm embrace, reveling in how safe he made me feel.

"Are you okay?" I whispered hoarsely into his chest. He brushed my hair, kissing my head.

"I'm fine, little assassin. I'm fine."

A gagging sound pulled my attention away from Ryland.

The five other men were choking, desperately grabbing at their necks and the tightening collar around them. I ran towards them, but it was too late. All five of them fell to the ground, faces blue and cold.

Dead.

Including the young teenage boy.

Tavvy released a sardonic laugh, clutching his belly. When I spun on him, eyes murderous, his laughter only intensified.

"You said release your mate," he pointed out between chuckles. "Not the other five prisoners."

THIRTY-TWO

Z

The strangest sense of loss plagued me that night and all through the next day. It was completely irrational, to mourn someone you didn't even know, but it was my reality.

The man's name was Jakob.

The boy's was Radon.

No matter how long I scrubbed at my skin, I could still feel tendrils of blood. I wished I could bleach my hands, my eyes, my mind. I may not have been the one to hold the sword, but it was my admission that had cost Jakob his life.

But Tavvy? He was behind the death of the other five innocent men.

I sat in the now pink water, staring at my pruned hands.

Would they always be a beacon of death, these hands? Would death always trail behind me like a lost, albeit obedient, puppy?

"You're not going to clean yourself like that."

Ryland's voice came from behind me, from the shadows converged in the corner of the room, but I didn't jump. I didn't do anything but sit in the sickly pink water.

The shadows steadily receded, revealing his face to me. I barely noticed it, barely comprehended what a gift that was.

He drained the water, perching at the edge of the claw-foot tub. Once the tub was emptied, he began to refill it, placing a hand beneath the faucet to check the temperature. Steam billowed, but I relished the blistering heat. I wondered if it could burn away all my sins.

"How long have you been here?" I didn't recognize my voice. It was croaky, almost as if I'd just gotten out of bed.

"Awhile," he admitted unashamedly. "I wanted to give you space."

"And now?"

"I want to take care of you." He practically breathed the words, his voice a purr.

When the tub was filled once more, he turned off the faucet and grabbed a clean rag off the bathroom counter.

"Talk to me," he pleaded, covering the rag with a generous amount of soap. Slowly, gauging my reaction, he brought it to my shoulders.

His ministrations were slow, cautious, but I leaned into him. Everywhere the rag touched, goosebumps erupted.

"I don't know why I feel so guilty." I stared pointedly ahead at the golden edged mirror, a beautiful adornment on the cream painted wall. I made out my reflection— cheeks sunken, eyes hollow, blonde hair tangled. I wondered if this was how I looked when Diego died, another innocent brutality of this war I knew nothing about.

Ryland moved the rag down my arms, paying special attention to each of my fingers. I'd never thought that bathing someone could be so erotic, but each accidental graze of his hand against mine caused my skin to burn.

He didn't interrupt me as I spoke, focused entirely on his task.

"It wasn't my fault. Not Jakob's death. Not Diego's. So why do I feel such staggering guilt?" I laughed humorlessly, watching Ryland move around the tub to wash my other arm. A part of me grieved the lack of his touch for that brief moment of separation.

Ridiculous.

Utterly ridiculous.

"But Jakob's eyes... He stared at me with hope, Ry. He truly believed that I would be his savior. But look at him! Because of me, he's dead. I may not have been the one to do the actual killing, but..." I trailed off helplessly.

I wanted Tavvy to bleed for what he'd done. I wanted him to suffer. The need was almost more compelling than the mage bond. It painted a beautiful yet macabre picture. Striding towards the smug asshole with my knife held firmly in my hand. Cutting through the tender skin of his neck. Smiling down at him, as he'd smiled down at the six men.

"I think..." Ryland began. He moved to sit inside the tub with me, still fully clothed. The water played with the edge of his shirt, gifting me briefly a view of his darkly sculpted muscles. "You feel guilty because you're a good person."

I snorted at his logic, but he continued before I could protest.

"You see the world the way the rest of us want to. Not in black or white or even gray, but in vibrant colors. You're able to separate the innocents from the predators. You recognize evil for what it is, and you wish to stop it."

His hands were wrapped around my calf as he scrubbed at my skin. Tiny bubbles appeared on my bare leg. Briefly, I wondered if I'd shaved recently. Why was that something I would think about?

I shook my head, the enticing aroma of my body wash finally reaching my nostrils. The scent was almost decadent. Pomegranates, I believed. Lupe's favorite.

"I've killed a lot of people in my life," I whispered harshly. I stared at Ryland, waiting for the moment when he realized what a monster I was and ran. His expression remained warm, if not slightly impassive, as he scrubbed the soles of my feet.

After a long moment of silence, his breathy confession breached the distance between us.

"So have I."

I gaped at him, his words sending me reeling. My eyes tracked each and every scar on his face, so many that his skin was discolored shades of white, red, and brown.

I hoped that the people he killed were the ones who'd done that to him.

Silence stretched between us, but it wasn't uncomfortable. Instead, I focused on his dark hand moving through the water and up my inner thighs. I held my breath, need and desperation causing my heart to hammer and breathing to speed up.

Despite my silent plea, he didn't touch me where I wanted him to.

He brought the rag to my stomach, and his thumb grazed my belly button. The only sound was my sharp intake of breath and the rippling of water.

The rag inched higher, higher, higher, until it brushed the underside of my breasts. This time, I couldn't contain the pathetic whimper that escaped me.

"Please," I whispered. My core was aching, and I rubbed my thighs together to alleviate the pain.

When he dropped the rag, I thought I was going to die. Literally die.

Die.

Guilt chewed away at me.

"Hey, stay here. Don't get lost in that mind of yours." Ryland cupped my face in both of his hands, eyes searching my own. Only when he found my assent, did he release my face.

And abruptly cupped my aching breasts.

I gasped, staring at his hand over my skin and loving the contrasting skin colors as his dark hand held my pale breast. His thumb grazed my nipple, and I jerked.

Keeping his eyes trained on mine, Ryland removed his hands and lathered them in soap.

"You don't see yourself clearly," he whispered, bringing his hands back to my skin. I groaned at the contact, the soft pad of his fingers and rough calluses of his palms eliciting sensations I'd never felt before. He paid extra attention to my nipples, pulling at them, twisting them.

"You don't either," I responded, slightly breathless. His hands lifted both of my boobs, scrubbing soap underneath them, before he dropped them, watching them bounce with heated eyes.

"What if I told you that the men I killed didn't deserve it?" His voice was broken. A stark contrast to the sure, domineering man who'd thrown a book at my face. "Would you leave me?"

His hands cupped water and dropped it onto my chest, washing away the soap. He did this three times before moving his hands to my thighs.

"Would you?" he whispered hoarsely.

"What if I told you," I countered, spreading my legs wider so he could fit comfortably between them, "that I killed an innocent person as well? Would you leave me?"

"Never." His answer was instantaneous.

His finger moved up my thigh, the touch reminding me of a first snowfall. Ironically, I couldn't help but think how the soft touch burned my skin.

One finger pierced my wet cunt, and I arched my back, moaning.

"Fuck," I whispered.

He brutally, savagely, fucked me with his finger, pulling it in and out of me. It was completely different from his soft hands and even softer words from only moments before. This was rough and brutal. Claiming. Punishing. That one finger was joined by two more. I had to give Ryland credit—he wasn't doing anything half-assed.

I was reaching the tip of a mountain, seconds from tumbling over. I had to decide if I was going to fall and trust him to catch me, or remain stranded at the top. My back arched sharply, fire racing down my nerves.

I pulled his face to mine, and our lips met in a desperate dance. He kissed me like rain falling on a spring day. Everywhere we touched, we dissolved into each other until there was no Z and Ryland, but one person.

Finally, I found my relief, sobbing. Ryland continued to finger fuck me long after my orgasm subsided. He pulled out slowly, lips tilted up in smug, male satisfaction against my own.

My stomach tightened with lust when I realized we were both bathing in my release.

Ryland pressed a kiss against my forehead, eyes burning with an emotion I recognized all too well.

"You won't become a monster, Z, because you recognize the monsters in others. Soon, you're going to recognize the monster in me."

His words took me back to his earlier question.

Would I still love him if he'd killed innocent people?

It had only just occurred to me that I'd never answered it.

Ryland's voice was self-deprecating when he spoke next. "This world is designed to bring out all our monsters. It's only a matter of time until you see mine, little assassin. Only a matter of time."

THIRTY-THREE

Z

By the time I left the room, my nerves had settled and I found that I could breathe.

Ryland had receded back into the shadows, a fact that saddened me. With time, he would be okay with showing his face to the world. Long, excruciating time.

Dair was uncharacteristically silent when I stepped into the main bedroom. He sat on the bed, arms crossed over his muscular chest and eyes contemplative. When he saw me, he sat up, a brilliant smile etching across his face.

It was nice to see such a smile. The mood with my mates had been tense and somber since the fight with the kraken and then the massacre in the dungeons. We all just wanted to go home, to escape.

To kill some damn mermaid princes.

"Z!" Dair rushed from the bed and grabbed my hand in his. "I want to take you to see my mom and sister today."

His words froze me in place. I blinked at him wordlessly.

"Excuse me?" I asked on a screech. Meeting his mother? That sounded more terrifying than fighting another kraken. Was there something wrong with me, something so deeply and intricately wrong with me, that made me fear opening myself up to these men?

"I want her to meet you," he said softly. His face softened in adoration, and I could see how much he loved his mom.

I wanted to say yes, to see the glorious smile I knew would cross his face, to feel his golden hand in mine as he tugged me out of the room.

But something was stopping me. Nothing large, but a diminutive clamp that tugged at the top of my heart. I knew that if I said yes, if I agreed to something so monumental, it would alter my life forever. I would no longer be "Z the assassin" or "Zara the assistant." I would be their mate, their lover, first and foremost.

Why did that terrify me so much?

Maybe because you surround yourself with death, I told myself snidely.

Staring into his brilliant blue eyes, I knew I had feelings for him and the others that surpassed even my fears. That thought cemented my resolve.

I loved him. Maybe it was the beginnings of love, the slightest trickling of rain before the downpour. Maybe it had progressed in the weeks I'd been at the capital. Either way, it was love. The strength of my conviction took me by surprise.

Fuck.

"Yes," I whispered. Did he see how much he meant to me in my gaze? Hear it in my voice?

"Yes?" He stared at me in disbelief. From his expression, it was obvious he hadn't expected me to agree. That disbelief changed to joy, and I was right. He flashed that brilliant smile at me once more.

I may have had six other mates, but to Dair, I was his only one. He stared at me as if he'd never seen a woman so beautiful before, so perfect, so deserving of his love.

Utter bullshit, if you asked me. I didn't deserve this man in front of me with his golden hair and golden face and a heart that made women everywhere weep. He was a good man. I'd known it from the first moment I met him, after he'd saved me from what might've been a disastrous and deadly fall. From the very first word, when he somehow saw through the mask and to the vulnerable, brokenhearted girl beneath.

Before I could say anything else, Dair rushed at me, grabbing my waist and spinning me in a circle.

He knew, just as I did, that my yes went beyond merely meeting his family.

"But first," I said, tapping his back. He immediately dropped me to my feet. "I want to see Slippy."

His nose crinkled adorably.

"That's an awful name for a scary ass monster," he pointed out.

I reached a hand up to smooth the skin between his eyes.

"He's the size of a small dog," I protested.

"He was once the size of a very large building. And he tried to kill us."

I waved a hand dismissively.

"Let bygones be bygones."

I didn't know what had possessed the kraken to attack us. Bash had deduced that it must've been a spell, designed specifically for me. To capture me.

It made me...sad.

Had Haven, the gorgon, been acting under a spell?

Bash must've somehow broken the spell on the kraken when he made it tiny. That was the only conclusion he could come up with.

Either way, both Dair and Bash had assured me that the sea monster wasn't a threat. The water had promised Dair, and Bash... Well, I wasn't sure how he knew, and he wasn't in the mood to share with me.

I hadn't seen the blond asshole since we'd left the dungeon.

Dair took my hand and led me down the hall. He stopped only a few doors down at the room I'd noted during my arrival.

Heat emanated from the open door, choking me. Sweat prickled at my skin.

The room was unlike anything I'd ever seen before, both beautiful and strange. Jagged, brown rocks lined the walls, melded together in a way that couldn't be natural. The flooring abruptly switched from wooden planks to sand, burning my toes. At the very edge of the sand was a small pool of water. Waves rippled the shoreline, but from what source, I couldn't tell.

Slippy chirped happily when he caught sight of me, clambering out of the water and rubbing against my feet like a cat.

If you hadn't seen a kraken before, consider yourself lucky. He was so ugly that it was borderline adorable. Long tentacles wrapped around my legs, but unlike before, it didn't hurt. His one eye stared up at me as if I'd hung the moon.

My stomach churned uncomfortably when I noted the dark lines grazing the white of his iris. From my arrow.

I wondered if he still felt pain.

"Do you have anyone who could look over him? Make sure we didn't do any lasting damage?" I asked Dair nervously, bending down to pick up the little guy. He cuddled beneath my chin, and I could've sworn that he was purring.

Dair stared at me strangely but conceded with a nod. "I can have the family doctor check him out. We have five, and at least one always stays here."

Five doctors.

I couldn't even begin to wrap my head around that, having spent years without any medical care at all.

"You be a good boy for when the doctor comes, okay?" I told Slippy sternly. The little asshole rolled his one eye as if he actually understood me. I gave him a disapproving frown. "I mean it. No fish for you if you misbehave. I'll feed you the shitty tuna from the marketplace."

That seemed to pierce his monster brain. His eye widened slightly, almost imperceptibly, and he wiggled to let me know he wanted down. I dropped him at the edge of the water, and he swam away without a glance back in my direction.

I feigned sniffles.

"They grow up so fast." I punctuated this statement by brushing away an imaginary tear.

Dair snorted, wrapping his arm around my shoulders and pulling me out of the hot room.

"And you're fucking weird. Come. Let me introduce you to my mother."

DAIR'S MOTHER lived in a tiny, bungalow style house a few miles off the main shoreline. The white paint looked freshly coated, and a long, wraparound porch held two rocking chairs. Hanging plants adorned the awning overhead. The ground was surprisingly grass, instead of sand like I'd expected, freshly manicured and bedecked in shrubs and what appeared to be tulips. The single tree I'd noted earlier stood proudly in the waning sunlight, a brilliant collection of green leaves intermixed with a deep burgundy and light orange.

It was an entire little world condensed onto a small island.

I shouldn't have been surprised that it was beautiful, the opulence of the house nearly unmatched. After all, the Mermaid Kingdom was just as wealthy as the Genie Kingdom.

The seductive pulls of envy couldn't be ignored, even by Dair's family.

I smiled as I took Dair's offered hand, stepping out of the boat. It was significantly smaller than the one I'd ridden with Bash, but it was cute nonetheless, with plush leather seats, a canopy overhead, and what Dair had called the captain's chair.

My mermaid mate had driven the boat with a skill and expertise that hinted at his years in the water, both swimming in it and riding over it. His cheeks were still flushed, eyes hooded, from the hour-long ride.

I wobbled the second I touched the grass, my feet and body adjusting to the steadiness of dry land. There wasn't a part of me that missed the rocking of the boat and the clenching of my stomach seconds before I expelled the contents of my lunch.

"Seasickness," Dair had told me.

"It's beautiful," I told Dair now, spinning in a circle. In every direction, I could see waves of water. There were no other islands in sight.

"Yes, it is," Dair murmured absently, but his attention was locked on me. He brought a hand up to cup my cheek, his thumb caressing my bottom lip.

The moment we were inevitably about to have was shattered by an earsplitting squeal. I immediately went on alert, pushing Dair out of my way and grabbing the dagger I always kept up my sleeve. Was it Aaliyah? Another monster? Tavvy?

My confusion turned into something akin to jealousy when I spotted Dair running to the water's edge and wrapping a girl in his arms.

She was beautiful, I noticed immediately. A sort of ethereal beauty you would read about in storybooks but never see in real life. Her hair was long and black, like molten obsidian stones, and cascaded around her porcelain skin.

I'd never seen a female mermaid before, and I couldn't help but gawk. Her tail was luminous, a rich purple that sparkled in the sunlight like thousands of diamonds. Seaweed wrapped up her torso, covering her breasts from view, thank God.

I saw red, literal red dots obscuring my vision, as she continued to hug Dair. I wanted nothing more than to stomp down there and rip her beautiful black hair from her scalp.

Muscles trembling in exertion, as if I'd run for miles and miles, I glanced down at my dagger. That wouldn't do.

I may have hated the girl still hugging and whispering to my mate, but I didn't want her dead.

Before I could think rationally, before I could piece together the clues that had been laid out in front of me, I bent down, took off my shoe, and chucked it at her face.

Not my finest hour.

The girl squeaked, batting at the air, and Dair released her, stepping back. His eyes were comically wide in his face as he stared back at me.

"I didn't even think to do introductions," he murmured to himself. His golden blond hair fell over one eye, and he brushed it away impatiently. "What with the mating bond still so new..." He took another deep breath, eyes flickering from the girl rubbing at her head and then back to me. "Z, this is Angelica, my *sister*." He stressed "sister" in a way that made me feel like an idiot.

My face flamed like there was a fire burning beneath the surface. My first time meeting a boyfriend's family, and I'd already fucked it up.

Note to self—don't throw things at females until you get the whole story.

I had a feeling I'd be breaking that rule more often than not. At least it hadn't been my dagger...

...that was still held in one of my hands, blade unintentionally pointed at the beautiful female. Angelica. Dair's sister.

I scrambled to shove it back in my sleeve, accidentally nicking my skin in the process.

"Angelica," Dair turned towards the ravishing female, "this is Z, my mate."

The girl's eyes widened slightly, and before I realized what was happening, she was scrambling to her feet, butt naked. In the next second, she had her arms wrapped tightly around me.

She looked a few years older than Dair, with a sort of elegance in her face that couldn't be found on a child. Full, pouty lips and a Roman nose befitting a princess.

But she wasn't a princess, I recalled. She was the daughter of Dair's mother and her mate, a commoner.

"It's so good to finally meet you," Angelica squealed, practically breaking my rib cage. I awkwardly patted her back.

"I'm sorry for throwing a shoe at you," I blurted. "I just saw you hugging him and—"

"No worries." She pulled back with a slight smile. "The first few years after you meet your mate are always the worst. Jealousy and all that shit." She waved a hand dismissively, that smile never leaving her beautiful face. "Dair would be just as bad if another man touched you who wasn't your mate. Isn't that right, little brother?"

She glanced over her shoulder at Dair the same time I did. His face had been soft as he watched me with his sister, but at her words, his expression hardened, eyes narrowing.

"No other man is allowed to touch you," he said coldly to me.

His possessiveness should've made me mad, but it only served to do the opposite. Liquid heat settled in my core, and I wanted to squirm.

Something that would've been quite awkward with his naked sister's arms still around me.

Angelica pulled away with a devilish smile. I wondered where she'd gotten her sense of humor from. Dair, though not cold, was one of my more serious mates. Kind, calm, collected. Those were just a few words in my arsenal to describe Dair Mermaid.

Dair strode briskly back towards me, as if he couldn't stand the distance that separated us, and interlocked our fingers. Or...

As if he was jealous of his sister hugging me and me hugging her back.

There was a soft noise from the front of the house, a nearly inaudible whimper, and I whipped my head in that direction.

A petite older woman stood in the doorway, hand clenched around one of the many white pillars holding up the awning. She was beautiful, with honey-toned blonde hair and deep blue eyes. Gray speared the roots of her hair, the only indication of her age. Her wide, petrified eyes surveyed everything and nothing all at once.

"Why is she here?" the woman asked harshly.

Dair held up his hands placatingly. "Mother, this is my mate, Z. We came here to see you."

He took a step closer, and she flinched. I recognized the movement—the reaction of a woman who'd been beaten and hit one too many times. Disgust and anger battled for dominance. I had no doubt in my mind who was behind her skittish reaction.

The mermaid king.

"It's safe, Mom. You can trust her." He met my stare pointedly, but I couldn't understand what he was trying to say.

"Juliet, you're safe," a different voice said. An older man stepped out of the house and placed his hands on her shoulders.

He had the same dark hair and blue eyes as Angelica. A soft smile graced his lips when he caught sight of Dair.

"Dair, my son, how are you?"

Dair smiled back at the man with love and warmth. It was the sort of look you would give to your dad...

Wait.

Understanding dawned as I flickered my eyes from Angelica, now fully dressed, to Juliet leaning against the man, and then to Dair.

This man was Juliet's mate, I realized. The father of Angelica. And apparently, the pseudo father to Dair.

No wonder Juliet was so nervous to see me, a stranger, on her island. The secrets held here were capable of killing them all. The mermaid king was ruthless, volatile. If he discovered his wife was still seeing her mate, living with him, he would not hesitate to kill them all.

"I'm Z," I introduced, moving to stand beside Dair. My mate gave me another long, beseeching look, but once more, I couldn't comprehend it. "Dair's mate."

Juliet stared at me for a long moment before tears pricked her eyes and her hand rose to her mouth. I had only a second to fear I'd said something wrong before she was pulling me into her arms with a soft sob.

"My dear girl," she whispered, rubbing a hand up and down my back. "I'm so happy he has you."

One glance to the side showed that Dair seemed just as stunned by his mother's reaction as me. I tentatively patted at the woman's blonde hair, resisting the urge to whisper "there, there" as I would to a crying toddler.

When she finally pulled away, her face was blotchy and swollen. She sniffled once.

From somewhere in the house, a baby began to cry. I stiffened.

A baby?

As the man kissed his lover's cheek and rushed back inside, I realized they were hiding more than just a hidden relationship.

If the king caught wind of this...

No, I decided resolutely. He never would. I would make sure of it.

"Come, my dear children," Juliet said, linking her arm with mine and pulling me inside. When Dair remained standing on the front porch, a dumbstruck look on his face, I pulled his arm and tugged him in after us. "Let's have dinner."

"And you can tell us all about how you met," Angelica added wickedly.

And so it began.

THIRTY-FOUR

JAX

Light penetrated the darkness I'd found myself in.

"Z?" I whispered desperately. I scrambled to my feet and placed one hand against the blood soaked walls. Even after all this time, they continued to bleed. And bleed. And bleed. And bleed. The enticing scent of copper permeated the air. I wanted nothing more than to press my tongue to the wall...

No! I told myself I would never feast on blood again, no matter how hungry I got.

And I was famished.

My stomach growled painfully, almost a reminder and confirmation all at once. Pain. It was all I ever knew. Normally, I could ignore it. Shove it under the rug and pretend it didn't exist.

This time, my need very nearly consumed me. It pelted me repeatedly in the face until I was dizzy with the madness of it all.

Thirsty.

Bleeding walls.

Drip. Drip. Drip.

The light was abruptly snatched away, and the darkness returned.

With a dizzying clarity, I realized I was all alone. Trapped in my own mind.

Trapped.

Blood.

Drip. Drip. Drip.

I curled into a ball and began to rock, whispering nonsense to myself in an attempt to calm my racing heart.

She'd done it. She'd left me, and she wasn't planning on returning. She'd taken my brothers with her, finally relieving them of the thankless task of watching over the crazed, eccentric vampire.

Alone.

So, so alone.

I called her name, but she never answered. It was only then that realization pierced me, a killing blow.

She wasn't coming back.

For the first time in my life, I was really, truly alone. Emotion clogged my throat, and I released a whimpering sob.

The walls continued to drip blood, taunting me. The urge to feed was nearly overwhelming.

Alone.

"You deserve it," I whispered to myself. Images of Sasha flashed through my mind, one after another. I hugged my knees tighter to my chest in a desperate attempt to tame the rising storm inside of me.

Alone.

And so I waited, with bated breath, for death to finally claim me.

THIRTY-FIVE

Z

"I like your family," I said as the boat sliced cleanly through the water. "They're...homey."

Dinner hadn't been as bad as I'd expected. After being peppered with rather embarrassing questions, we'd sat together around the table for a home-cooked meal of fish and clams. It struck me as odd that they were eating their brethren, but I didn't complain. The food was delicious.

Dair's youngest sister, only a year old, was named Shelly, after the seashells she'd immediately grabbed to play with after she was born. Juliet had apparently kept up her relationship with her mate, even after marrying the mermaid king, unbeknownst to him. This was a crime punishable by death.

I discovered through our conversations that Juliet's mate's name was Pearce. I also discovered that they had a second home at the very bottom of the water.

A wistful part of me wanted to see the castle in the

water, something that sounded like it came out of a fantasy book, and Dair assured me he would find a way.

After hours of senseless chatting and another hour of them in their mermaid forms, we left with our bellies full and chaste kisses to our cheeks.

"Homey." Dair snorted at my description of his family. "I've never heard that one before."

"Your mother and father really love each other," I mused, and that was what Juliet and Pearce were to him —his parents. Pearce may not have been blood, but I could see the familial love between the two of them. Dair thought the world of the man with the boisterous laugh and sharp-witted tongue.

He needed that. Dair needed a father figure who looked out for him, who loved him unconditionally, who remembered silly aspects of his life such as his favorite dessert—which was clam cake.

"You were glorious with them," Dair whispered. He moved away from the steering wheel to stand directly in front of me. His hot breath fanned my face. "Shelly adored you. I've never seen her laugh so much before. Angelica and Pearce loved you as well. I've never seen my mother so taken with a stranger before."

"Do you bring a lot of strangers to your house?" I asked, only half joking. The thought of him introducing another girl to his parents filled me with unease.

"No."

And then he was kissing me, or I was kissing him. At that point, it didn't matter. We were devouring each other, telling a story with our lips alone. My soft, supple body fit perfectly against his hard one, and I wrapped my arms around his waist.

"You're mine now," he whispered roughly. Before I could comment, could agree, he snaked his hands beneath my ass and hoisted me up. My legs instinctively wrapped around his waist as he held me. "Because now that you're mine, I'm never letting you go."

With those words, I was crushed tighter in his arms, our lips once more chasing each other in an endless race. My body melted against his.

He moved forward until my back hit one of the leather benches. With a gentleness that belied the euphoric energy in the air, he pressed me down, immediately covering me with his long body.

I tore my lips away from his, only long enough to breathlessly say, "The ship..."

"It'll be fine."

And then he was kissing me once more. Our tongues tangled together, hands desperately grabbing at any bare skin they could find. One of mine caught the edge of his shirt, pulling it up so I could lay my palm flat against his abdomen. His muscles were hard beneath my hand, flexing. My other hand touched his corded bicep.

"My love..." he whispered into my ear. His teeth grazed my earlobe before lowering. His tongue brushed the sensitive skin of my neck, my jaw, before claiming my lips once more.

And they were his to claim. There was no doubt in my mind.

His. Theirs.

Mine.

Dair pulled back suddenly, balancing over me on his elbows. His tender eyes traced my features reverently.

"Tomorrow, things are going to be different," he told me. "I'm going to be different. But my feelings for you are not going to change, do you understand?"

His words brought more confusion than understanding, but I nodded anyways. His lips twitched slightly, but my answer was apparently sufficient enough. Or his need matched my own.

His look of amusement was replaced by one of veneration.

With a desperate gasp, he pulled my lips into a bruising, possessive kiss. I rivaled his own neediness by ripping at his shirt so I could touch more of his skin.

Each of his muscles was defined, a delicious trail of golden hair leading into the waistband of his pants.

Movements jerky, he helped me out of my shirt and bra, sitting back for a moment to admire me. My stomach fluttered at the heated look in his eyes, and any self-consciousness dissipated in that moment.

He was mine, as surely as I was his.

"You're so damn beautiful," he whispered in awe. His tongue took its time memorizing each crook and crevice of my body. My back arched when he sucked on my nipple, his hand leaving my hips to knead my neglected breast.

His lips moved down my stomach, tongue swirling in my belly button, before he reached my pants. Meeting my eyes, he pulled the pants and then my panties off my legs. I lifted my ass to help him remove them completely.

Bare in the moonlight, I didn't feel vulnerable. The

way he stared at me went beyond mere love. I would almost describe it as worshipful...and that scared the crap out of me. I didn't deserve to have a man as good as Dair look at me with such warmth and love. It very nearly took my breath away.

His hot breath hit my dripping wet core, and I whimpered.

I was so needy, so ready for him.

"You're perfect," he whispered, one finger settling in my slick folds. His finger had just barely begun its ministrations before it was replaced by his hot mouth.

All coherent thoughts fled from my mind as Dair devoured me. My hips bucked of their own accord, desperate to ride Dair's face. His tongue and teeth nipped at my bundle of nerves, alleviating the ache only slightly. I was seconds from the impending explosion, seconds from losing myself in his mouth.

The second I would've crumbled over the edge, he lifted his lips from my core and captured my mouth in another searing kiss. I tasted myself on him, a fact that nearly sent me spiraling.

He pulled away, briefly, and I heard the sound of his pants being removed. I had only a second to appreciate his long, golden length before it was sheathed inside of me.

I moaned at the sensation, one of being too full yet not full enough.

"Dair," I whispered. I needed him to move, to send me crashing and tumbling over that edge. I needed it more than I needed air to breathe.

I'd given him everything, and I wanted him to do the same.

"My love," he whispered, eyes pinched closed. Pure, unadulterated pleasure crossed his face. That look alone was nearly my undoing. It told me everything he wasn't saying.

"Move," I ordered breathlessly.

Dair complied, slowly moving his hips. He wanted our first time to be slow and sensual, but that soon changed. He couldn't seem to control himself as fucked me relentlessly, tiny spurts of air leaving his lips.

"Yes, yes," I shouted into the night air. Each buck of his hips sent me closer to that edge. He lifted my legs suddenly, angling himself so he was deeper inside of me. The tip of his cock pounded my clit, and I cried out.

I pulled his lips to mine in a feverish kiss, desperate to feed both his and my insatiable hunger.

I reached the precipice with a loud scream, my orgasm crashed around me. Dair continued to move inside me relentlessly until he, too, spilled his seed. I shuddered in his strong, powerful arms, my body depleted of any and all energy.

"Fuck," I whispered. Dair chuckled breathlessly, planting a kiss on my bare shoulder. He was still inside of me, and I could already feel him getting hard once more. In the next moment, he had his strong forearms beneath my ass hoisting me up and his mouth on my clit, sucking and licking.

It was unlike anything I'd ever felt before.

I placed my hands on his shoulders to maintain my

balance as he expertly held me in the air, devouring my pussy.

Minutes later, I exploded into his eager mouth and he lapped up every last drop. Through it all, his strong arms didn't waver once...though I wasn't a light girl by any means. Spent, I collapsed into his arms, and he pressed a kiss to my temple.

"I love you, Z. More than I've ever loved anyone or anything before." His words were earnest. Beautiful.

His hand stroked my sweat soaked hair as he held my eyes. I knew he wasn't expecting a reply, but I wanted to give him one anyway. I wanted him to know how much he meant to me. How much I adored him. His gentle smiles and soft hands. The laughter always dancing in his eyes. The pain I could see behind that laughter.

"I love you too," I whispered into the silence of the night.

His smile was unlike anything I'd ever seen before. Nothing could be more beautiful. All of his previous smiles paled in comparison.

There, with the water rippling against the side of the boat and the birds cawing overhead, we were content to hold each other.

With our bodies, we showed each other how pure and wonderful love could be.

IT WAS hours later when we returned to the dock. Blissful hours of memorizing each other's bodies, discovering what we liked.

I felt sated in a way I hadn't been in a long time, not since my time with Killian. In those moments, all fear and anger and hurt had disappeared completely, leaving only Dair and me.

I felt safe in his arms. Loved. Treasured.

With great reluctance, we cleaned each other up and set course for shore.

I remained curled in Dair's arms as he steered the ship. He stayed true to his word. Now that he had me, he wasn't letting me go.

Only the moon guided us as we departed the boat. My legs felt like jelly, but this time, it wasn't just because of the ship.

Stumbling, I couldn't help the very girly giggle.

I felt like a schoolgirl with a crush. Young and in love, the familiar feelings of elation coursing through my veins.

Dair met my smile with a blinding one of his own. I didn't think I would ever get tired of seeing that, especially aimed at me. It was as if the clouds parted and the sun appeared.

"You're beautiful," I told him seriously.

"I love you," he replied.

He hadn't stopped saying that.

Each time, it sent delightful tingles down my body.

He suddenly lurched forward, eyes glazed, and I let out a surprised scream, staggering under his weight. His heart still beat steadily, and I nearly collapsed in relief. Gently, I placed him on the ground and spun to meet our attacker.

I lunged forward with my blade extended, only to

stop short seconds before I would've cut the offender's neck.

What the hell?

My eyes were wide, feet paralyzed with fear, as I met Tavvy's blue eyes.

"Beautiful, you know you can't hurt me." He shook his head disapprovingly and took a step closer. His hand cradled my head, and he brought his lips a hair's breadth away from mine. I was trembling with the need to stab him, to push him away, but I couldn't.

I was trapped with a psychopath and no possible way to defend myself. My body physically wouldn't let me harm him.

His tongue licked a long trail down my face, and I shook with revulsion and anger. And fear.

An all-encompassing, all-consuming fear.

Before the ball, I'd thought I would be able to fight him and escape, but I now knew the truth—I was entirely at his mercy.

All I could see penetrating the darkness were his bright blue eyes and blinding white teeth as he smiled.

"My dear, I think it's time we had a chat."

THIRTY-SIX

Z

"You don't want to do this." I hated how my voice shook.

Tavvy's fingers were rough under my arm as he led me up a stone staircase and into a dilapidated hut at the base of the clifftop.

It looked to be a small store, unoccupied, that sold seashells, glass wind chimes, and rental boats. Moonlight pierced through the open window, illuminating everything in vivid detail.

I was tossed to the ground like a rag doll, and I let out an instinctive grunt of pain.

"What do you see in my brother?" Tavvy's cadence was harsh, broken, manic. He took a step closer to me, and I braced myself for pain. The man did not disappoint when he swung a fist at my face.

Pain erupted behind my eye, so intense that I gasped.

"Why him?" he continued. He sounded and looked completely unhinged. His eyes were wild, wild, wild as they swept over my face. "Why does everyone love him more than me? Why can't I have a pretty mate? Why don't you love me?!" The last statement was accompanied by a kick to my ribs.

Maybe it was foolish to poke the beast, but if I couldn't fight back physically, I would get in his head.

"Because you're a psychopathic asshole!" I hissed. Blood dribbled down my chin, but I ignored it. "Because you're evil. And an ugly bastard as well."

The next kick was enhanced with his mermaid magic. I flew through the air, hitting a shelf that held glass statues of animals. I collapsed on the floor, and glass rained down on me. Shielding my head did little to stop the onslaught of pain from tiny nicks as glass cut up my arm.

"You're a fucking coward, Tavvy," I managed to say through clenched teeth. Pain radiated throughout my whole body. "That's why no one loves you."

He was in front of me a second later, hand tangled in my blonde hair as he pulled me to my feet. Pain emanated from my scalp, and I cried out.

"All I wanted was for you to be mine," Tavvy whispered brokenly. "Why can't you just be mine?"

Before I could reply that I could never belong to such an asshole, he kissed me.

Kissed me.

His tongue prodded the seams of my lips, but I kept my mouth closed. Disgust churned in my stomach. Disgust and an incandescent fury that threatened to burn me alive. I hated him.

Hated him.

It was on the opposite end of the spectrum of what I

felt for his brother. I loved Dair intensely, with all I had to offer, and I hated Tavvy just as much. It was a pendulum that swung in both directions—one side hate, the other love.

But I couldn't stop him, couldn't push him away, couldn't even angrily bite down on his lip like I wanted to. My only course of action was to hold myself perfectly still, muscles rigid, and hope that whatever he did would be quick.

A searing slap sent tendrils of pain down my left cheek. My head snapped to the side with the force of his hit.

"Why won't you kiss me?" Tavvy screamed, spit hitting my face.

If goading him didn't elicit the reaction I wanted, I would try stony silence. Again, my thoughts shifted back to the image of a pendulum. One extreme followed by another.

"Answer me!" He shook my shoulders. Crazed. Desperate.

Envious.

The man was overridden by the sin he was born with, an inherent part of himself. He couldn't control his nature, just like I couldn't control being born with blonde hair.

It wasn't the sin that made people act like monsters, it was how people wielded them.

Tavvy's hands clumsily pulled at my shirt, and I once more held perfectly still. My eyelids were squeezed shut, blocking out his hideous face and cruel smirk.

I knew what was going to happen. I knew it, and a little part of me died inside because of it.

"You're mine," Tavvy whispered hotly, tongue lapping at my neck.

One second, he was touching me, and the next, his body's weight left mine. I peeled open my eyes, scarcely believing what was happening.

Another face hovered a hairsbreadth away from my lips.

He was an avenging angel in the flesh. A being materialized straight from heaven to smite the creature who dared to harm me.

Dair's eyes flashed with a rage unlike anything I'd ever seen before. It burned me, burned my very soul, and was exactly the balm I needed. He would protect me when I couldn't protect myself.

"How did you...?" I couldn't finish my sentence, my eyes taking in his face. He looked positively murderous in the sliver of moonlight, his eyes flaming with an elemental fury. A darkness emanated from his eyes like a spilt bottle of ink. He looked like a monster.

My monster.

"I told you," he whispered roughly. His hands grabbed something behind him, but I couldn't see what it was. "I'm not letting you go."

One of his hands held both my wrists together as he led me back a step, and then another. He brought my wrists to a wooden post.

And then abruptly tied my hands to the post, the rope sinking into my skin and no doubt leaving red gashes. I couldn't even fight back at first, the shock I felt at his actions leaving me speechless.

"Dair!" I hissed, pulling at the rope. It held. "Dair!" My voice was a screech, an accusation, and a condemnation all in one. Still, my mermaid prince didn't falter under my glare. There was no sympathy or guilt in his blue gaze. Only resolution.

And it was then that I understood.

"Dair!" I kicked at the post, wiggling my wrists futilely. Without a word, Dair grabbed my dagger from my sleeve, being extra careful not to cut me, and then reached behind me to grab my sword. His eyes were dark when he finally faced his brother.

Tavvy rolled to his feet, blood gushing from his nose. It gave me great satisfaction to see him injured, though a part of me screamed in fury.

I had to protect him. I had to...

No!

I tried to ignore the mage spell. My mind knew that I didn't want to protect such a monster, but my body refused to listen to me. It struggled helplessly against the bindings in a desperate attempt to get to Tavvy.

"What are you doing, little brother?" Tavvy asked gleefully. He either wasn't aware or chose not to care about the blood staining his palms as he opened his arms in a large, swooping motion. "We're family. You share your mate with those...*friends* of yours. Why can't you share her with me, your brother?"

"You're not my brother." Dair's voice was dark and raspy, an inarticulate growl.

In the next second, Dair had Tavvy on the ground, punching him repeatedly in the face. The sword clattered as Dair dropped it, his need for vengeance, for the satisfying sound of flesh hitting flesh, overcoming his logical reasoning.

I began to struggle in earnest. I needed to get to Tavvy, I needed to protect him.

The need was almost uncontrollable. Sweat dripped down my forehead, and not just from my struggles.

My body and mind warred for dominance, each one believing itself to be right. I knew, innately, that I didn't want to help the monster bleeding on the floor, but my body refused to listen. And if it listened, it didn't obey.

"You. Hurt. My. Mate," Dair seethed between blows. Tavvy released a manic laugh.

"I would've done more than hurt her," he rasped out. "I would've stuck my cock into her sweet cunt."

His words pierced a part of my brain, the part that warned against helping such a monster, but it didn't completely override the need I felt to protect him. I needed to get to him. I needed it more than I needed air to breathe.

His statement had the desired reaction from Dair too. His movements became erratic, just sloppy enough for Tavvy to slide smoothly out from underneath him and jump on his back. Dair fell to the ground, twisting. Their positions reversed, Tavvy began to level punch after punch to my sweet mate's face, cackling beneath his breath.

I couldn't help Dair. My body refused, but my mind stayed sharp. They could take away my body's autonomy, but they couldn't take away my voice. I would not be silenced.

"Get angry, Dair!" I shouted. "Get fucking enraged. He hurt me! He hurt you! Fight back! Fight back!"

Even as I screamed this, my body worked to break free and fight for Tavvy. Fight *against* my mate.

I hated myself.

My wrists were red and raw, but I did not relent. It was a helpless feeling, these contradicting emotions battling inside of me. A part of me wanted to stay tied up forever, while the other part wanted—no, needed to break free. Protect Tavvy.

No! Protect Dair!

No, Tavvy!

"Think of all that he's done to you!" I screamed at Dair. I couldn't see his face, but I could hear his moans of pain. That sound would forever haunt me. "Fight back! Fight fucking back!"

My words must've pierced the darkest recesses of his brain. With the next punch, he gripped Tavvy's fist, twisting it with a roar. There was the satisfying crack of bone breaking and Tavvy crying out.

Dair stumbled to his feet. His beautiful face was bruised and bloody, but his eyes continued to gleam with a malicious glint I'd never seen before.

Tavvy lunged at Dair, but neither he nor I noticed the dagger held tightly in Dair's hand. The blade cut through skin.

Tavvy's eyes widened, shock evident on his pale face. He hadn't expected Dair to actually do it, to actually kill him. His body lurched forward, and Dair none too gently placed him on the ground.

The dagger protruded from the center of his stomach. Blood pooled on the ground, the color so dark, it was almost black.

A strangled laugh escaped Tavvy.

"I didn't think you had it in you, little brother," he whispered hoarsely.

No! I struggled earnestly against the ropes, ignoring the pain and the voice telling me that Tavvy wasn't the one I needed to protect.

Dair moved away, only for a second, and returned with my sword. He held the weapon in a tight grip, the blade pointed at Tavvy's throat.

"Dair!" I screamed helplessly. He needed to lower the weapon, he needed to...

I let out a scream of agony.

One of my wrists was minutes, if not seconds, from breaking free. I knew, without a doubt in my mind, that the second I was free, I wouldn't hesitate to hurt Dair in order to save Tavvy.

Ignoring my screams, Dair pressed the sword further into the other man's skin.

"What did you mean earlier?" he asked darkly. "About us not being of royal blood?"

Tavvy's howl of laughter turned into a guttural moan as blood poured from his lips. He was blinking rapidly, as if struggling to stay awake.

I could sense he was seconds from death. It pierced my heart, this pain I couldn't understand.

So close...

I wiggled my wrists once more.

"I meant what I said," Tavvy answered cryptically. "You aren't related to the king. None of you are."

"Explain." The sword dug deeper into Tavvy's neck, and the psychopath once more released a crazed laugh.

Tension flooded my muscles. All I could see was red. How dare he hurt Tavvy? Threaten him?

One of my wrists slipped free, and I hastily worked on untying myself from the pole.

"I always suspected it, but this only confirms it." Tavvy's voice was losing its maniacal edge as death claimed him. He blinked rapidly. "Your mom..." He coughed violently, more blood sputtering from his chapped lips. "She was never pregnant."

"What?"

"If the rumors are true" —another hacking cough— "you and those men you call your brothers magically appeared. Out of thin air."

Dair momentarily lowered the sword, face slack with shock and unhealthily pale.

I wrenched my hands free of their prison in the same second Dair lifted his sword and cut off Tavvy's head.

THIRTY-SEVEN

DAIR

B lood.

It coated my skin, contaminated my lungs, filled my nostrils. I stared down at my soaked hands, unable to believe that these same hands, these unremarkable limbs, had been a harbinger of death.

I'd killed a man. And not just any man, but my blood brother.

Or not my blood brother, if I believed the nonsense Tavvy had spouted.

I shook my head as if that gesture could clear my thoughts.

Slowly, I turned to face my mate. I didn't want to see the expression on her face—the horror and disgust towards a man willing to kill his own brother.

Her face was spotted in bruises, a fact that only served to enrage me further. If Tavvy weren't already dead, I would've killed him again.

Z's wide, terrified eyes flickered from my blood-stained body to Tavvy.

"Stay back," she whispered hoarsely the second I took a step towards her. The blood drained from my face. I would rather be stabbed repeatedly in the chest, fight a thousand Tavvys, than have her look at me like that.

With fear.

"I don't know..." She gritted her teeth together. "I don't know if the spell is going to expect retribution. I don't want to hurt you anymore, but I'm not sure..." Her face was pinched. "The spell wanted me to hurt you to protect Tavvy. I'm not sure if I'm going to hurt you now that Tavvy's dead."

She held up red, bloody wrists and took a tentative step towards me.

Relief filled my chest, this instantaneous buoyancy that had me floating. She didn't hate me, didn't fear me.

She feared herself.

One second, she was surveying the store, expression pensive and slightly cautious, and the next, she was in my arms. I hugged her to me, molding her body to my own.

We were both bloody, injured, and admittedly fucked in the head, but in that moment, we had each other.

The rest of the world didn't matter.

I DIDN'T KNOW who was more shocked when we arrived home, dripping in blood and holding Tavvy's body in a bag. The twins were the first ones to see us, and they threw us scathing glares.

They wouldn't mourn their older brother. They

would, however, mourn the power Tavvy's presence gave them.

Lupe must've scented the blood, as he came barreling out of the house next, eyes frantic. Ignoring me, he grabbed Z gently, as if she were fine glass seconds from breaking. They began to whisper to one another, voices hushed, and I turned away to give them privacy.

"What the hell happened?" Ryland asked. He hovered just behind Z, shadows continually appearing and disappearing around him in his agitation. A dark hand reached out to touch her, but he pulled it back, granting Lupe the time he needed to get his beast under control.

I mechanically explained to him the fight with Tavvy. How could the best memory of my life, Z's confession of love and our bodies moving as one, be tainted by my worst memory? I didn't think anything could compare to the fear and rage I felt when I saw Tavvy's hands on her.

And the sword slicing through his head...

Nausea swirled within me, and I couldn't stop myself from vomiting in the nearby bushes.

A memory burned itself in my brain, searing.

The sword had gotten caught on something, bone more than likely, when I'd tried to cut off his head. I'd meant to quicken his death, to grant him relief from the agony he was experiencing. But I had only prolonged it. It wasn't a clean slice through skin. It was jagged and brutal, and I would never forget the pain in his eyes.

Z's small hand touched the bottom of my back, but even her comfort couldn't stop the storm raging in my mind.

A murderer. I was a murderer.

"I need to heal you guys," Bash said tersely. He stood in the doorway, body rigid and his focus on Z. However, he didn't step towards her. He didn't hold her like I knew he wanted to.

"Dair first," Z answered immediately, and I couldn't help but smile. If she thought there was a chance in hell Bash would heal me before her, she was crazier than she looked.

Bash continued to stare her down, his typical no-nonsense stare. When Z saw he wouldn't relent, she released a huff and wobbled up the front steps.

Both Ryland and Lupe rushed to steady her.

She was even more injured than I'd realized. If I'd arrived even a second later...

No, I didn't want to think about that. I shot those thoughts from my mind vehemently.

What I needed was a scorching hot shower, a chance to wipe the excess blood off my body. I also needed to swim in my mermaid form. Already, my twelve hours as a human were coming to an end, the familiar itch begging to be scratched.

A part of my curse. Twelve hours as a human. Twelve as a mermaid.

Tavvy had always preferred his human form.

Tavvy...

I could still hear my brother's laugh. I didn't think that sound would ever fade completely.

At the end of the day, he was just a sick, twisted boy in desperate need of help. Did that make me feel guilty for killing him? No, absolutely not. Did I feel guilty because I didn't feel guilty? Yes.

"You know you're going to be punished when you get back," one of the twins, Idol, said.

I sighed.

My legs were a gift, and like with any present, they could be ripped away.

At least I'd enjoyed them to the best of my ability while I had them.

THIRTY-EIGHT

Z

There was a sort of tension in the air. A sickly cloud that hung ominously over our heads. Not palpable, but just foggy enough to be notice-able. A mist floating over the land.

The tension remained as we pulled up in front of the capital, parking near the stone fountain.

Two familiar figures were waiting for me when we arrived, and I unbuckled my seatbelt and flung myself at them.

Both sets of arms immediately wrapped around me before Devlin pushed me away with a scowl.

"What the fuck happened?" he whispered, hand tracing the bruises and cuts on my face. I captured his hand and gave it a reassuring squeeze, knowing that he needed it.

Bash had tried to heal me the best he could, but he'd quickly tired.

"I sense something in you," Bash had said suddenly during the healing session, brows creasing. My mind had immediately drifted to Zack and his talk of poisons. When Bash had waited for me to answer with a raised brow, I'd meekly shrugged in feigned cluelessness.

Despite my protests to take a break, he'd continued with a renewed vigor until he abruptly slumped forward, passed out. Still, I was ten times better than I had been before. I couldn't imagine what my other mates would've said if I'd come back without any healing.

"I'll explain everything," I promised Devlin now.

Keeping my hand in his, I turned towards my incubus. His red hair was tangled, and he had dark shadows beneath his eyes. My brows furrowed at the helpless expression on his face, the need to comfort him driving me.

"What's wrong?"

Before he could respond, the doors were pushed open and the mermaid king stepped outside. His blond hair was swept away from his face, once more revealing eyes a spitting image of his son's. Or...not his son's. Those eyes fixed on me with a predatory gleam.

I straightened under his gaze. It was time that I proved myself. It was time that I demolished the game board, emerging victorious.

I was no one's fucking pawn.

"I completed your task," I said, refusing to tack on the dreaded "Your Majesty" at the end. If he noticed my intentional slip of protocol, he didn't react. His eyes continued to glimmer in the sunlight.

Everything was painted in a pale pink and orange, the sun just barely cresting the horizon. It was another reminder of how little I'd slept the last few nights. My sleepless days were finally catching up to me—my body was tired and weary.

I'd tried to eat on the car ride back, but everything landed like lead in my stomach, tangling with the ball of nerves and fear.

I waited now, listening to my mates move behind me. It was Ryland who appeared a moment later, Jakob's red-haired head in his hands. Without preamble, he tossed it at the king's feet.

"Very good," he practically purred, surveying the man whose only crime was defending the woman he loved. My throat tightened with emotion, making it impossible to release anything louder than a croak.

"I completed your task," I repeated. "I'm done."

"You're not done," he countered. His lips were still curved upwards in a cruel smirk. He was a beautiful man seeped in poison. Everything about him was dangerous, exuding raw power. Even his smile held thousands of hidden meanings.

I waited silently for him to continue, hands on my hips. My posture screamed disobedience. Rebellion. With one eloquent quirk of my brow, he knew I wasn't a toy he could play with.

Still, he would try. He would mold me and break me until I was unrecognizable. Through it all, he would be wearing that damn smirk.

"You still have six other tasks to complete," he said, turning on his heel. I wasn't worth the attention he'd given me, apparently. Asshole. "The next task will begin tomorrow. Sleep while you can, my daughter."

Before I could react to his admittedly terrifying statement, the king stiffened as something was thrown at his feet. Only his head moved to survey the second head rolling beside the first. The king's eyes were blank, expression carefully impassive, as he stared at his eldest son's severed head.

Dair stood a foot away, breathing heavily. His hands were balled into fists.

After a long moment of staring, the mermaid king began to chuckle. It was so unexpected, so sudden, that all I could do was blink at him. His first reaction to seeing his dead son's head was to laugh?

"Son, son, son," he tsked at Dair. "I didn't know you had the balls to do it."

As if Tavvy's head were nothing more than a soccer ball, he kicked it out of the way. Guilt, for the first time, clawed at me.

Maybe guilt was too strong a word. It didn't fully encapsulate what I felt. It was...sadness.

Nobody had loved Tavvy. Even his father had discarded him the second he was no longer useful. He'd lived in a world, in a family, that had deprived him of love at every turn. It was no wonder he'd turned out the way he had. That wasn't to say I excused any of his actions, because I didn't, but it made me wonder how Dair would've turned out if he'd been raised solely by the king. No Pearce, Angelica, and Juliet. No Ryland, Bash, Killian, Jax, Lupe, or Devlin. Alone. Unloved. Unwanted.

Maybe things would've been different for Tavvy if he'd been loved. Maybe.

But I couldn't focus on the maybes without

completely spiraling down a hole I wasn't sure I could crawl myself out of.

"Dair," the mermaid king said, redirecting my attention to the matter at hand. I wouldn't grieve or mourn for Tavvy, but I would remember him. It was the only consolation I could offer.

"Yes, father?" Dair's voice was resigned. Already, he knew what his father was going to say. My hackles rose, hair standing on end.

"You know what has to happen now, don't you?"

Dair's face was pinched tight. I didn't like that, not one bit.

"Yes, Father."

"Meet me in my office in five minutes." Without another word, he moved up the stairs and disappeared from view. The second he was gone, I spun to face my mermaid mate.

"What does he mean?" I asked breathlessly. My hand wrapped around his corded bicep. "What's going to happen? Are you going to be punished? I can take the blame. He doesn't have to know it was you."

"With the mage spell, who else would it be?" He tried to smile at me, but it didn't reach his eyes. "I accept what's going to happen, Z. And I think you do too. You just don't know it yet."

"Know what?" My voice was desperate. High-pitched.

Dair cupped my cheek with his palm.

"I promise you, I'm going to be okay. We're going to get through this." His words did nothing to calm my racing heart. I tried to think of what the mermaid king could do to him, what the mermaid king must've already done to him, if his haunted expression was any indication, but I came up blank. The knowledge was there, right there, but it remained just out of reach. It burned the tip of my tongue...

Dair grabbed my ass suddenly, and I wrapped my legs around his waist as he kissed me. A quick, desperate kiss that spoke louder than any words ever could.

"I needed to do that one more time." His tone took on a hushed murmur so soft, I wasn't sure if he'd intended for me to hear it. He placed me back on my feet.

"Wait! Dair!" But he was already racing off, his golden hair disappearing inside the large wooden doors.

How many more monsters did we have to fight? We'd already killed so many.

Thousands of monsters in this world, and the worst was my mate's own flesh and blood.

I shook my head, coming out of my daze, when Killian put a hand on my shoulder to capture my attention. I turned to meet his anxious, slightly frantic gaze.

"What's going on?" I asked.

"I tried to find him." His stutter was more pronounced than before, and he absently scratched at one of the many tattoos adorning his arm. "I looked and I looked and I looked. He's gone, Z. He's gone."

"Who's gone?" I whispered, but a part of me already knew. A part of me had felt his absence acutely when I'd stepped out of the car.

Searching once more, just to be one-hundred-percent certain, I felt my body fall. Fall. Fall.

The day had been long and daunting, but I'd survived.

This? I wasn't sure I could come back from it.

Because my mate was gone.

Jax was no longer in the capital.

EPILOGUE
JAX

The bugs whispered to me. I couldn't discern exactly what they were saying, but the meaning was clear.

Alone.

Alone.

Alone.

They were practically screaming it at me.

Light pierced my eyes, and I lifted my hand to block the worst of it. A dark silhouette came into view, kneeling down in front of me.

"Z?" I whispered, hope clenching my heart. But if you clenched a heart too much, it broke. And that was what happened to me.

My heart...it shattered.

It wasn't Z looking back at me, and it wasn't Sasha. No, this woman with the red hair and sky blue eyes was unfamiliar.

"She left you, Jax. Even if she didn't leave you now, she would soon. I can see the poison running through her body. She can try to deny it all she wants, ignore it, but it will come for her. She's going to leave you, and she might not even have a choice," the woman said soothingly. She reached a hand out to touch me, and I flinched, curling against the far wall of my cage. I didn't want her touching me. I didn't want anyone except my mate touching me.

The woman stood, pursing her lips. She surveyed my skittish form with not a small amount of distaste.

"Do you want your mate back?" she asked softly. "Do you want Z and your brothers?"

"Yes," I whimpered. The walls were bleeding all around me, and I just wanted it to stop. Z was the only one capable of stopping it.

I needed her.

"Then we'll get her." The woman smiled suddenly, but it only made me more uneasy. Restless. Cornered. "You'll bring her to me, won't you, Jax? You'll be an obedient monster."

Blood.

Drip. Drip. Drip.

Alone.

So alone.

The woman lunged at me suddenly, lips still curled into that beautiful, sardonic smile. I only had a second to cry out Z's name before a dagger was in my heart.

Drip. Drip. Drip.

Blood. Blood.

"You'll be the best monster," she whispered into my ear. "Now sleep."

And I did.

ACKNOWLEDGMENTS

As always, it takes a team to make these books.

First, I would like to say thank you to my family. Thank you to my mom and dad for loving and supporting me unconditionally (even if I never let you read my books). I would also like to thank my sister for allowing me to kill her off in every novel of mine. Love you, sis. Thank you to my younger siblings and my grandparents.

I would also like to thank my author girls. You know who you are, and without your support and encouragement, I don't know where I'd be. Special shout out to Clitterati. I love drinking the Kool Aid with you ladies.

Thank you to my alphas: Kelly, Elena, Heather, Phylicia, and Sarita.

Thank you to my betas: Kelcey, Haley, HarleyQuinn, Katie, Michelle, and Rachel.

Finally, I would like to thank my readers. You guys have been incredible. I wouldn't be where I am today without you guys taking a chance on me. From the bottom of my heart, thank you. Thank you. Thank you.

ABOUT THE AUTHOR

Katie May is a reverse harem author, a KDP All-Star winner, and an USA Today Bestselling Author. She lives in West Michigan with her family and cat. When not writing, she could be found reading a good book, listening to broadway musicals, or playing games. Join Katie's Gang to stay updated on all her releases! And did you know she has a TikTok? Yeah, me either. Follow her here! But be warned...she's an awkward noodle.

Tory's School for the Trouble (Bully Horror Academy Reverse Harem)

1. Between

2. Beyond (Coming Soon)

Supernaturalette (Interactive Reverse Harem)

1. Introductions

2. First Dates

3. Group Outing

4. Game Night

5. Exes

Kingdom of Wolves (Shifter Reverse Harem Duet)

1. Torn to Bits

2. Ripped to Shreds

CO-WRITES

Afterworld Academy with Loxley Savage (Academy Fantasy Reverse Harem)

1. Dearly Departed

2. Darkness Deceives

3. Defying Destiny

Darkest Flames with Ann Denton (Paranormal Reverse Harem)

1. Demon Kissed

1.5. Demon Stalked

2. Demon Loved

3. Demon Sworn

STAND-ALONES

Toxicity (Contemporary Reverse Harem)

Blindly Indicted (Prison Reverse Harem)

Not All Heroes Wear Capes (Just Dresses) (Short Comedic Reverse Harem)

Charming Devils (Bully/Revenge Reverse Harem)

Goddess of Pain (Fantasy Reverse Harem)

Demon's Joy (Holiday Reverse Harem)

www.ingramcontent.com/pod-product-compliance
Lightning Source LLC
Chambersburg PA
CBHW021438310726
48971CB00005B/1414